To An...

Thank y...

Best wishes.

UNFINISHED BUSINESS

Retribution and Reconciliation

Ray Dan Parker

Books by Ray Dan Parker

The Tom Williams Saga
Unfinished Business: Retribution and Reconciliation

Coming Soon!
The Tom Williams Saga
Fly Away: The Metamorphosis of Dina Savage
Pronounced Ponce: The Midtown Murders
Last Gleaming: Love and Death in the Age of Pandemic

For more information
visit: www.SpeakingVolumes.us

UNFINISHED BUSINESS

Retribution and Reconciliation

Ray Dan Parker

SPEAKING VOLUMES, LLC
NAPLES, FLORIDA
2023

Unfinished Business

ISBN 978-1-64540-909-0

I dedicate this work to the memory of my father and my sister.

Prologue

ATLANTA (April 9, 1968)

I'd been on the road seven hours but still felt wired, perhaps from the third cup of coffee I downed with my supper at a roadside diner, perhaps the leftover adrenalin from the past two days. Though it was only Wednesday, I'd already had a long week.

When my editor offered me the chance to cover Dr. King's funeral, I jumped at it. It was the kind of story for which any young reporter would gladly give his firstborn. I finished it before leaving Atlanta and called it in from a pay phone. I felt good about it, but there was something missing. For me the assassination and the ensuing riots awakened old nightmares, memories of a boyhood friend and a Saturday night lynching.

All week I'd looked forward to going home. Tonight, though, as Interstate 75 unwound before me like an old black-and-white newsreel, the scenes played out again, the small-town setting, my family, now mostly gone, and that night ten years ago when I lost my two closest friends.

I took the Cordele exit.

Normally I wouldn't come this way, but I decided at the last moment to drop in on my grandmother. This had once been the most direct route from Atlanta to Tampa. Nowadays, however, the interstates hummed with traffic, tourists heading south to the Gold Coast, the Sun Coast, the Palm Coast, *any damned coast*, but certainly not Monrovia, Florida. Nestled in a very different part of the state, Monrovia was a place tourists seldom saw, unless a car broke down or a cop stopped them.

The sky hung clear and bright but for some puffs of white against a star-studded, indigo canopy. Along the way I passed cotton, peanut, and soybean fields. Moonlight flickering through the passing trees created a hypnotic strobe. The speeding shadow of my Mustang convertible made a sharp contrast against the luminescent blur. Beneath the rushing wind, I could almost hear the low murmur of voices from the fields, songs and chants of people long dead, their mortal remains lying out there somewhere behind the small churches and homesteads.

I like travelling at night. The air is cooler. There's less traffic and fewer police. The road beneath me felt smooth, like a bobsled run. I let down the top and felt the wind whip through my shoulder-length hair.

The V-8 engine thrummed as bugs splattered the windshield. I'd have to wash them off when I got to my grandmother's house.

Four hours earlier I had rolled out of Atlanta to the sounds of Jimi Hendrix and Cream on a local FM station, but in South Georgia all I could find were clear channel call-in shows on WSB AM and Fort Wayne's WOWO, mostly rants about the war in Vietnam, campus demonstrations, the presidential primaries, and the riots following Dr. King's assassination. I finally picked up a faint signal high up on the dial. From out of the ether came Steven Stills and Buffalo Springfield singing "For What It's Worth."

Farther down the highway I passed a vintage Chevy pickup as though it were standing still. Somewhere south of Albany, the Cokes and the coffee finally kicked in. I stopped to pee at a wide spot near the entrance to an unpaved driveway.

Straight, flat blacktop stretched into empty darkness in both directions. In the bright moonlight to my left lay a field with what looked to be forty or fifty acres of soybeans or peanuts. The tree-lined driveway made a broad curve into the distance. There, under a tall pecan tree, stood an unpainted wood-framed house with a rusted metal roof. A bare yellow bulb glowed on the front porch, and a whippoorwill whistled from somewhere across the field over the cacophony of crickets and cicadas. An old dog barked from the shadows beneath the house.

Across the road, the lights of a large fertilizer plant winked at me above a distant tree line. Its massive, gleaming cylinder seemed out of place here in the middle of nowhere, like the vanguard of some alien invasion. I considered pulling out my Nikon. I could snap a couple of pictures, doctor them up later, and perhaps write an alien abduction story for a grocery store tabloid.

As I stood in the darkness swatting mosquitoes, I thought about my girlfriend Colleen. We met a few months ago at a cocktail party in Tampa. I called her last night to tell her about my detour to Monrovia, that I wouldn't be back for a couple of days.

"I could clear my calendar," she said, "and drive up there. You keep telling me about your grandma. I'd like to meet her."

"Thanks, but I'm not sure you're ready for the rich cultural experience of Monrovia. You might never go home to Boston"

"Seriously, it's not that far. I could be there in a few hours."

"Monrovia may be in the same state, darling, but it's a world away from Tampa."

"Tom Williams, are you afraid I'm going to meet some of your inbred relatives, or perhaps one of your old girlfriends?"

"Yes."

"Which, the relatives or the old girlfriends?"

"Is there a difference?"

She laughed. Though we'd dated for such a short time, this was the woman I wanted to be with for the rest of my life. Last night I asked her to marry me. She said she'd think about it.

As I gazed across the emptiness around me, I wanted nothing more than to be dead-heading down I-75 back to Tampa, but there were things I needed to do. I assured her I'd be back by Monday.

***

At seventy-eight, my grandmother had grown frail. I could hear it in her voice when I spoke to her on the phone. I hadn't seen her since Christmas and felt guilty. She was my only remaining family besides an aunt and uncle in Pensacola. I considered calling her from Atlanta to say I was coming down but decided to surprise her… in case I changed my mind.

The moon hung low on the horizon when I crossed the Florida line. In the east the sky had grown pale. In the predawn light the world materialized before me like a black-and-white photo in a developing tray. Each turn in the road awakened another memory… a collapsed tobacco barn, Burma Shave signs, ads for alligator farms and a billboard for the Cheyenne Barbeque Ranch in Perry where my parents took me when I was little. The boy on the Coca Cola sign with his white, swept-back hair and bottle cap hat grinned at me through rusting bullet holes like an old friend. But as I passed him, his smile became a sinister image, something more akin to a sneer.

I passed the Jefferson County courthouse, antebellum mansions and fast-food restaurants of Monticello. Forty-five minutes south, I turned left onto a smaller road. A green and white sign read…

MONROVIA
20 MI.

Known locally as Tallahassee Highway, its pavement lay broken by countless log trucks and blistered by the relentless Florida sun. Weeds reached through the cracks like bony fingers clambering out of graves. The rutted-out shoulders were washboards. Palmettos and moss-draped pine trees closed in on both sides. In places they stood so tightly the rattle snakes, possums and armadillos could barely get through. There had been a time, not long ago, when this was all farmland, but in recent years it had reverted to forest, thanks to timber subsidies, falling tobacco prices, and rising labor costs.

By the time I reached the Pelahatchie River I knew my return to Monrovia had little to do with visiting my grandmother. The realization came to me like a low but urgent conversation from another room. It murmured through the rafters of old haylofts where I'd played as a child.

There was something else too, something lurking in the deep pools of my memory like a boogey man in the back of a child's closet. I couldn't quite see it, but I knew it was there.

Of one thing I was certain. My coming here was no last-minute whim. It was the culmination of events stretching back more than a decade.

I slowed to a stop and gazed into the river's dark, languid currents. A short distance away they passed beneath a canopy of overhanging trees and into a tunnel of absolute blackness. Overtaken by momentary vertigo I had the feeling I might fall into that tunnel, like Alice down a rabbit hole. But, *unlike* Alice, I knew exactly what lay at the bottom.

I drove on.

Moments later another green and white sign caught my headlights:

MONROVIA
10 MI.

Book One

Back Story

Chapter One

MONROVIA, FL (September 15, 1945)
Pug Donovan – *Tampa Sentinel*

Theirs was a generation suspended in time, but now they are awakening, like Rip Van Winkle, to a world changed in so many ways.

Three and a half years ago young men and women from across America set aside jobs and families, placed their lives at risk, and took up the defense of liberty and this great land of ours. Others served at home in factories and on farms producing weapons and materials needed for the war. Now those who, by the grace of God, survived will return to their hometowns, communities like this small tobacco farming hamlet in North Florida.

Just as Asia and Europe will never be the same, neither will the United States. No one could have stated this more eloquently than Marine Lieutenant Sam Williams, who returned early this week to a tumultuous hero's welcome. Standing beside him on a hastily erected bandstand were his lifelong friends and comrades-in-arms, Bill Emmett and George Martin. The three received early medical discharges due to injuries received at the Battle of Iwo Jima.

It seems the entire town of 5,000 souls turned out to greet them as Monrovia's mayor, Bernard Kelly, proclaimed a special day in their honor.

I was four years old when my dad returned from the war. Rereading this newspaper clipping, now yellowed and brittle with age, I struggle to recall that day, the sun-drenched courthouse lawn, the crowds fanning themselves against the heat. How much I remember and how much came from second-hand stories I have no idea.

He must have seemed a stranger to me. In December 1941, when he and his friends shipped out to Parris Island, he couldn't have known that my mom was pregnant with what would be their only child.

Following his return, we moved into a small, white asbestos-shingled home in Warren Heights, one of many post-war neighborhoods popping up around the country. There we lived until the year I turned eleven.

In 1952 Jasper County Sheriff Mark Anderson announced he wouldn't seek reelection, and my dad agreed to run. His only opponent was Howard "Cuz" Willingham, a policeman from nearby Mabry. My dad won easily.

He promised the voters an end to the bootlegging, gambling, and prostitution that were common throughout the county, where damned-near everything was illegal. The voters had heard such pledges before from politicians who, once in office, promptly forgot them. They assumed my dad was no different. They assumed wrong.

The day after he took his oath, my dad and his deputies set to work, shutting down stills, gambling halls, and brothels. Among those arrested were many prominent citizens. Convictions were few and sentences light, but the new sheriff continued his crusade.

Just before dawn on May 2, 1953, the criminal elements of Jasper County struck back, as buckshot shattered my parents' bedroom window. My dad sprinted into my room and pulled me from my bed as the window above me exploded from a second blast. But for a few cuts from broken glass, we were okay, physically at least.

The next day my mom and I went to stay with her sister Phyllis in Pensacola while my dad repaired the damage. He and his deputies went back to work, more determined than ever to put an end to the reign of crime. Two weeks later, with several of Monrovia's less upstanding citizens behind bars, my mom and I returned.

We arrived from Pensacola by train on a bright Saturday afternoon. My dad drove to the depot to meet us. To celebrate our homecoming, he and my mom dropped me off at my grandparents' farmhouse outside Monrovia and drove to Tallahassee for supper at the Silver Slipper restaurant, where they'd gone when my mom was a student at Florida State College for Women. They never made it.

In my last memory of my them, they stood in my grandparents' dimly lit doorway, my mom kissing me on my forehead, her brown curls tickling my cheek, my dad tousling my hair and saying, "Tommy, be a good boy, now. Mind your grandmama and granddaddy."

***

Just before daybreak there came a soft knock. Unbeknownst to my grandparents, I was already awake. I heard them answer it and opened my bedroom door just enough to see who was there. A uniformed sheriff's deputy, soaking wet, filthy and exhausted, stooped slightly as he peered through the rusted screen. He had curly blonde hair and seemed very upset.

"Mr. Clarence, Miss Edna, I'm afraid I have bad news." His voice choked so that I could barely hear him. "We found Sam and Jean's car at the bottom of the river below the Pelahatchie Bridge. It looks like they hit a deer and went over the side... I'm afraid they're gone."

My grandmother collapsed in the doorway. The deputy helped my grandfather carry her to her bed. When my grandfather came to tell me, I didn't know what to say. I ran from the house and hid in the barn. Calling after me, he stood in the yard for several minutes, then went back inside.

By afternoon the house had filled with people, speaking in hushed tones, yet loud enough for me to hear them. Some had spilled out onto the porch. I came closer and hid beneath a window. They said how horrible it was that I'd lost both parents and what a loss it was for the community. They wondered how such a thing could happen. My dad was a safe driver. It had been a clear night with a full moon.

I peeped around a bush and saw Clara O'Connor, a friend of my mom's, sitting on the white porch banister, her eyes red from crying. Clara taught English at Monrovia High. She folded her Kleenex, put it away and fumbled through her pocketbook for a pack of cigarettes.

The deputy, Win Stevens, had returned, wearing a clean uniform. He stood across from Clara and, without looking, pulled a nickel-plated Zippo from his pocket. He flipped it open with one hand and lit her cigarette.

"How the hell could this happen, Win?"

"I have no idea, Clara," he said quietly, "but I sure plan to find out."

"Do you really think it was an accident?"

"No."

She fixed him in her gaze. "It was those damned moonshiners."

"Yeah. Well, knowing that and proving it are two different things."

***

The next morning my grandmother dressed me for the funeral and fussed at my grandfather to hurry up. Gray clouds gathered, and a slow drizzle set in as mourners arrived. A warm, misty breeze blew through the old farmhouse. It slowly stirred the lace curtains and the cut flowers perched on the sideboard.

People arrived, dressed in black. Crowded into the small living room, they filled every piece of furniture. Latecomers stood wherever they found an empty spot. They made small talk, as if to avoid the real reason they were there and somehow postpone the inevitable. My aunt Phyllis arrived late the night before with her husband Frank. She retreated to the back bedroom, unable to speak to anyone.

The hearse from Spooner Funeral Home rolled into the front yard. Through the living room window, I watched as two somber looking men emerged and slowly climbed the steps. I recognized Tony Spooner from church. He wore an immaculate black suit, starched white shirt, and silver cuff links, his hair a gleaming mass of gray, swept back with tufts of white at the temples. He appeared to have spent hours carefully plastering each strand in place.

"Miss Edna," he said in his low, sonorous voice, "we're ready now. If y'all don't mind, you and Mr. Clarence and Tommy can ride up here with me."

The cars formed a procession, their headlights on, and pulled onto the narrow highway. I rode in the back seat of Spooner's car, seated between my grandparents, a box of tissues in my lap. My Sunday suit had grown an inch too short in the sleeves and pant legs.

Through the rear window of the hearse, I could make out the matching oak coffins, one bearing an arrangement of spring flowers, the other draped in an American flag. It seemed unreal to me that they carried my parents, that they were going away forever.

As we followed Pleasant Springs Road into town, vehicles pulled aside. Citizens, Black and white, lined the sidewalks, men with their hats removed, women with tears streaking their faces. At Broad Street we turned left and made the slight right onto Mabry Road. A half mile down on the right, we turned into the long, sandy drive that led to the New Hope Baptist Church.

It was a simple, white frame structure with a plain square steeple topped by a gunmetal gray cross. It stood tall and slender in a clearing

11

surrounded by graves. Our pastor, Don Fullerton, waited at the top of the steps, a large, floppy brown Bible clutched in his folded hands. The double doors stood open, and from inside came the strains of "Nearer My God to Thee."

Fullerton followed the caskets and pallbearers down the aisle in front of us. There two low pedestals draped in black awaited them. We took our places on the front pew.

Behind us sat three rows of sheriffs, deputies, and local police from surrounding towns and counties, all decked out in dress uniforms. Every pew had filled. The doors at the back remained ajar for those who stood on the steps gazing in.

"Brothers and sisters in Christ," Fullerton began, "we come together today to say goodbye to two wonderful friends, a son and daughter, a husband and wife, a mother and father. We cannot possibly know what purpose our Lord had in mind, calling them home at this hour, but we can rest assured in the faith that we shall all be with them, some glorious day, in that blessed land beyond pain and death and sorrow, if we but put our trust in Him. While we mourn their loss, let us also celebrate their lives. Sam Williams was a hero to his country and our community and a model for all in his Christian faith. Jean, through her gift of teaching, touched more lives than we will ever know… I was talking with Sam just last week, and he said to me, Don…"

The man droned for what seemed like hours. I squirmed on the hard, wooden bench, stared at the high ceiling of whitewashed tongue-and-groove and watched a June bug crawl across the dais in front of the small pulpit. There were more hymns and prayers and scripture readings. The funeral ended with everyone singing "Amazing Grace." Then some men, all friends of my dad's, carried the two caskets out to the small cemetery in front of the church where two open graves awaited them, and set them atop metal frames.

The skies cleared. The weather turned hot and steamy. Birds chirped and insects buzzed, oblivious to the solemn occasion. As I stood beneath that green tent staring into those holes in the sandy clay, it seemed that everyone around me faded away.

Following the funeral, mourners returned to the farmhouse for lunch. Hours later Bill Emmett and George Martin remained in our sparse living room talking to Clarence and Edna.

Emmett leaned forward and clasped my grandmother's hands in his. "I just want you to know," he said, "we'll do whatever we can to take care of your needs. I've set up a trust fund for Tommy, to help with his education, and several of Sam and Jean's friends have already contributed to it."

"You could help a lot more by telling me how my son and daughter-in-law got killed." It was the first time my grandfather had spoken all day.

"Clarence!" My grandmother gave our guests an embarrassed look. "You'll have to excuse us, Bill. This all happened so quickly, and we're still in shock. We haven't had any time to think about Tommy's future. We appreciate your kind offer and all the things you did to help us with the funeral expenses. Sam and Jean were truly blessed to have had friends like you and George."

George shifted uncomfortably in his chair and stared at his shoes. "It was the only thing we could do, Miss Edna, under the circumstances. We're going to miss Sam and Jean very much. They were such good friends."

In the coming days our Superior Court judge, Cephas T. Adams, appointed as sheriff Cuz Willingham, the man my dad had defeated. Willingham's first act was to fire my dad's deputies and hire his two incompetent nephews.

Chapter Two

At the age of eleven I went to live with my grandparents on their farm. I'd spent summers there when I was younger… when my parents were still alive. But it took time for me to see Clarence and Edna Williams as my new parents. They'd seemed so strong and active when I was little. But as I grew older and taller, they grew small and frail.

Sometimes my grandfather and I would throw an old baseball back and forth in the yard. He taught me how to pitch using an old truck tire hung from a tree limb to simulate a strike zone. He would wrap the small fingers of my right hand around the ball with the thumb, index and middle fingers along the seams. "Now hitch up your left leg like this, turn your body and shoulders like so, and step toward the plate. Point right at the middle of that tire and chuck it right through the hole. Don't try to throw it hard, just fast and smooth."

In the evenings he and my grandmother would sit by the fireplace staring at some distant point neither of them seemed to recognize. The dancing light outlined every crease in their faces.

Once, as she cleaned out an old chest of drawers, my grandmother came across a hickory slingshot that had belonged to my dad. She stared at it a long time, and then looked away as she handed it to me. "I guess this is yours now," she said, her voice barely audible.

I slept in my dad's old room, with the same furniture and many of the same toys and souvenirs he'd had as a child. On the wall were his old pictures. His trophies sat on the bookshelf above his desk. To me it was still his room, and I half expected him to walk in, eleven years old like me, and ask who I was and what I was doing with his stuff.

***

I began to have nightmares in that room. The details varied, but the setting was always the same. I'd gotten lost in a swamp or a wooded area running away from men who'd done something horrible. They wore cloth sacks over their heads, ragged holes for their eyes and mouths. Dogs howled after me as I ran blindly, limbs and briars tearing at my face.

There was something else in those woods, something even worse than my pursuers, some unseen monster waiting around the next turn. I'd awake, my sheets drenched in sweat.

As I got older the dreams became less frequent. For years I attributed them to the loss of my parents. But then I began to wonder if it were something else, concealed somewhere in the back of my mind, a truth so horrifying I'd buried it. It weighed on me like a bag of cement.

***

In my earliest memory of Jimmie Lee Johnson, from before my parents died, we were both five years old. Jimmie was an inch shorter and several pounds lighter but remarkably strong and quick on his feet. He was the youngest of six kids and the only son. His mother, Ida, worked for my grandparents, cleaning house, washing clothes, and cooking our meals.

She must have been about forty at the time, but to me she looked older. Her husband, C. W., left her for a younger woman right after Jimmie was born. Now she supported herself and her family on what little she earned and the small amounts her children made in the tobacco fields. Her oldest daughter, Ruby, cared for the younger kids while Ida worked.

Sometimes Ida would bring Jimmie to work with her. My mom would drop me off, and we'd take turns jumping from the loft into a tall pile of hay. I'd ride my bicycle around the yard, with Jimmie on the handlebars screaming at the top of his lungs. We became best friends.

There were two things my grandmother and Ida forbade. We couldn't ride our bikes on the highway, and we couldn't go fishing by ourselves for fear of drowning, getting bitten by a snake, or whatever. But, when no one was looking, Jimmie and I forgot those rules.

We came home one Saturday afternoon, riding our bicycles down the two-lane road carrying stringers of fresh-caught bream. When my grandmother met us in the yard I told her we'd found a safe fishing spot at a hunting club near the Little River. For some reason, this only upset her more and led to the only belt whipping I ever got.

At age six Jimmie and I went to our "separate but equal" schools. Jimmie still came to the farm on Saturdays. Sometimes my white friends would visit, and we'd show them the fishing spot we'd found.

The year my parents died I began working in my granddaddy's tobacco fields. He no longer talked about the farm someday being mine. The next year he sold his packinghouse, and in 1955, when I was thirteen, he stopped growing tobacco altogether. He said it wasn't profitable anymore, which was probably true, but the reality was his heart was no longer in it. Most of his employees, Jimmie and I among them, went to work on another farm owned by Max Brabson.

I turned fifteen in the summer of 1957, not knowing that would be my last year working in tobacco. I'd grown taller and leaner. The old shirts that once belonged to my dad now hung on my frame like clothes on a scarecrow, and the faded work pants were two inches too short.

Jimmie and I no longer worked in the fields but in the barn with about twenty-five other people. The women ran heavy string through the stems and tied the leaves to wooden slats. The barn foreman counted the sticks and punched a numbered card at each table. At the end of the day, he'd collect the cards and Max would tally up their weekly pay at twenty-five cents a stick.

Children too young to work in the fields carried the sticks to old men who handed them up to guys like Jimmie and me. We placed them on rafters above us to cure. We'd climb sometimes as high as thirty feet, straddling a four-foot gap with nothing between us and the ground but dust and heat and the odors of human sweat and fresh tobacco.

For all this work a grown man might make, at most, eighty dollars for a fifty-hour week. For his family to survive on such wages they all had to work, even the youngest.

Chapter Three

In the mid-summer of my fifteenth year Panky Carter came to work for Max. She had a smooth complexion, long, slender legs, tight little hips and a reputation that seemed to precede her. She moved with the ease and grace of a cheetah, her hair plaited half-way down her back.

Her arrival had an immediate effect. The young men grinned and made lewd comments. The women shook their heads and grumbled, but Panky ignored them all.

One day, as I climbed down from the top of the barn, my lunch pail in hand, a voice startled me. I assumed everyone else had gone outside to eat beneath the shade of the spreading live oak.

"Hey white boy." I turned and peered into the semi-darkness. There she sat on a low wooden sill, back against a post, her short cotton dress pulled up on her smooth mocha thighs.

I took an appreciative look and smiled but said nothing.

"You like what you see?" She smiled, revealing a row of straight, white teeth. Firm, round breasts and dark nipples pressed against her flimsy cotton dress. Even in the dim light, I could see there was nothing beneath it but a nubile sixteen-year-old body.

Caught off-guard, I stammered, "Sure! Why not?" Having nothing else to say, I turned and half-stumbled out of the barn. I tried not to think about her as I dug into my bologna sandwich and downed a thermos of sweet tea. If anyone saw me talking to her, I'd never hear the end of it.

A couple hours later the tea hit my bladder. I yelled up to Jimmie, "I'm going out." I climbed down and got one of the older men to take my place.

At the edge of the woods a narrow, sandy path cut through a black-berry thicket. Trod by countless workers over the years, it led to a dense area that served as the farm's latrine. I stepped carefully to avoid rattle-snakes.

A twig snapped behind me. As I spun around, Panky stepped lightly into the shadows and stopped a few feet away from me. We stood there for what seemed an eternity. Neither of us said a word.

"Are you going out too?" I asked stupidly.

"What do you think?"

"Oh! Okay." I turned and continued into the woods. The path divided several times before crossing a shallow creek, but, without looking back, I knew she was still behind me.

It wasn't until we reached a small clearing that she spoke again. "I reckon this is as good a place as any." She hiked up her dress and squatted to pee, looking up at me with a child-like grin.

I had no idea what to say. I turned to pee in the bushes but for some reason couldn't manage. When I glanced back she was studying me.

"You ever been with a woman before?" she asked.

"Yeah... Sure," I lied.

"You ever been with a Black girl?" A faint smile played at the corners of her lips.

"Uh, no"

She stood and unfastened her dress. It dropped softly onto the carpet of pine straw. Strands of sunlight slanted caressed her naked body. "You gone take your clothes off or just stand there looking?" She came closer and thrust her face up into mine.

I tore clumsily at my shirt, nearly popping a button. She knelt, spread the dress carefully and, in the middle of it placed a red-and-white checked bandanna she'd pulled from her pocket. She lay across the dress with her ass on the bandanna. I crouched over her and took in the full length of her thin body. Her breasts flattened as she lay back. The short, thick pubic mound felt soft to the touch as my fingers sank into her. I stared into her dark eyes, leaned forward and kissed her hard on the lips. We stank from having worked and sweated all day, but neither of us cared.

As I thrust into her, I pushed up so I could gaze down the full length of our bodies. Despite my summer tan, I looked like a ghost next to her. She closed her eyes, parted her lips, arched her back and let out a barely audible sigh. When I could no longer move inside of her, I fell away. Panting heavily, I gazed into her face. Her eyes still closed, her head tilted back, her chest rose and fell.

She rolled toward me and smiled. "You need some more experience, white boy. We'll have to come back here again. Now you get on back to the barn. I'll be along in a little bit. And *don't you tell a soul.*"

"I won't." I stopped for a moment and tried to think of somthing else to say. "Listen, do you suppose maybe, sometime, we could get together…"

Her eyes flashed. "And do what? What we gone do? I'm gone be your girlfriend?" She smirked. "You gone take me to the sock hop at the country club? We gone hang out together at the Burger Shack?" She shook her head in disgust. "Where you from anyway?"

I felt like an idiot. I pulled my clothes on and I stumbled down the path. Then I remembered the reason I'd gone out in the first place. I turned, unzipped my fly and again experienced intense pleasure as I relieved myself. This was *much* better than any wet dream.

When I got back to the barn the man who'd filled in for me gave me a smoldering stare but said nothing. He climbed down and returned to his place beside the wagon, emptying the tobacco that had just come in from the field.

"Where the hell you been, man?" asked Jimmie. When I didn't answer, he grinned at me, "You better not let old Max catch you. He'll fire yo ass for sure."

***

The following afternoon we were hanging the lower tiers when there came the low rumble of an approaching storm. Jimmie stood a few feet above me looking down. As I reached up to him I felt a prickling sensation on the back of my neck. His eyes widened and he yelled something about my hair. As he lunged at me I heard what sounded like an explosion.

I landed in a tobacco wagon with Jimmie's weight on top of me, hitting my head against a wooden rail. The breath ripped from my lungs, and I blacked out.

I came to in the emergency room at Jasper Memorial with Homer Green, our family doctor leaning over me. The ceiling tiles spun lazily overhead. My chest burned. The room reeked of antiseptics. My grandparents stood quietly in a corner.

Without warning I turned my head and puked onto the linoleum floor. I closed my eyes and lay quivering for what seemed like an eternity.

"Just relax, son," the doctor said. "You'll be okay. You're lucky you and that boy fell into that wagon. The tobacco saved your life."

I wanted to tell him it was Jimmie who saved my life but was too sick at my stomach to speak. I lay there and prayed for God to make it all go away.

***

Jimmie was thirteen when he first got in trouble with the law. One afternoon as he rode his bike past a small grocery store on the lower end of Broad, another Black kid ran out with a carton of cigarettes. Jimmie ignored him and rode on.

He was about a block away when Deputy Bubba Jeter, nephew of Sheriff Willingham, pulled him over. "Hang on there, boy. Where you going in such a hurry?" He grabbed the bicycle by its handlebars.

"I'm going home."

"Yeah. Sure, you are. Why don't you tell me where you hid them cigarettes?"

"What you talking about? I didn't steal no cigarettes. That other boy did it."

"Get in the car, boy."

Jimmie had to leave his bicycle behind and ride to the jail in the back of the Jeter's car. He knew it wouldn't be there when he returned. Ida had saved all year to buy it for him for Christmas. Now she had to pay more money to get him out of jail for something he didn't do.

Ida couldn't afford a lawyer, so she appeared before Judge Adams and pleaded with him not to send her only son to Florida School for Boys in Marianna. Adams reluctantly agreed and made Ida pay for the cigarettes.

From that day on, whenever anything happened, the sheriff or one of his nephews would pick up Jimmie for questioning. It gave them something to do while they ignored the bootleggers and fireworks dealers who paid handsomely for protection. By the time we were sixteen Jimmie had been arrested five times and had spent several months in Marianna. He had a knack for being in the wrong place at the wrong time.

Tobacco farming in Jasper County came to an end in 1967. A federal court determined that Jasper County's pay scale and working conditions were unacceptable and that children shouldn't be working in the fields and tobacco barns.

The farmers, most of whom hadn't made a profit in years, couldn't afford the higher wages or the loss of young workers. They tried other crops, tomatoes, peanuts, and even poinsettias. None of them succeeded, and one by one they did the only thing they could do. They converted their fields to timberland and laid off their workers. The barns and packinghouses fell into disrepair, and by 1968 the principal sources of income in Jasper County were welfare checks, food stamps, and, ultimately, drug-dealing.

None of us could see this coming in that summer of 1957. Nor did I know that three of the most important people in my life would be dead within the year.

Chapter Four

The fall of 1957 began my sophomore year at Monrovia High. With the tobacco season over, I took an after-school job bagging groceries at Swift's IGA. From there I'd ride my bike home, have a late supper, and do my homework until I fell asleep.

Late one afternoon I got a frantic call at work from my grandmother wanting me to come home right away. She wouldn't say what the problem was, but somehow I already knew. I put my bike in the back of old man Swift's truck, and he drove me out to the farm.

I arrived to find Doc Green standing in the doorway with my grandmother. She was sobbing, her face buried in her apron. My grandfather had died from an apparent stroke. Like my grandmother he'd never gotten past the loss of their son.

If I was certain of anything at all, as I stood there on that porch with my arms wrapped around my her, it was that no one in this community really cared what happened to us. Ever since the deaths of my parents it seemed we'd become increasingly isolated. The only people likely to visit us were Ida, the preacher, the doctor, and maybe a couple of neighbors.

I've never been so wrong about anything in all my life. Within an hour a throng had gathered in our living room, many of them people I knew only in passing. Others I hadn't seen in years.

As the crowd grew inside the small house, I had to get off by myself, so I went out in the back yard. For a long time, I sat alone in the tire swing my granddaddy had hung for me. I stared at the waning moon peeping over the treetops. Finally, I recovered my composure and went back inside to face these people I'd known all my life and had so badly underestimated.

I lay awake that night, exhausted from crying, the house unusually quiet. I'd become so accustomed to my grandfather's snoring in the next room that I couldn't sleep without it. A large owl hooted from the tree outside. I gazed up and saw his moonlit shadow on the wall.

Even now I can still close my eyes and see my grandfather. It's late afternoon, and he's walking through the waist-deep corn field beside the house checking each stalk for bugs or blight. He's wearing bib overalls, mud-covered work boots, and a blue, pin-striped cotton shirt. He stops for a moment, removes his sweat-stained hat and mops his brow. His matted hair, thinned on top, reveals a freckled scalp.

I'm pulling weeds nearby. He turns to me and calls out in a voice so deep it seems to roll in from somewhere beyond the hills, "Alright, Tommy, that's it. Let's go inside and get cleaned up for supper."

***

My grandmother sold the farm to Bill Emmett and bought a small home on a shady street near downtown. It sat on a corner lot and had a red brick exterior with white trim and a large magnolia that filled our summer nights with the fragrance of heaven.

We moved all our belongings in the back of our old truck. I carried most of them up to the attic, knowing we'd probably never use any of them.

Now that we lived closer to church, to school and to the IGA, I could get around more easily on my bicycle. It seemed that I'd worked all my life, first in tobacco and now at Swift's, something I'd always taken for granted. My parents and grandparents took care of me when I was young. Now it was my turn to help care for my grandmother.

I had another motivation as well. In a year I would turn sixteen, I'd have a driver's license, and I didn't want to have to take girls out on dates in my granddaddy's old truck. The car of my dreams was a two-tone Bellaire convertible with big, Lifesaver tires.

On weekends I'd push my granddaddy's old mower around to neighbors' houses and cut their grass. At five dollars a yard, even after I paid for gas, oil and repairs, I made more money than I'd ever earned in tobacco or at the IGA. By that spring I was so busy I was turning down new customers. I still had schoolwork to do, as well as my job at the store.

Each day I'd come home from school or work and, tired as I was, pull out the mower and cut a neighbor's yard before dark. I'd push it home under dim yellow streetlights to find my grandmother waiting with supper on the table.

"Tom Williams," she'd say, "you're going to work yourself into an early grave if you don't stop. You need to slow down and relax. Have some fun with your friends. What are you punishing yourself for?"

Sometimes I'd lie awake at night asking myself that same question. Was I punishing myself for something? Did I think I was somehow responsible for the deaths of my parents all those years ago?

I didn't need the money for college. By now the savings account and stock set aside for me had grown to where it would easily pay for my education, but I kept putting away more, just in case. The image of all that money became my security blanket. I'd think about it every time I awoke in the middle of the night in a cold sweat. When the school year ended, I took a part-time job as lifeguard at the country club pool.

The summer of 1958 was the perfect moment in time to be a fifteen-year-old kid of modest means. Every Sunday I'd dress up in the same uncomfortable plaid jacket, brown slacks, white short-sleeved shirt, and red clip-on tie. During the week my standard attire was a t-shirt, blue jeans, and black-and-white, high-topped Keds, just like all the other James Dean wannabes.

With considerable effort and a handful of butch wax I could style my hair into a flattop, but my t-shirts never quite fit the way I wanted them to. No matter how many pushups and sit-ups I did, or how much I worked out at the high school gym, I'd never look like Charles Atlas on the back of the Superman comics. Instead, I grew taller and skinnier.

***

I got a phone call one evening in late July from Dana Padgett, a young housewife two streets over wanting me to mow her lawn. Her husband, Mike, owned the local radio station, purchased, according to local gossip, with money given him by his rich mother.

The Padgetts had moved to Monrovia from Westchester County, New York. He was about forty, and she was thirty-two. Anxious to make a good impression in the community, he finagled a country club membership by running free ads for influential local business owners. Now he was too busy working on his golf game to take care of his yard or, as I would later discover, Dana.

Like most of the male populace of Monrovia, I'd noticed her many times, especially at the swimming pool in her form-fitting two-piece bathing suit. She would arrive each Saturday, promptly at noon, while her husband was out on the course. She'd wait for the perfect moment, when every eye in the place was on her, to remove her white terry cloth robe. She had the flawless complexion of a porcelain doll and eyes of periwinkle blue.

Her shoulder-length blonde hair and classic features gave her a look of child-like innocence. I can still picture her standing at the edge of the diving board, gazing down in quiet anticipation, her face illumined by the sunlit water, her wet bathing suit clinging to her firm body like cellophane.

27

I arrived at the Padgett home that first day to find Mike pulling out of the driveway. He had the canvas top down on his Austin Healey, his golf bag resting on the passenger seat. He wore Ray-bans and enough Vitalis to make sure every hair on his head remained in place when he got to the club. From his car radio Jerry Lee Lewis blasted "Great Balls of Fire."

I waved. He barely glanced at me, gunned his engine, and laid rubber as he drove away.

The two-story home was a portrait of Dana. With its white stucco and red terracotta roof it stood tall and slender, slightly hidden by a cover of cedars. Gently arching doors and Palladian windows graced its front. Its grounds and carefully arranged gardens were immaculate. French doors on the back opened onto a brick patio with a gas grill and wrought iron furniture. The detached two-car garage matched the stucco and tile. A high privacy fence and Leland cypresses surrounded the back yard.

I knocked, and Dana answered wearing a short white tennis skirt and matching blouse that fit tightly across her chest. She'd pulled her hair back into a ponytail, accenting her long slender neck. She spoke as though she were out of breath.

"Hi!" she said with a distracted smile. She brushed a stray lock from her face as she spoke.

"Hey! I just wanted to let you know I was here."

"Thank you." An awkward silence ensued.

"I'll, uhm… go ahead and get started."

"Let me know if you need anything." She didn't go back inside right away. Instead, she stood in the doorway and studied me as I cranked the mower. I looked back. She still wore that faint smile. I stopped for a moment, half waved and began mowing. Moments later I looked back to find she'd gone.

Someone else had cut the grass recently, and I finished the front and back in less than an hour, so I decided to edge the walkways with a tool I'd found in the shed. On one side of the patio a brick planter filled with mint and snap dragons ended beside a small fishpond full of hyacinths. Gold, white, and speckled carp moved languidly beneath the plants.

At first I could barely see them through the glare reflecting from the dark water. Then a cloud passed over and I stared into its depths. It seemed bottomless, as though the fish had swum up from the deep recesses of the earth drawn to the sunlight.

Standing there, gazing in fascination, my t-shirt soaked through in sweat, I heard the French door open behind me. I looked up to see Dana holding two glasses of iced tea on a silver serving tray. In each was a sprig of mint, which must have come from the planter. She looked like a mirage in the shimmering heat and for a moment I thought I was halluci-nating.

"You must be exhausted," she said with a beatific smile. She spoke quietly with the slightest trace of Midwestern accent, like Grace Kelly. "Why don't you come in, sit down, and have some tea?"

"Sure. Thanks."

The air conditioning reached out to embrace me as I stepped through the doorway. I took off my shoes and socks and left them outside. The cream-colored tile felt cold beneath my bare feet. I felt like a field hand at a formal dinner. A marble-topped counter separated the den, common-ly known as a Florida room, from the kitchen. A vacation picture of Mike and Dana on a Colorado ski slope hung from one of the oak paneled walls. On another was a picture of them on some Caribbean island. An arrangement of sunflowers stood on a glass topped table in a tall Oriental vase.

Above the fireplace hung a tarpon, about five feet long, beneath it a black-and-white photo of the fish hanging by its tail from the end of a boat. Mike Padgett smiled as he stood beside another man, Latin in appearance. He wore a Panama hat, wraparound sunglasses and a plain, white linen shirt.

Scattered around the room were various civic awards, golf plaques, and letters of appreciation, a veritable shrine to the man's ego. Notably absent from this tableau were any books. The only reading material in the room was a stack of home decorating and sports magazines on the coffee table.

"Your shirt is drenched. I'm running a load of clothes," she said. "Why don't you take it off and let me throw it in with the whites." Dana stood barefoot in the kitchen, her toenails painted a bright red. She'd exchanged the tennis outfit for a man's dress shirt, pale blue pinstripe, size Large. On her left ankle was a tiny gold chain. As far as I knew that was all she wore.

I had no idea what to say. "Um … I… I don't know," I stammered.

"Come on. It's just your shirt. I've seen you without it at the swimming pool." She arched one eyebrow as she spoke.

"Okay."

Brushing against me on her way to laundry room, she said, "Ooh! You're all sweaty. Why don't you go up to the bathroom and rinse off while I fix you something to eat?" She gazed up at me and ran her fingers lightly across my chest.

My only thought was that this had to be a dream. I said nothing. Instead, I climbed the carpeted steps to the guest bath, stepped inside and closed the door. With its pale blue wallpaper decorated with white seashell patterns, matching tile and fixtures, the place was like nothing I'd ever seen. On the vanity sat a jar of multi-colored, sweet smelling bath soaps. The neatly folded monogrammed towels looked as though no one had ever touched them. I closed the side door leading to a guest bedroom.

I stood for several minutes feeling stupid. Finally, I stripped, folded my nasty clothes atop a wicker hamper and stepped into the bath enclosure. For a moment I became light-headed. *"What the hell am I doing here?"* I thought.

I adjusted the shower to lukewarm and let it run over my hair and face. I applied shampoo from a bottle I found on a ledge above the tub. It smelled of pineapple and tropical flowers.

As I rinsed there came a soft click of the bedroom door closing. I turned as the frosted glass slid back and Dana stepped into the shower beside me.

The sight of her naked was everything I'd imagined on those bright Saturday mornings when I'd watch her standing there on the diving board. By now I *knew* this was a dream, but I was going to enjoy every bit of it before I awoke.

Her skin was the color of fresh cream from the nape of her neck to the tips of her tiny feet. Her breasts curved upward slightly, and her ruby colored nipples seemed to stare at me in surprise. She'd taken her hair down, and it fell in soft curls over her shoulders, catching the droplets of spray. "I thought you might like some help," she said.

She glided toward me and pressed her body against my chest. Reaching behind me she picked up a bar of soap, rubbed it between her hands, and ran it lightly down my back all the way to my butt. Then she began on my front. She gazed down with lips parted. "See, you're getting cleaner already."

I was breathing heavily as she embraced me and began to caress me with her lips and tongue. When she pressed her soft, wet mound against me I was afraid I'd come right there in her shower. She reached behind me and shut off the water.

We grabbed a couple of towels, dried ourselves off and ran into the guest bedroom. Dana pulled the old-fashioned quilt from the brass-framed double bed and let it drop onto the floor. I flipped onto my back amid the soft sheets as she climbed on top and began working her hips back and forth as though riding a horse. All too quickly it ended. She trailed her long hair across my chest and collapsed on top of me, breathing heavily.

"Tell me," she asked, "was this your first time?"

"Uh, yeah" For some reason that sounded better than the truth.

She rose up on her side. "You know what? I like you a lot." She ran her hand all the way down my chest. "I can see now that my yard is going to need a lot of mowing. And this part," she said as she took me into the palm of her hand, "will be our little secret."

"Sure." What else could I say? I still expected to awake and discover this had been nothing but a wet dream.

"You don't have a problem with that do you? I mean, you being a good Baptist kid."

"I guess it's okay… as long as we're not dancing."

Her laugh had a high-pitched nasal quality like that of a little child.

"Aren't you afraid we might get caught?" I asked. "What if your husband comes home and catches us?"

"Don't you worry. My husband is very predictable. If he's not out playing golf with his clients, he's off somewhere fishing in the gulf with his business associates from Miami." She shrugged. "If he can't take care of my needs, then I'll find somebody who will."

"If you're not happy, why do you stay with him? Why don't you just leave?"

"Sure! And do what? I married him right out of high school. He was handsome and adventurous and had all that money. I've never had a job in my life, and I'm certainly not going to work at a checkout counter or a diner.

"Besides, I could never have a life like this on my own, not even with alimony. I'd have to find someone else to take care of me. So, unless you suddenly come up with a fortune," she said as she ran her fingers through my hair, "we'll just have to keep meeting like this. I'll make sure you have plenty of money to take care of your little lawnmower."

"Did you ever think of having kids?" I have no idea why I asked such a stupid question. I suppose I wanted to find out more about her.

Her face darkened as she looked away. "We tried once, but I lost the baby. The doctor told me I'd never have children, so I gave up trying."

"I'm sorry."

"Oh, don't be. It's just as well." She gave me a rueful smile. "Mike Padgett is all the child I can handle."

I thought of how young she looked and how old she must feel. Her marriage hadn't turned out as she'd planned, and this house with all its décor was nothing but a gilded cage.

That's when I heard the front door shut, and my heart stopped.

From downstairs came Mike's voice. "Hey, Babe, do you know where my other sunglasses are? I broke these."

"I'm not sure, honey." Her voice caught for a moment. "I think I saw them in one of the drawers in the kitchen."

"What are you doing up there?" His voice was closer now. Was he at the bottom of the stairs?

"Oh, I got hot and sweaty from working around the house, and I thought I'd take a shower. Let me throw on something. I'll be right down."

She was already out of the bed and pulling on her robe. Quietly, I rolled off onto the carpeted floor and squeezed under the bed as she whipped the quilt back over it, not bothering to straighten out the rumpled sheets. She ran on tiptoes back into the guest bath, grabbed

Mike's sunglasses off the counter, where they'd been all along, and closed the door to the hallway. From under the bed, I watched her as she threw some water on her hair from the bathroom sink and wrapped a towel around it. She glanced back at me through the bathroom doorway with a sly grin.

"Here. I found them. I'll bring them down."

He was coming up the stairs. "You're showering in the middle of the afternoon?"

"Yeah… I got all sticky working around the house. I was cleaning up behind you, you big slob."

"Yeah, well that's your job, isn't it?"

"Yep, you're absolutely right. I'm just your little hausfrau, a regular June Cleaver."

"Where's that yard boy? He left his mower on the patio."

The door from the bedroom to the hallway stood ajar, and I could see the corner of Mike's pants leg at the top of the stairs. On the bathroom floor, barely out of sight, lay my blue jeans and belt. I prayed he didn't have a sudden urge to pee.

"Oh, you mean Tom?" Dana said. "I think he got thirsty and walked up to the corner to get a Coke."

"Alright. Just make sure you don't pay him too much. Three bucks is plenty."

He turned and went back downstairs. I let out a deep breath when I heard the front door slam and slid out from under the bed. If I'd had any misgivings about sleeping with this guy's wife they were long gone.

Dana bounded back into the room and climbed onto the bed beside me. She laughed and tried to tickle me as we rolled back and forth under the sheets. Before long we were making love again.

I mowed a lot of yards that summer, but none paid as well as Dana's. I was sure no one had any idea what we were up to, until the day another customer mentioned that she'd seen me at Dana's house. "Looks like you're taking mighty good care of her," she said with a coy smile.

"Yes ma'am. She likes to keep her yard cut pretty close." I've never been a good liar and my expression must have given me away. I began to worry that somebody would find out about us, and that it might get back to her husband. I worried even more about my grandmother finding out. It would kill her.

Despite the guilt and the fear, perhaps because of it, I couldn't stop seeing Dana. Over the short span of that summer, she gave me more pleasure and showed me more ways to give pleasure than I'd ever imagined. I lay awake at night, thinking about her, wishing she were with me, and fell asleep dreaming of her. In a couple of years, if I could last that long, I'd turn eighteen and take her away from all this. There was no way she'd stay with that sack of shit she'd married.

I was clueless. I had no idea how dangerous this was, or how dangerous Dana might be. It never even occurred to me she might be sleeping with someone else. When other guys made sly comments about her it was all I could do to keep from decking them. Instead, I kept my mouth shut and smiled.

Even now, as I look back and wonder what kind of thirty-two-year-old seduces a fifteen-year-old kid, there's still a large part of me that misses her so badly it hurts. I still dream about her. I wake in the morning and wonder if any of this really happened. What I remember most after all these years is the way she giggled like a little girl when I tickled her and trembled like a small bird when I held her close.

Chapter Five

Clara O'Connor was another of my customers that summer. She taught English lit at Monrovia High and lived a few blocks west of us in a small craftsman bungalow with a broad front porch. Clara had been a close friend of my mom and often spoke of her. She would become the greatest influence on my young life.

Her front lawn was small, enclosed in a white picket fence and shaded by several large trees. The back was larger and more open. I'd mow the grass while Clara weeded the flower beds and pruned the shrubs. Her hands were large for a woman's yet well-formed. The muscles stood out in a vivid detail that reminded me of Michelangelo's *David*.

When we finished our yardwork, we'd sit on the porch as evening fell, admire the sunset and wait for the fireflies to come out. We spoke of everything from politics to literature and religion. She was the first person in my life who ever addressed me as an adult. She seemed to sense the things that interested me even before I did.

I'd sit on the swing while Clara leaned against the railing and puffed on a cigarette. She always smoked outside, even though she lived alone. She'd sit for a while without saying a word and then turn and speak suddenly as though already in the middle of a conversation. Once, as we sipped sweet tea and munched on lemon cookies, she brought up the subject of my future.

"You're going to be a junior next year, and the year after that you'll graduate." She let out a long slow curl of smoke and watched as it rose. "You know, it's not too early for you to be thinking about college. Where do you suppose you'll go?"

"I don't know. The University maybe"

"Excellent! Your parents would be proud. Have you thought about a major?"

"I'm not sure, but I've decided I want to be a newspaper writer."

In all the time I'd known her I don't believe I'd ever seen Clara smile, but for a moment the corner of her lip seemed to move. She encouraged all her students to write, no matter what their career plans might be. "So, I guess you don't plan to come back here then." She took another drag from her cigarette.

"I don't think so. There's not much to write about in Monrovia."

"Oh, I wouldn't be so sure of that. There's always something to write about, but if you're as smart as I think you are, you'll get the hell out of this town and never look back."

"I still have my grandmother to think about."

"You could come home to visit her. You don't have to live here. Your grandmother can take care of herself. I can look in on her from time to time, and she still has Ida. If you stay here and make the mistake of marrying one of these little mealy-mouthed girls you'll be stuck in Monrovia forever."

"Well, I'm not planning on doing that," I laughed.

"I guess not. You don't seem to have much time for dating anyway, with all the work you do."

"Nope." I thought of Dana and decided to change the subject. "How about you? Have you ever thought of leaving Monrovia?"

"I've thought about it a lot. In a few years I'll be able to retire. I'd like to move to Sanibel... It's a small barrier island off Sarasota. I could live near the beach and spend time over in town at the artist colony."

"Are you actually ready for retirement?" I asked.

"Oh, I will be soon. I have a close friend who could move down there with me. I doubt you know her."

"That's nice," I said. "Listen, I need to go. My grandmama will have supper on the table. Thanks a lot for the tea."

"Before you leave I have something for you. It's a novel by Ayn Rand, *Atlas Shrugged*. I just finished it last night. It's rather long, but I believe you'll enjoy it."

I followed her inside and waited as she disappeared into a bedroom. The living room and dining area extended across the front of the house with low ceilings and exposed beams matching the dark pine floors. Bookshelves, crammed full, covered every inch of wall. There were more books stacked on tables and on the mantle. Above the fireplace hung an autographed photo of Gertrude Stein and her secretary Alice B. Toklas.

When Clara returned I thanked her. "I'll get it back to you as soon as I finish it."

"No rush. I guess I'll see you next week then."

"Sure."

***

August arrived, and I began to look forward to a new school year, not so much the prospect of returning to the classroom as hanging out with people I hadn't seen all summer, the few with whom I'd built a friendship.

I'd known Jenny Maxwell since first grade but seldom spoke to her. She came into the IGA one afternoon while I was bagging groceries.

"Hello, Tom, how has your summer been?" Her bright smile reminded me of an Ipana toothpaste commercial. She always spoke in complete sentences, concise and grammatically correct, as though she were writing an essay for Clara. Her straight black hair, held in place by a white barrette, flipped up at her shoulders.

"Fine... how was yours?"

"It's been fabulous!" She was the only girl I ever knew who used words like "fabulous." "My parents and I just got back from our cabin at Montreat. Before that, I went to music camp at Agnes Scott College earlier in the summer."

"That's great, Jenny." I fumbled for something else to say. "I guess you're looking forward to school starting back."

"Absolutely... It will be so great to see everyone again."

I carried her groceries out to her parents' wood-paneled station wagon and went back inside. As I turned and watched her drive away, I decided to ask her out.

I hadn't lost interest in Dana. She gave me something I wasn't likely to get from any of the girls at school, especially Jenny, but I could no more invite Dana to the sock hop than I could Panky Carter, and I wasn't going to spend my Saturday nights at home with my grandmother watching re-runs of *Gunsmoke*.

I wanted a girl I could take to movies and football games and hang out with at the Burger Shack. Jenny was perfect. She was nice looking and had a sweet personality, but when I thought of sex I always pictured Dana.

On my sixteenth birthday my grandmother took me to the Florida Highway Patrol office where I passed my driver's license exam. I drove my granddaddy's old pickup, which now looked as though it might fall apart in the road. If Jenny and I were going to cruise the town with our friends, I had to get myself a nicer ride.

The car I wanted sat on the lot at the local Chevrolet dealership, which George Martin had bought out in 1955. Every Saturday I'd go by to look at it and make sure George hadn't sold it.

Over the summer I'd saved more than a thousand dollars from my work, and in a few weeks I'd have all the money I needed. My grandmother offered to help me buy it and Bill Emmett was willing to lend us the money, but I refused them both. This would be my belated birthday present to myself, and I was determined to buy it with my own money. Everything seemed to be going my way.

Little did I know.

Chapter Six

Nothing I cared, in the lamb white days, that Time would take me
Up to the swallow thronged loft by the shadow of my hand,
In the moon that is always rising,
Nor that riding to sleep
I should hear him fly with the high fields
And wake to the farm forever fled from the childless land.
Oh, as I was young and easy in the mercy of his means,
Time held me green and dying
Though I sang in my chains like the sea

"Fern Hill"
Dylan Thomas

I'd worked six days a week since school let out, and in mid-August I decided to take one Saturday off. As lifeguard at the country club, I had weekday golf privileges. Sometimes the pro would let me play on Saturday mornings provided I finished up before the members arrived. Now that I had a driver's license I could go out there on my own.

It was eight a.m., two weeks after my sixteenth birthday. I parked the old truck next to the pro shop and pulled my golf bag out of the back. The clubs had belonged to my dad, and I'd taken good care of them over the years. The way they felt in my hand and the smell of the leather grips reminded me of him.

The parking lot was empty, and there was no one in sight, but I had the feeling I was not alone. A light patch of ground fog hovered over the putting green and the air smelled of fresh mown grass. As I swung the bag over my shoulder a tingling sensation ran down the back of my neck. I swatted at a bluebottle fly as it buzzed past. The air hung thick and still, portending another hot, sticky day. I thought I'd play nine holes, hang out at the pro shop for a while, then slip over to Dana's before Mike returned from out of town.

Suddenly, Benny Stillman, the groundskeeper, bolted out from behind the cart shed at the edge of the woods. He crossed the parking lot to the pro shop and a moment later returned with the club pro, Victor Molina. Neither of them spoke or acknowledged my presence. Curious, I fell in behind them.

Behind the cart shed a narrow path led into the trees. A few feet beyond, in a thicket beneath a large pin oak lay a fresh pile of leaves. As I came closer I heard the hum of swarming flies, and a sickening smell overcame me. I edged toward it, denying with every step the reality unfolding before me.

At first the only thing visible beneath the leaves was a human foot. I recognized it right away from a tiny birthmark on the inside of the arch. Benny stood off at a distance and stared at the ground as Victor pulled back the overhanging limbs. He looked like he'd been caught doing something wrong and was afraid someone would punish him.

At first I took her for someone else. She lay there on her stomach with her face, turned toward me, tinged in purple. Her eyes bulged, her tongue lolled between swollen lips, and dark bruises encircled her neck.

As the stench of human waste came over me like a wave, I turned and lost my breakfast. I looked up, and the tree limbs above me began to turn. The flies became dark specks as I fought to remain conscious. Somehow I managed to stumble back to the parking lot where I collapsed onto the pavement in the shadow of the truck and closed my eyes. I sat there for a long time, my body convulsing in dry heaves.

Every time I thought I might regain control I saw her again lying among the leaves, the bluish cast, the bulging eyes, the swollen tongue and dark, circular bruises on her neck. A shutter came over me and I began to choke. What kind of animal could do something like this to someone as sweet and beautiful as Dana?

She had been the most alive and energetic person I'd ever known. Now she lay there naked in the dirt and the rot, discarded like a bag of garbage carelessly tossed by the side of the road. Though I'd lost both parents and my grandfather, until now I'd never seen a dead body. The funerals I'd attended had all been closed casket affairs.

I was still sitting there with my head down and my back up against the left front tire of the truck when the ambulance arrived followed by three sheriff's vehicles. Car doors opened and slammed. The voices of Cuz and his nephews trailed into the woods.

Sometime later a shadow passed over me. I looked up into a florid face. It wore the look of a tired bloodhound. His mouth hung agape with a bead of spit stuck in one corner. He had thick, poorly formed lips that never seemed to fit properly, like two slabs of bologna sliding around on a mayonnaise-slathered piece of white bread. He had the vague but arrogant smile of the blissfully ignorant, the confidence of one to whom all things are as simple as he is.

"Boy, you alright?" Cuz asked.

I couldn't bring myself to speak to him. I looked down at my reflection in the spit shine of his black uniform shoes.

"What do you know about this, boy?"

I managed to shake my head.

"Now don't you go anywhere, you hear."

He stepped away for a moment to speak with Benny and Victor. The stupid shit kept eying me suspiciously as Benny explained that I'd arrived *after* he found the body. A few feet away ambulance attendants loaded Dana's nude corpse onto a gurney and covered it with a stiff white sheet as Willingham's nephews gawked. If the two of them had

had cameras I'm sure they'd have taken pictures. By now they'd so thoroughly trampled the crime scene that a competent investigator, had there been one in Jasper County, would never have found any usable clues.

The sheriff sauntered back over to where I sat. "Alright, you can go now."

As I got up and slowly climbed into my truck I watched the ambulance pull away. I drove back to the house and took a hot shower to get the smell of vomit off me and the sour taste out of my mouth. When I'd dried off and dressed, I found my grandmother on the phone in the hallway talking to somebody about the murder. Already the news had spread. I told her I was going back out and left before she could say anything.

By noon everyone in Monrovia knew about Dana. In a town where practically nothing happens, something like this could consume conversations for years. The last concern on anyone's mind was getting the facts straight. There would be rumors that Dana's husband had killed her, or that Benny had killed her. There would be some, no doubt, who, for no reason, thought I'd killed her. The last thing I needed was to listen to ignorant gossip.

I was pretty sure her husband had nothing to do with this. As far as I knew he had no idea what Dana and I were up to. He was off deep-sea fishing with his buddies from Miami and wasn't due back until that afternoon.

When I saw her two nights earlier I asked Dana if we could get together the following evening, but she said no. She was meeting an old friend. I didn't want to seem jealous or nosey, so I didn't ask who it was. Now I wished I had.

I was angry and afraid, but there was nobody I could speak to. As far as I knew no one knew about us, and I intended to keep it that way.

As I cruised aimlessly through town I avoided eye contact with everyone I saw. I drove past Dana's house and found the street filled with cars. Her husband had returned home early to find his wife dead, and everybody who knew him was there. George Martin and Bill Emmett stood in the driveway deep in conversation, wearing dour expressions. I ignored local custom and sped away before either of them spotted me.

I never liked Mike Padgett, and there was nothing I could do for Dana now. I couldn't stand the thought of being around all those people. They'd take one look at me and wonder what the hell was wrong. By now my grandmother would be there, and the last thing I could do was face her at a time like this. I went home and changed into some old shorts, a T-shirt, and a pair of low-topped sneakers.

***

Two years earlier I'd played junior varsity baseball and took up running as part of my training. Despite my granddaddy's best efforts, I was never any good at it and quickly lost interest, but I kept up the running as a way to blow off steam.

My favorite route was a deserted stretch of dirt road on the back side of our old farm. It was Bill Emmett's property now, but I knew he wouldn't mind. I never could figure out why he bought the place. He damned sure wasn't a farmer. The tobacco shades were gone now, the barns fallen into disrepair, and the fields had become cow pastures, rented out to a dairyman down the road.

It was early afternoon, and the sun was directly overhead. I mopped my brow as I ran the three and a half miles to where the road abruptly ended at the edge of the woods. With every step I saw again the wreckage of Dana's body, murdered and dumped like refuse.

I turned back the way I'd come, oblivious to the heat and the clouds of gnats. At one point I glanced down to see a track left in the sand by a rattlesnake.

I was almost back to the highway when I rounded a curve and looked up to see our old farmhouse. I slowed to catch my breath, took off my T shirt and wrung out the sweat. I decided to go inside and look around.

In the front yard the tire swing my granddaddy hung for me was gone now. All that remained was the rotted loop of cotton rope. It had cut deep into the bark of the stout limb. The screen door hung from its hinges, and the house stood open. The white paint on the siding had peeled away, and several windowpanes were missing. Bill had left the house vacant for more than a year, and it was already falling apart.

I stepped gingerly across the porch, avoiding the soft spots on the floorboards. The leaves and dust inside lay so thick the floor was indistinguishable from the ground outside. A kudzu vine had made its way through a window and was now halfway across the living room. Golden specks of dust waltzed in the dazzling sunlight. The corners, by contrast, were pools of unfathomable darkness as my eyes slowly adjusted.

There were marks on the walls where our family pictures had hung. I gazed at my reflection in an old mirror above the mantle. I couldn't believe this had been my home for so many years. As I wandered through the house it was as though I'd stepped into a strange dream.

My old bedroom seemed smaller. I tried to imagine it as I remembered it, all my furniture, my toys, and the clothes in the closet. I stood in the corner where my bed had been, closed my eyes and travelled back to a night only a year ago. Again, I saw the splash of moonlight against the wall and the shadow of a large owl on a tree limb outside.

Ida once told me that every place has its own magic. The magic comes from our memories of people who've lived and died there. It's there whether we feel it or not. I had no idea what she was talking about.

I stopped believing in ghosts when I was seven years old and my mom told me they weren't real. My Sunday school teacher said that people who were saved went to heaven when they died, and everybody else burned in hell. I asked Ida about that.

"Where do you think heaven and hell is, boy?" she asked me as she leaned over and gazed into my face. "Do you think heaven's up in the sky?" She crooked one finger toward the ceiling. "Or that hell's down under the ground? There ain't nothing up in the sky but the sun, and the moon and the stars, and there ain't nothing in the ground but dirt. Naw suh. Everybody who's ever lived on this earth is still right here, all around us. Some of them are in heaven alright, and some are in hell, but they're all right here and they're looking right at us."

I never believed any of that. Ida told me wild stories all my life, perhaps to scare me into behaving. But now, as I sat in my old bedroom, I wasn't so sure. If my parents and my granddaddy were here, I wondered what they were thinking. They couldn't possibly understand how I felt about Dana or the pain inside me now.

I wondered where Dana's magic place might be. Would she have gone back to her white stucco home on Magnolia Drive with the patio torches and the fishpond? Was she lying there, just like I remembered her, among the starched white linens, the cut flowers, and the scented bath soaps? I could still feel and smell them every time I thought of her.

Wherever she was, there was one thing I knew for sure. She couldn't possibly be back there in that pile of leaves behind the golf cart shed where some animal had dumped her. There was no way in hell she could be there. Whatever her weaknesses may have been she was a decent and beautiful person and she deserved better.

The events of the past hours finally descended on me. I collapsed to the floor, and buried my face. For the first time since my grandfather died I began to cry.

Amid all this a brief memory flashed across my mind. It lasted but a moment, then disappeared. It was a frame from a nightmare I'd had many times as a child.

I'd climbed out the window in this very room, and Jimmie and I had ridden off on our bikes while my grandparents lay asleep. In my dream there were men with cloth sacks over their heads gathered around a fire. I heard the voice of a woman screaming as these men without faces did terrible things to her.

I shuddered violently and I opened my eyes. I told myself none of this was real. It had just been a bad dream. It never really happened.

Why couldn't Dana's murder also be a dream? Why couldn't I wake to find that she, my parents and my grandfather were still alive?

Gradually the tears washed away the shock, and in its place burned an anger like none I'd ever known. I had a focus now. If it took me the rest of my life I'd find the son-of-a-bitch who killed Dana. I'd strangle him with my bare hands, exactly as he had done her, and I'd dump his ass somewhere in a garbage pile for the flies and the maggots.

Slowly I picked myself up and walked back outside. I wandered down the road toward the distant woods, gazing at clouds gathered on the horizon. The breeze picked up and a thick, gray film spread across the sky.

I reached the point where I'd parked my truck and was about to climb inside when I saw a plume of dust moving toward me around a curve in the road. A silver Lincoln pulled up, and the passenger window came down with the soft whir of an electric motor. Inside, staring at me was the face of Bill Emmett.

He was in his forties now and had gained weight. His face had the roundness of a full moon. He had an extra chin, and his mid-section hung out over his belt. Graying strands of hair lay plastered across his forehead a vain attempt to hide the receding hairline.

"Your grandmama told me you'd be out here," he said. "She wants you to come home right away."

I stood there dumbstruck. I never told her I came out here to run. I wondered what else she knew about the places I went and the things I did. Why would she send Bill Emmett out to find me?

"Tom, I thought you might want to know. They caught that boy who murdered Dana Padgett."

This was too good to believe. Willingham and his nephews couldn't catch a cold.

"It was your buddy, Jimmie Lee Johnson."

For the second time that day I felt as though someone had sucker punched me. The blood rushed to my face, and I screamed "Bullshit!" I pounded the top of his car, turned away and stared out across the cow pasture. My breath came in short gasps. It was bad enough that Dana was gone, but there was no way Jimmie could have killed her.

"Now, just calm down a minute, son. They know he did it. Somebody saw him walking down the highway this morning about a half mile from the country club, and they called the sheriff's office. When the deputy picked him up, they found a necklace on him that belonged to Dana. They think he raped her, killed her, and stole the necklace."

"Wait a minute. Somebody just happened to see Jimmie walking on the road right after Dana died, and they called the sheriff's office because they figured he was the murderer, before anybody even knew that a murder had happened. And who the hell said she was raped?"

"Well...they don't really know... They just found her naked."

"That doesn't mean she was raped. That sheriff's a regular Dick Tracy isn't he! And how does he know that necklace belonged to Dana?"

"Somebody recognized it and said it belonged to her. It had this funny looking little green stone. I think it was jade, shaped like a broken-off piece of a heart."

I started to speak, but the words caught in my throat. I knew that necklace. She never took it off, even when we were making love. I was too upset that morning to notice it was missing. I asked her once if Mike had given it to her.

"Hell no," she laughed. "That bastard never gave me anything but his checkbook and his name." She didn't say who gave it to her, and I never asked.

I still couldn't make sense of it. I shook my head and stared at the ground. I didn't think Jimmie even knew Dana, and I'd never seen him anywhere near the country club. I glanced up to see Emmett staring back at me.

"Look, I ... I'm sorry, Bill... I've got to go."

I jumped into my truck and cranked the engine. As I turned and headed back to the highway I glanced at Bill. He sat there gazing at me, the dust settling on his leather upholstery.

Chapter Seven

Collier Street ran so narrow behind the Jasper County Courthouse that cars had to pull off the road for oncoming vehicles to pass. Roots of overhanging trees buckled the pavement causing it to heave like the ocean in a storm.

On the north side stood the county jail, a plain brick, two-story box of a building shaded by surrounding trees. Its cracked and pitted red-brick exterior supported a gray shingled roof covered in green mold. Front steps of poured concrete led to an oaken front door that had worn and peeled repeatedly over the years. Rather than sanding it down to the wood and refinishing it, maintenance workers simply scraped and re-varnished it until it has taken on the texture of an alligator hide. Here and there drips had hardened into beads like frozen tears.

In 1958 this jail, like everything else in Jasper County, was a segregated institution. White prisoners occupied the downstairs cells while Black inmates crowded the upstairs. Regardless of race they all entered through the same rear door.

A pair of deep ruts filled with crushed oyster shells ran down the right side of the building to an open, gravel-strewn parking lot in the back. Beside this narrow alley a large live oak straddled the property line and encroached on the used car lot next door. Its branches reached out as if to embrace and comfort those incarcerated inside.

The sun had begun to set by the time I arrived. I parked the truck a block away and walked to the jail.

As I climbed the steps, Sheriff Willingham met me at the doorway. "What do you want, boy?" he asked, glowering down from the top step, clearly impressed by the extra stature it gave him.

"I came to see Jimmie Lee Johnson."

"You just go on back home, boy. This ain't none of your business."

"But Sheriff ..."

"Go on. Get the hell out of here, before I arrest you too."

I started to argue with the asshole but thought the better of it and walked away.

An hour later I made some excuse to my grandmother and left before she could ask questions. This time I parked in a darkened corner at the IGA down the street where no one would notice. The store had closed early, for some reason, and the streets were empty. I walked the seven blocks to the jail.

To its left stood an abandoned home. I stopped and looked back, as though I'd forgotten something. There was no one behind me. It was early, but the entire town seemed deserted. I strolled down the darkened driveway that ran behind the house.

The back yard was so overgrown I could barely pick my way through the briars. A tall wooden fence separating it from the parking lot behind the jail strained under the weight of a rambling Wisteria. I pried back two of the planks and squeezed through.

Three Sheriff Department cars sat in an orderly row near the back door. From inside came the sound of a radio and the soft voice of Patsy Cline. There were voices, Cuz and his nephews probably, but I couldn't understand what they were saying.

Taking one last look to make sure no one had seen me, I circled the rear of the building, careful to avoid the pool of yellow light spilling from the back porch.

The branches of the live oak were low enough for me to climb. I shimmied out on an upper limb to within three feet of a barred second-floor window, trying not to look down.

"Jimmie," I whispered. No one replied. The cell was dark, but for a faint glow emanating from the hallway. "Jimmie!" I called a bit louder and waited.

I figured this cell must be empty. What I could do I had no idea.

I was just about to slide back down the limb when a low, sandpapery voice called out, "Who dat?"

Startled, I nearly fell out of the tree. It didn't sound like Jimmie, and I wasn't sure what to say.

"Who dat out there?"

"I'm looking for Jimmie Lee Johnson."

There was a long pause. "Jimmie!" he murmured.

Fast-moving clouds parted overhead. Jimmie's face appeared in the window of the next cell. At first I didn't recognize him. In the moonlight I saw his right eye had swollen shut, his lips puffed out and bleeding.

"Tom is that you?" he whispered. "You crazy motherfucker! What you doing out there?"

"I had to come see you, and the sheriff wouldn't let me in. Jimmie, what's going on here?"

"They say I raped that white lady and killed her."

I lay there clinging to the tree limb, aching all over.

"Tom, I didn't do it. You know that. These crackers just snatched me up 'cause I was close by. I never even seen that lady."

"Jimmie, they say you had her necklace in your pocket."

"That's a damned lie! They had it themselves. Now they gone put all this on me."

"Why, Jimmie? Why would they do that?"

"I don't know. They just do. Sheriff and his boys always been out to get me. You know that."

"Do you have a lawyer?"

"Now where the hell am I gone get a lawyer?"

"Sheriff!" shouted a drunken prisoner downstairs. "Sheriff, come get this boy out of this tree."

Willingham yelled from the front room, "Shut up, Frank, and go back to sleep."

"You better get out of here, Tom," said Jimmie, "before the sheriff catches you."

"We've gotta do something, Jimmie."

"You can't do nothing, man. Now just get the fuck out of here. Go on home." His voice caught. Tears streamed from his eyes.

"Sheriff," the drunk yelled again, this time louder, "there's a boy up there in that oak tree, and he keeps waking me up."

A light came on in the downstairs hallway. As I scrambled down the tree, I saw Willingham standing in front of the drunk's cell and froze. He was looking down at the prisoner. "Now, Frank," he said, "I want you to shut up. You're just having DTs again."

"I'm telling you, sheriff, he was up there in that tree, talking to one of them niggers upstairs."

Willingham's gaze slowly rose toward the window as I dropped to the ground.

I couldn't chance getting caught in front of the jail, so I sprinted around back. A high chain link fence stood between me and the used car lot. My only way out was the way I'd come in. A flood light came on as I squeezed through the gap in the planks, bathing the entire parking area.

"Hey, boy!" the sheriff yelled. "You stop right there."

I prayed he hadn't recognized me. I didn't need problems with the law. If I could just get away for a moment maybe I could figure out a way to help Jimmie. I knew the sheriff couldn't catch me. The least of my worries was him squeezing his fat ass through that small hole and coming after me. One of the nephews shouted something from around front. He'd run out onto Collier Street to cut me off in case I doubled back. I crossed the abandoned property and scrambled over another fence, oblivious to the thorns tearing at my face and clothes.

A narrow alley led to an unpaved street lined with unlit tarpaper shacks. I stepped cautiously, fearing I might trip over something in the darkness. From a nearby henhouse came the cackling of chickens. A dog barked from beneath one of the houses and a man yelled something from inside. I ran back to the IGA parking lot and jumped into my truck.

Sitting there, catching my breath, I pulled thorns from my flesh and clothes. Spots appeared before my eyes. Gazing up and down the street, I saw no sign of the sheriff or his deputies. I figured they must have given up and gone back to the jail.

As I cranked my engine and started to pull out, another pickup passed on the street. In its cab were three men. In the back sat five more. It turned down Collier toward the jail with its headlights off. Behind it came seven more vehicles. Some of the men wore felt hats pulled down low. Others wore hoods. They all appeared to have guns.

This was not good. I pulled in behind the last truck as it passed, never questioning where it was going. When we arrived at the jail, men poured out and ran up the steps. One carried a long rope, about an inch thick, with a noose tied in one end.

Willingham stood in the doorway, his nephews cowering behind him. "Now what are you boys doing here?" His voice shook as he struggled to convince himself he was in control. He had that same stupid grin I'd seen at the country club that morning. He was scared shitless.

The men in front of him carried guns and they all began to yell at once. One of them, the apparent leader, screamed at Willingham to get out of his way.

Willingham seemed to know him despite the hood hiding his face. Later he'd swear he didn't. Neither he nor his nephews reached for their guns.

55

There was no way I could get through that crowd. Instead, I dropped back into the darkness and ran around the building, finding no one there.

From the back door I could see all the way down the hallway to the front. The sheriff, his nephews and an aging trustee stood with their backs to me. The crowd argued and yelled from the foot of the steps. I could see the tops of their heads but not their eyes and was sure they couldn't see me.

To open Jimmie's cell door, I had to get the keys, which I'd seen hanging in the front office earlier. I padded down the hall, crouching low and staying close to the bars so no one could see me from the front. I didn't look inside any of the cells for fear an inmate, like the drunk I'd heard earlier, might give me away. None of them made a sound.

The sheriff's office had a large window facing out onto the street. The hallway was a good twelve feet from the front door. Reflected in the windowpanes the keys dangled from a nail just inches away. I knelt, slipped my arm around the corner and grasped them as gently as I could so as not to make a sound.

Outside the mob grew louder. One man shouted, "We're gonna hang that boy, Sheriff, and there ain't a damned thing you can do about it. Get the hell out of our way, or we'll hang you and your nephews with him."

I sprinted down the hall toward the stairway at the end. *Then my luck ran out.*

From behind me came the echo of running feet. "Hey, boy, what're you doing there?"

As I reached the stairs a sharp blow caught the back of my head and a light exploded inside my skull. Total blackness overcame me, and the last thing I heard was the clatter of the keys hitting the floor.

Floating in a dark void, I heard voices as if from another room. I couldn't understand what they said. Footsteps reverberated on the linoleum floor and up the staircase. I could no longer remember where they were going.

The sounds faded and I found myself in a place so bright I couldn't make out anything around me. Gradually the light dimmed.

A distant voice called out, "Tommy." It was my mother.

"Where am I?"

"Tommy… Tommy, you have to go back. You don't belong here, not yet."

I had no idea where "here" was, but part of me wanted to stay. Part of me wanted to wake up. And every bit of me wanted the past twenty-four hours to go away.

Time passed. There were new voices, softer and somewhere just above my head, a man's and a woman's. As I awoke my stomach lurched into my throat. I tried to open my eyes but instead turned my head and puked.

I had no idea where I was or what had happened. At first, I thought I was at home in bed. I tried again to open my eyes, but the overhead lights shone so bright I had to close them. Waves of pain tumbled through my head like an empty beer can bouncing down a highway. I almost passed out again.

The man's voice said, "Watch out there, Tom. Just lie back down. You're not going anywhere yet."

It was Doc Green. "You took a nasty bump and you're dehydrated from throwing up. We're going to take you to the hospital now and get some fluids in you. You know, I'm not always gonna be around to patch you up every time you get into one of these scrapes. You're gonna have to take better care of yourself."

Though he tried to comfort me, the strain in his voice was obvious. It sounded like a distant echo, the noise a tin cup makes when it falls onto a tiled floor.

I tried to turn away from the harsh overheads, but all I could do was roll my head to one side, something I instantly regretted. For a moment I could almost focus. I was on my back in a jail cell lying on a bare, blue-and-white-striped mattress. Overcome by the smell of urine and stale sweat, I tried to throw up again, but all I could manage were dry heaves. Then it came back to me, where I was and what had happened.

When I finally opened one eye, I made out the shapes of three faces, swimming slowly in circles above me. Doc Green crouched beside me. "Here, let me take a look at you." He pried open each lid and flashed a light in my eye.

Beside him in a folding chair sat my grandmother, and behind her stood Sheriff Willingham. His grin had gone now. In its place was an embarrassed and frightened look I'd never seen. His face had a greenish cast, the way the sky looks just before a tornado. In that moment I knew that Jimmie was dead. In less than twenty-four hours I'd lost my two best friends.

I closed my eyes again and prayed quietly. After what seemed an eternity, four hands slowly lifted me and lowered me onto a stretcher. My head spun faster. I opened my eyes for a split second. Two Black orderlies in starched white uniforms wheeled me headfirst down the hallway toward the back.

As I passed one of the cells a grating, nasal voice rang in my ears like a spoon against the metal bars. "That's him, Sheriff. That's him. He's that boy what was up in the tree out there talking to that nigger they hanged."

"Now, Frank, am I gonna have to come in there and beat your head in?" Willingham asked in a low voice. He was right next to the gurney. He leaned over me so close I could smell the bourbon and cigarettes on his breath. "I saved your life tonight, boy," he whispered. "Now you just remember that. Those men were gonna string you up right out there with your friend. I was the one who stopped them. I was the one who pulled you out of their way. I saved your life." He almost pleaded for me to believe him. It was just as well that I couldn't reply.

The ambulance faced the street with its rear doors open. The orderlies jostled the gurney as they tried to roll it over the crushed shells and gravel. Finally, they gave up, lifted it, and carried me the few remaining feet. They folded the wheels under it and placed me inside.

In those days Jasper Memorial Hospital had only two ambulances. Somehow, I knew this was the one that had carried Dana's lifeless body only hours earlier.

Just before the door closed I made the mistake of forcing my eyes open one more time. They had parked beneath the live oak. So long as I live I will carry that image of Jimmie illuminated by the taillights of the ambulance, swinging barefoot from the same limb I'd climbed onto less than an hour earlier. From the darkness nearby I heard Ida and Ruby wailing and sobbing.

Chapter Eight

For the next four days I was a guest of Jasper Memorial. It was Monday before I could manage the short walk down the hall to the lobby. My only guests were my grandmother and our pastor, Don Fullerton. My Aunt Phyllis phoned from Pensacola to see how I was doing.

People around me spoke in hushed tones or gave me strange looks. Others would shut up and look the other way when they saw me coming. Nobody mentioned Dana's murder or what had happened at the jail. Maybe they thought by ignoring these things they could make them go away.

On Wednesday morning I left the hospital under strict orders from Doc Green to go home and take it easy. By late afternoon I thought I would lose my mind. I felt better physically, as long as I avoided the swollen knot on the back of my head. Ida was still at home grieving for her dead son, and my grandmother fussed over me constantly.

I waited until she went back to the kitchen and then got up slowly and put on my clothes. I shouted from the living room that I was going for a walk, hoping I could get out the door before she stopped me.

As I backed onto the porch there came a familiar, cheerful voice. "Well now, it seems that you're going to live after all." Jenny Maxwell stood at bottom of the steps.

"Hey." The late afternoon sun in my eyes made me wince.

"I thought I might come by and see how you were doing. I want you to know that I think it was a very brave and very foolish thing you did."

"Well, it didn't exactly work, did it?"

"It's not your fault, Tom. At least you tried." Her voice softened as she reached out and brushed her hand across my face. "Are you up for a walk?"

I glanced back through the living room window. My grandmother stood in the dining room doorway. She gave me an exasperated look, turned and walked back into the kitchen without a word.

"Sure."

I moved slowly at first, not yet certain how my legs would hold up. The fresh air and soft breeze felt good on my face. We saw neighbors in their yards. Some smiled and waved, but they made no effort to speak to us. They were getting on with their lives, ignoring the fact that two innocent people had been murdered in this small town only four days earlier.

They, no doubt, believed that Jimmie had killed Dana. I'm sure there were those who thought Dana brought it all on herself by the way she dressed and acted. They found comfort in their ignorance.

"I don't get these people," I said. "They don't give a damn."

"What do you expect, Tom? Nobody wants to believe this sort of thing can happen in a town like Monrovia. And when it does happen, they don't want to face it or even think about it. They just want a simple explanation that makes it easy for them to believe it's all over and done. Most of these people are decent enough. They probably have no idea who lynched Jimmie, and they actually believe that he murdered Dana."

I eyed her sharply. "What do you think?"

She looked away from me and her expression changed. "I think something is definitely wrong here, but I just don't know what anybody can do about it."

"How can those assholes get away with this? This isn't the thirties, you know. Why isn't the FBI down here investigating?"

"Actually, there were a couple of FBI agents here yesterday questioning Sheriff Willingham."

"And …"

"And I'm sure nothing will come of it. The sheriff issued a statement to the newspapers, saying he had no idea who the members of the lynch mob were. The ones he saw were all wearing hoods. The FBI agents may come back and ask more questions, but they won't get anything out of him. You know things are pretty bad when even the sheriff is afraid of the crooks."

"Are the reporters still here?"

"No. I think someone convinced them to leave town. The only story I saw was on the back pages of the *Times-Union*. They referred to Jimmie as a *suspect* in the murder of Dana Padgett."

Gently I took her by the shoulders. I turned her to me, looked into her eyes and spoke distinctly in low tones. "You and I both know Jimmie was innocent. I'm going to find out who killed Dana, and who was behind this lynching, and when I do …"

"What are you going to do?" She put her arms around my waist and stared up at me. "Be careful, Tom. If you start asking too many questions something bad could happen to you. I just couldn't bear the thought of that."

I was taken aback by her concern. "I'll just have to take that chance. I can't sit back and let those animals get away with this, and the sheriff sure as hell won't do anything. When I find out who did this, Jenny, they're going to pay."

"Then you'll be no better than they are."

"What do you expect me to do? How can you stand to live in a town like this?"

"I can't."

I stared back at her in shock. I'd never pictured Jenny Maxwell wanting to live anywhere else. Her family and friends were here. She'd always seemed like one of those people for whom the highway stopped at the Pelahatchie Bridge.

"Someday I'm going to marry someone, Tom, and when I do, I'll move as far away from here as I can."

She studied the ground at her feet for a moment then gazed back into my eyes. "You were in love with her, weren't you?" There was no accusation in the way she said it, just a flat, casual tone, as if she were asking me the time of day.

I turned and looked down the street at the late afternoon sky. It took me a couple of minutes to reply. "Yeah, I guess I was. How did you know?"

"I didn't until now."

"My God, that's all I need. I'm sure the whole damned town's talking about me and Dana."

"No. I don't think so. I guessed it from the look on your face. Besides, why should you care what people think? Most guys your age would be proud to have people know that they'd had an affair with the lovely Dana Padgett." She gave me a wry smile. "A thing like that could do a lot for your reputation." We turned and walked on.

"Look, Jenny, I'm sorry... I don't know what to say."

"It's okay, Tom. You don't need to say anything. You're a very special person to me and always will be. We've been out together... what, twice now? I just hope someday you can find some peace from all of this and come to terms with all you've been through. Otherwise, this will eat away at you until it kills you. You have to put it behind you and move on."

"Just like that? You expect me to forgive and forget?"

"I'm not asking you to forget. I seriously doubt you could do that. But you must forgive whoever did it, not for their sake, but for your own."

"Yeah, that sounds great! I'm not sure I can be that unselfish."

"Unselfish? Forgiving those who wrong you is not only right. It's the most selfish thing you can do. After all, you're the one who really benefits. This anger of yours is like a giant tumor. It will kill you."

"So, what do you expect me to do? How can I not be angry?"

"Well, to start with you can take ownership of your emotions."

"I can what?"

"You're angry because you choose to be angry. I know you have good reasons, but you can just as easily choose not to be angry."

"And how, exactly?"

"By admitting to yourself that there's nothing you could have done to stop the murders of Dana and Jimmie"

"Yeah. Sure."

"You have to admit to yourself that it's not your fault."

"I didn't say it was my fault." I realized I'd practically yelled at her and immediately said I was sorry. I didn't want to talk about it anymore. I stared into her eyes. They were the pale blue of a swimming pool on a bright summer day. Her alabaster complexion set off tiny freckles that dotted the bridge of her nose, and the corners of her lips curled into a beatific smile. I pulled her to me and kissed her. I didn't give a damn who saw us, or what they thought. I'm not sure why I did it, but it felt like the thing to do at the time.

If Jenny was shocked by my sudden affection, she didn't show it. She looked up at me for several minutes without saying anything.

When we reached Broad Street, we strolled past the shops across from the courthouse and stared in the windows. We avoided the jail, and I tried to put it out of my mind. It had rained earlier, and, under a blue sky and golden sunset, downtown Monrovia had the clean, fresh look of a Norman Rockwell painting.

A small group of men stood in front of the East End Barber Shop. They spoke just low enough that I couldn't hear them and clammed up as we approached. One of them was Bill Emmett, who gave me a broad smile and walked over to shake my hand. The other two stood by and looked on, their faces expressionless.

"Good afternoon, Miss Maxwell!" said Bill. "Tom, it's good to see you up and around, son." He took me by the shoulder with an earnest look. "You feeling better?"

"I'll be alright, Bill." I glanced at the two men and nodded but got no response. "Jenny and I are just out for a walk. I needed the exercise."

"That's good. That's good. I sure am glad to hear it. Well… you take care of yourself, hear?"

"Thanks, Bill. You do the same."

Jenny and I turned and crossed the street. Bill returned to his friends.

***

By the end of the week, I was well enough to drive out to see Ida. She had buried her son on the previous day, but there was still a dozen or so people at her house. The small yard was full of cars, and I had to park my truck in front of a neighbor's place down the road.

I tread carefully on the porch, as some of the boards were rotten and gave way under my feet. Peering through the rusted, torn screen door into the darkened living room, I could barely make out the faces staring back at me, but I could read clearly the suspicion written on every one of them.

"What do you want?" a man's voice growled at me from inside.

"I came to see Miss Ida."

He started to say something else when another voice called out, "Tom!" It was Ruby. "Come on in, Tom. I'll go tell Mama you're here. From the small bedroom in the back, I heard Ida crying. I felt awkward under the stares of the half dozen people seated there. I began to wish I hadn't intruded.

An old woman leaned forward from a chair in the corner and squinted at me. Cotton stuffing ballooned from its torn and stained fabric. The skin on her face crinkled like fine wrapping paper and her mouth opened to reveal what was left of dark stained teeth. "Ain't you the one tried to get Jimmie Lee out of that jail?"

"Yes ma'am."

She stared for a long time, her eyes narrowed. "I ain't never heard of nobody doing nothing like that. You are one crazy-ass white boy. You know that?"

I couldn't tell if she meant it as a compliment, but I thanked her anyway. I smiled and thought of the many times Jimmie had told me the same thing.

In the corner sat a man so wide it took two chairs to hold him. He wore a white three-piece suit and cordovan wingtips. He muttered something under his breath as he stared at me.

Ida came out for a moment. I hugged her and told her I was sorry. I couldn't think of anything else to say.

I nodded to Ida's guests and turned to leave. As I did, another face emerged from the gloom, that of Panky Carter.

Chapter Nine

My junior year began Tuesday, September 2, that Monday being a holiday. On the following Saturday I finally purchased the Bellaire convertible from George Martin. As I was underage, my grandmother went with me to sign the paperwork. She drove the truck home while I went by to pick up Jenny.

"Tom," Jenny said. "I have a wonderful idea! Let's drive up to White Springs for a picnic. We can pack a lunch and dine by the river. What do you think?"

"Sounds good to me"

With considerable effort and assurances that I was a careful driver Jenny convinced her parents to let us go. She packed some sandwiches and a thermos of iced tea while I called my grandmother and got her permission.

***

The Stephen Foster Memorial at White Springs, named for the composer of such minstrel ballads as "Oh Susannah" and "Old Folks at Home," was about an hour from Monrovia.

Jenny and I spread a blanket in the shade of a weeping willow where we ate our lunch and watched the Suwanee River swirl past. Neither of us said anything for a long a time.

"So," she finally asked, "are you happy with your new car?"

I gave her a bright smile. "It's great… and I get to drive it around with the cutest girl in town beside me." From where we lay, I could see it in the near corner of the parking lot, gleaming in the midday sun.

Whether I was happy or not was a much tougher question. Leaning back against the blanket, I felt the grass crinkle beneath me and smelled its sweet aroma. I closed my eyes and let the sun warm my face. A shadow passed over. I opened my eyes as Jenny leaned close staring intently. A smile fluttered across her lips.

"Well, I'm glad." She stroked my chest and kissed me softly. "You know you're such a sweet guy, Tom, but you seem so distant. What's bothering you?"

"Nothing's bothering me."

"You don't hang out with other people, except when you're with me. It seems all you want to do is work and study. You're a great runner, but you don't play football, basketball, or any other team sport. You could at least go out for the track team. They could use someone like you."

"Maybe I don't want to play a team sport."

"Your daddy was one of the best football players Monrovia has ever known."

"Well, I'm not my daddy, okay?"

I caught myself. "Look, I'm sorry. I shouldn't have snapped at you."

"That's okay, Tom. I didn't mean to upset you. I just want you to be happy."

"I know you do, and I appreciate that. It's just that… you're the only person I want to hang out with. Hell, you're the only person I can talk to, besides Clara, and, well… she's a little old for me." I smiled and wrapped her in my arms. "Is that okay with you?"

"I guess that's okay." She slid down onto the blanket and laid her head on my shoulder. The upturned curl of her hair tickled my face. "Where do you see us going, Tom?"

I groped for some innocuous, noncommittal answer. "What do you mean?"

"I mean, where do you see us two years from now, after we've graduated?"

This was not exactly a 'How do you like your new car?' question. It had all manner of implications and perils. The simple truth was that no matter how much I cared for Jenny, no matter how comfortable I felt with her, we came from different worlds. I had no mental image of us spending the rest of our lives together. I had places to go and things to experience. I couldn't imagine her wanting to come with me. I couldn't lie to her, yet I couldn't bear the idea of hurting her.

We laid back and looked for images amid the gathering clouds above. I nuzzled her hair with my nose. The aroma of tropical shampoo reminded me of Dana.

"I don't know, Jenny. I mean, I'm going to Florida and you're going to Agnes Scott. Gainesville's a long way from Atlanta. I just wish there were some way we could continue to see each other…"

I let it hang there, hoping she'd grasp the hopelessness of the situation.

She took a deep breath. "I guess you're right. There's a part of me that wants to shout that I'll change my plans and go to Gainesville just so I can be with you, but we both know better. Even if my parents would allow it, which I doubt, I'd be passing up an opportunity that means so much to me. I'd always feel like I'd given up my dreams just to help you pursue yours. In time I'd come to resent that, and perhaps even resent you, and that wouldn't be fair."

I knew I could count on her. Jenny was the most sensible girl I'd ever known. With her head resting on my shoulder, it was all I could do to keep from letting out a sigh of relief. And yet, at some level, I knew someone had laid a treasure at my feet and I was walking away from it.

We lay there quietly for a long time, exhausted from so much meaningful conversation. Through closed eyes I felt another shadow pass. A cool breeze stirred, and for a moment I reveled in it. Then reality hit me in the face, literally, as a raindrop smacked me on the cheek.

"My car...!" I shouted. I'd left the top down and my brand-new upholstery would be soaked. I slid my arm out from under Jenny, leapt to my feet and grabbed the picnic basket. She picked up the blanket and other loose items and followed.

In the short time it took us to get to the car the rain grew to a steady downpour. I vaulted over the driver's side door, without taking time to open the other side for Jenny. I cranked the engine and closed the roof.

She climbed in and we sat looking at each other. The flip of her hair was gone now. It hung straight to her shoulder. A spray of raindrops dotted her face. Our clothes were drenched. A drop hung momentarily from the tip of her nose and then fell into her lap. She crossed her eyes watching it. We broke into laughter at the same time.

"That's a good look for you," I said, and pushed her wet hair back from her face.

She poked me in the ribs and then grasped my face in both hands. Pulling me close she kissed me hard on the lips.

"You're incredibly beautiful," I told her, "and the most wonderful girl I've ever known."

She smiled, but as she turned away tears glistened in her eyes.

On the way back to Monrovia we made small talk for a while, and then, apropos of nothing, she asked, "What do you dream about?"

"You really don't want to know what I dream about."

"I want to know everything about you, Tom Williams."

I stared at the white line ahead. "Sometimes I dream I'm wading through a swamp, waste-deep in black water and hyacinths. There are cottonmouths and alligators surrounding me, and I don't know where to go. In the distance I see my dad coming toward me in a flat bottom boat, pushing it with a long pole. He's calling to me, but he'll never get there in time. The gators are circling closer … and then I wake up sweating and shaking. The crazy thing is I'm not afraid of snakes or even gators when I'm awake. Hell, I've been fishing in these swamps more times than I can remember."

"Maybe there's something else you're afraid of and you don't know what it is, so you see snakes and alligators instead."

"What do you dream about?" I had to change the subject.

"I dream of all sorts of things… Sometimes I dream I can fly."

"Wow! What's that supposed to mean?"

"Who knows? Maybe it means I want to spread my wings and fly away from Monrovia."

We laughed. That dream was the one thing we had in common.

***

Jenny and I dated through most of our junior year. She went to church with my grandmother and me on occasions. The lady on the pew in front of us would nearly break her neck turning around to look at us. To her this must have seemed like a serious relationship. But in the entire time I dated Jenny I never once pictured us as a married couple with children and a white picket fence like her parents.

Ted and Betty Maxwell were the two most genial people I'd ever known, but when it came to protecting Jenny they might as well have been Dobermans. I had to have her home by ten and they'd wait up until we got there. If even once we'd been late that would have been the end of our dating.

I'd pull up in front of their house and hop out of the car to open the door for her. Any making out or long discussions had to take place somewhere else. From the street we could see her parents sitting in their living room in their bath robes, flickering television images reflected in their faces. To this day I believe they could see us outside in the dark without bothering to come to the window.

Ted Maxwell was one of three doctors in Monrovia and had a very successful practice. Slight of build, he favored brown loafers, short-sleeved white shirts, and wool slacks. He wore beige sweaters on all but the hottest days and reminded me of Robert Young in *Father Knows Best*, only younger.

Betty was a petite blonde who must have been quite pretty in her day before the worry lines and the weight gain. When I visited it was always Betty who met me at the door, gushing with enthusiasm and offering me an overstuffed, high-backed wing chair in the living room. There I'd wait for Jenny to make her entrance. It was unthinkable that *she* should meet me at the door. It would've been un-ladylike and would have made her appear overly eager.

Jenny would descend the stairs, greet me with a smile and seat herself on the opposite side of the room in her mom's chair. We'd talk about the weather and the latest news while the ever-attentive Betty ran back and forth with sweet tea and cookies which I politely declined. I was sure no one had ever actually eaten in this room.

The Maxwells had a rat terrier who watched me even more closely than Betty, alternately barking or taking refuge in Jenny's lap. I'd smile and make little noises at him, all the while contemplating just how far I could drop-kick him.

By spring Jenny and I drifted apart. I'd never thought of this as anything more than a deep friendship and told myself that was all she expected.

Whether that was true, I'll never know. Jenny showed a genuine interest in me, but never expressed anything more serious. When we finally broke up we promised to remain close, and for a while we did. Over time, however, we saw each other less and less. We'd stop and talk, but never for long. I'm sure she had tired of my brooding over the deaths of Dana and Jimmie. She needed, and deserved, someone more fun to be with.

In my spare time I tried to find out everything I could about Dana's murder, but there was no one I could talk to. Benny Stillman and Victor Molina had found her, but Benny was afraid to discuss it, and Victor just wanted to forget about it. I doubted they knew any more about the matter than I did.

Even if I'd had the guts to sit down and talk to Mike Padgett, I couldn't. A few months after the murders he sold his house and the radio station and left town.

Often I'd see someone who looked like Dana or Jimmie, perhaps on a crowded sidewalk. In the early months after the murders, I'd awaken in the morning thinking it had been nothing but a bad dream. Then the images returned, Dana lying in the pile of leaves, Jimmie hanging from the live oak.

Chapter Ten

Dearest friends, tonight we gather for our last time as the Monrovia High Class of 1960. This is the moment we've long awaited, anticipated, and perhaps dreaded. We've known each other all our lives. I doubt any of us even thought of this night twelve years ago, in the fall of 1948, when that school bell rang and we filed in off the playground for our first-grade classes, but here we are at the culmination of those twelve years, our graduation commencement...

—Jennifer Elizabeth Maxwell;
Valedictorian, Monrovia High School Class of 1960

I spent my senior year working and studying harder than ever, mostly for lack of anything better to do. I ran every day regardless of the weather. It helped me tune out the world and forget, if only for a moment, the things I'd seen. Otherwise, I'd have gone nuts.

On the one occasion I tried to discuss the killings with Clara, she said Jimmie and Dana were gone and nothing I could do would bring them back. I'd be better off, she said, focusing my talents on things I could change. She made me promise that when I graduated, I would leave Monrovia and never look back.

It was the easiest promise I ever made. Two days before the commencement I'd already packed. I considered skipping graduation, but I knew how much it meant to my grandmother. I sat through a three-hour ordeal in that stifling auditorium before the principal finally got to the W's.

The only part of the ceremony that meant anything to me was Jenny's valedictory address. She showed tremendous courage in the things she said and ignored catcalls from some of our classmates. As I gazed at her I couldn't believe I'd once dated someone so brave and beautiful. I thought of how proud I was to have known her.

When it was all over I took my diploma, flipped my tassel, and gave Jenny a long farewell hug. I waved at my grandmother and kissed Monrovia High goodbye.

***

Through most of that summer I stayed with my Aunt Phyllis in Pensacola and worked for her husband, Frank, in his pharmacy. Frank and Phyllis lived in a 1950s middle-class neighborhood north of town. Over the years, as the pharmacy prospered, they replaced their asbestos siding with aluminum and added a master bedroom, bath and family room on the back.

The other houses on the street changed little over the years. They were practically identical and sat on small, square lots laid out on a grid. Years later, when I first heard the song "Little Boxes" by Pete Seeger, it was the image of that neighborhood that came to mind.

Though I hadn't seen them in recent years I had fond memories of Frank and Phyllis. They sent me Christmas and birthday presents and vacationed at the coast with us several times before my parents died.

The beaches from Apalachicola to Pensacola are among the most beautiful in the world. The Atlantic shores have higher waves, and the ones further south longer swimming seasons, but the sugar-white sand and crystal blue water of the Panhandle more than compensate.

Frank's pharmacy sat on a corner of Gadsden Street. It had a large soda fountain and a lunch counter which, like others throughout the South in those days, was for white patrons only.

I'd come in early in the morning, clean up before we opened and re-stock the shelves. Then I'd work the lunch counter until two, wash the silver and glassware and change into my swim trunks in the stock room. From the pharmacy it was a fifteen-minute drive across the bay to Perdido Key.

One afternoon in late July I was on my way there with the top down and the sea breeze caressing my face. The sun shone high and bright in the sky. I hadn't quite reached the bridge, but from atop a rise I could glimpse the endless, blue water. Sidewalks teemed with vacationers shopping for floats, towels, and suntan lotion. On the radio the Ventures played "Walk, Don't Run," one of the greatest beach songs of all time.

When the song ended an announcer came on with a brief local news and weather report. His voice sounded oddly familiar. I was about to change the channel when he said, "This is your host, Mike Padgett. And now, continuing our countdown, here is Ben E. King singing "Save the Last Dance for Me." I jammed my brakes and made a U-turn to the sounds of blaring horns and curses from angry drivers.

The station was just outside town on US 90 near the backwaters of the bay. I passed it every day on my way to work. A low, white stucco affair, it sat at the edge of a stand of pines with an asphalt parking lot not much bigger than a postage stamp. The tall, orange and white tower commanded the skyline for miles around.

The cool embrace of its air conditioning welcomed me as I strolled into the tiny lobby. A blonde receptionist with perfect, white teeth greeted me from behind a low desk. She wore a starched, white button-down shirt open to her navel, revealing what appeared to be an orange bathing suit top. Her matching orange shorts looked like someone had painted them on her. She must have been all of sixteen.

"Welcome to WUTF Radio. How may I help you?" she said with a broad smile.

I stood for a moment, not knowing what to say. In my swim trunks, sunglasses and flip-flops I must have looked like a tourist who'd taken a wrong turn on his way to the beach.

"I was wondering if I could speak to Mr. Padgett."

"He's in the control room at the moment, but I'll let him know he has a guest. I'm sure he'll be right out. Just have a seat over there. Can I get you a Pepsi?"

"No thanks."

I sank into a lime green vinyl couch beside a potted palm. The room had no windows. Light from outside filtered in through a curved, glass block accent wall that formed the corner of the building. Over the intercom Roy Orbison sang *Only the Lonely*."

Moments later, as though in response to some silent cue, the girl rose from her chair and disappeared through a doorway. She returned with Mike Padgett in tow.

He'd gained weight in the two years since I'd last seen him. The slicked back hairline had receded, and gray strands gathered along his temples. But he had the same arrogant, condescending smile. "Good afternoon. Is there something I can do for you?" He'd no sooner said it than his expression evolved from puzzlement to recognition, irritation and hostility. "What the hell do you want?"

"Look, I'm sorry to bother you. I just thought maybe there was somewhere we could talk."

"Talk about what? I have nothing to talk to you about, least of all my late wife or that piss-ant town of yours."

It had taken me half an hour to get there in traffic, and I'd spent all that time thinking about what to say. I'd never been good in awkward situations.

"Mike, I hate to bring up bad memories. It just bothers me that someone could do something like that to D…, your wife, and get away with it."

He was incredulous. "Are you suffering from amnesia?" he screamed. "It was that nigger friend of yours who did it. That fucking animal got exactly what he deserved."

Behind him the receptionist's eyes widened. She slid down in her chair as if about to crawl under her desk.

"Jimmie didn't do it, Mike. He was just a convenient fall guy for the sheriff, and you know it. All Willingham wanted to do was close the investigation as quickly as possible. He couldn't have cared less who the real murderer was. Hell, he probably *knows* who did it. Jimmie had no reason to kill your wife or anybody else." I paused for a moment then added, "I was just wondering if you might know anybody who did have a reason."

"What… do you think I killed her?" He moved a step closer. For a moment I expected him to take a swing at me.

"No. I don't. I just thought… Look, I'm sorry I bothered you." I felt like a fool. I turned and sidled toward the door just in case he decided to jump me.

He started to and stopped. His shoulders sagged, and he seemed to age another ten years. "Look, I knew she was running around on me. Everybody in town knew it." He paused a moment and glanced back at his receptionist. His voice softened. "But I didn't kill her. I never even raised a hand against her. I loved my wife very much." His eyes teared up. "If I ever found out who was screwing her I'll probably kill *him* instead."

I could see he meant it and was glad he didn't know who that guy was. Now I felt like an asshole for what I'd done and for coming here and bothering him.

He eased down onto the green couch and put his hands over his face. "I went to the bank one day," he said, "and discovered she'd taken out a large sum of money. I walked in and found her packing. We had a big argument. She swore she wasn't having an affair. She just needed to get away for a while.

"Of course, I didn't believe her. I'd seen the way other men looked at her. As far as I knew she was screwing all of them. We talked for a long time and finally she unpacked. She told me she'd changed her mind and would stay. Maybe I'm gullible, but I believed her. Anyway, I went out of town the next day on a fishing trip. When I got back, she was dead. After that all I wanted to do was get the hell out of that God-forsaken hole and start over somewhere else."

I moved to put my hand on his shoulder but stopped. "Mike, I... I'm sorry. I should never have come here. I promise I'll never bother you again." I turned and left him sitting there.

That afternoon as I sat on the beach and watched the slow, smooth curl of the waves I ran over again in my mind the things he'd said. I was no closer to finding out who'd killed Dana and probably never would be. Mike Padgett had moved on, and it was my turn to do the same.

Chapter Eleven

For the rest of that summer, I worked in the pharmacy and relaxed on the beach. I found a new radio station and never saw Mike Padgett again. In the fall I left for Gainesville where I began my freshman year.

I wrote for the campus newspaper and took pictures with a Nikon I bought at a pawn shop. I covered political campaigns, including the Kennedy-Nixon election and saw both candidates when they visited the state. In October 1962 a friend and I drove to Tampa with a couple of sleeping bags. We took pictures of troop trucks streaming into MacDill Air Force Base in response to the Cuban Missile Crisis. On November 22, 1963, I was in psychology class when an administrator appeared at the doorway, her eyes filled with tears. President Kennedy had been shot in Dallas.

Upon graduation, for want of anything better to do, I enlisted in the Coast Guard. My first stop was basic training at Cape May, on the southern tip of New Jersey. One evening, as we fell in for supper, our company commander made a brief announcement.

"Gentlemen, early this morning the destroyer USS Maddox came under fire from North Vietnamese patrol boats in the Gulf of Tonkin. I don't have the details yet, but she was on a reconnaissance mission near a group of South Vietnamese islands."

The Chief had drilled us all day. It was suppertime, and I was hungry. My only thought at that moment was "What in the hell does this have to do with me?" If only I'd known.

In the spring of 1965, the Treasury Department dispatched Coast Guard Squadron One to Vietnam. It comprised forty-seven officers and 198 enlisted men, among them one Petty Officer First Class Thomas S.

Williams. For some unknown reason this dumbass never learned the cardinal rule of all military services, *Never volunteer for anything*.

That night I called my grandmother from a pay phone.

"Hey, Grandmama. I'm in California. In a few weeks we ship out to Southeast Asia."

There was a long pause on the other end. "Tom, what have you gone and done?"

"It's a job, Grandmama. Somebody's gotta do it."

"It's a job where people get killed, Tom! It's a war, for Pete's sake!"

"Technically it's not a real war."

"Yeah, well *technically* they'll be shooting real bullets at you."

"I'll be okay, Grandmama. I swear!"

Another long pause. "I've lost my husband and my only child." She spoke more softly, her voice cracking. "You're all I have left, Tom ... You remember that."

"I will, Grandmama. I'll be alright."

When we arrived at Da Nang on July 24 I ran into an old shipmate from Cape May, a tall, freckle-faced North Carolina redneck named Kevin "Sandy" Sandifer. We were never buddies in boot camp, but I was happy to see somebody I knew.

Over the next fifteen months we patrolled the Vietnamese coast. We stopped and searched junks and fishing vessels for small arms and supplies bound for the VC. Most days we were bored shitless. The occasional incidents were minor, and overall, we were successful in our mission.

On shore leave we'd hit the bars in Da Nang. One night, Sandy and I picked up a couple of girls in a dimly lit bar. Our entertainment that evening was a Vietnamese man with an electric piano. He tried to play Beatle songs over the din of drunken sailors and Marines. A couple of wire service correspondents sat in one corner writing accounts of battles they'd probably never seen.

Sandy had been drinking scotch and sodas for hours. I'd have to steer his ass back to the base, hopefully without running into shore patrol. I nursed a gin and tonic while one of the girls sat in my lap. The other leaned against Sandy, who had one hand halfway up the slit in her silk dress.

He picked up his drink, downed it, and stared at me through bleary eyes. "Now, why in the hell … did you volunteer for duty in Vietnam?" He pronounced it "Vee-yet-namm," the way Lyndon Johnson did.

I gave him a wry smile. "I guess I'm here to defend democracy, like everybody else, how about you?"

"Hah!" he snorted and nearly fell out of his chair. "I came here so I could shoot some gooks… present company excluded," he added as he looked at the girls.

Neither of them said anything.

I'd known bigots like Sandy all my life. To him these people were all the same unless he wanted to screw one of them.

The girl leaned over, nibbled on his ear and whispered something. He dug into his wallet and handed her twenty dollars.

She said something in Vietnamese to the girl on my lap, who ran her hand over my crotch and said, "We be back real soon. We go powder our noses."

They disappeared while Sandy continued to drink. When neither of them returned, I coaxed him into a cab and took him back to the base.

A week later, Sandy and I returned. We were a block away when a young man on a bicycle deposited a large satchel near an open doorway and rode off. Seconds later an explosion reduced the building to rubble, killing fifty-two people, among them twelve sailors and marines.

My ears rang for days, but neither of us suffered permanent injury.

Unfinished Business

***

On October 14, 1966, my luck ran out. At about 1500 hours we spotted an aging junk with what appeared to be four men and a woman. I grabbed my M-16 and took up position on the port bow as we pulled alongside. An old man sat in front. He grinned as he squinted into the sun, his eyes narrow slits in a craggy face. A black hole gaped at me where there should have been teeth.

I smiled back and waved. Behind him two men were coiling rope. Another sat in the stern. Everyone seemed friendly. A young woman waved at me from the wheelhouse.

Suddenly from the corner of my eye I saw one of them slide his hand under a tarp. In a fluid motion he pulled out an AK47 and opened fire.

On instinct I hit the deck. Pain seared through my right thigh. Above me a 50-caliber erupted. I looked up to see Sandy. Though I couldn't hear him over the gunfire, I read his lips, "Die you mother-fuckers!"

As quickly as it began it was over. I struggled to sit up, squeezing my leg and staring in disbelief. Purplish blood poured from a ragged tear in my denim pantleg revealing torn muscle tissue but no indication of arterial bleeding. A corpsman was there before I knew it. He wrapped my belt above the wound while another seaman lifted me from the deck.

The last thing I saw before I blacked out was the remains of the man who'd shot me, his face a red, pulverized mass, the back of his head gone, gray and white brain matter littering the ropes and canvas where he lay.

Tossed about like rag dolls were four other people, various body parts missing. The shattered deck was awash with blood. A row of holes dotted the hull just above the waterline as she listed to port. Amid all this carnage lay the body of a small child I hadn't noticed earlier. He couldn't have been more than four.

I awoke at a U.S. hospital in Da Nang, still groggy from morphine. Three weeks later an Air Force jet evacuated several of us to a San Francisco hospital known, unofficially, as the "Pussy Palace." Sadly, for me it never lived up to its name.

There I underwent physical therapy and, with the help of a cane, gradually regained my ability to walk. I transferred across the bay to Alameda, where my Vietnam tour began two years earlier. There I received an honorable discharge and a Purple Heart, which I later gave to my grandmother. After all I'd put her through, I figured she deserved it more than I did.

Like everyone else, I'd grown up in a black-and-white world. We watched black-and-white television. The good guys wore white hats. The bad guys wore black. Our communities and schools were segregated into Black and white. Our newspapers had no color, except for the Sunday comics. This shaped our view of the world. There was right and there was wrong. Most people knew the difference… or said they did. When you did something you weren't supposed to, you prayed for forgiveness and hoped like hell you didn't get caught.

The events of my high school years and my experiences in Vietnam changed all that. I came home from war, as my dad had, years before, to a world forever changed.

It was the "sixties." Everything was in color now. Barriers crumbled. Things we'd always done in secret, we now did in the open.

Chapter Twelve

"We are the unwilling, led by the unqualified, to do the unnecessary on behalf of the ungrateful."

—Popular wall poster in 1968 depicting US soldiers in Vietnam

I returned to Monrovia in July 1967 on a commercial jet out of San Francisco, compliments of the U. S. Coast Guard. There's an old joke that if you die in the South it doesn't matter whether you go to Heaven or Hell, you'll have to make a connection in Atlanta. I arrived at Hartsfield International Airport on an early morning flight and changed to a much smaller plane bound for Tallahassee. I knew I was there when we flew in over the cornfield at the end of the runway.

I was a month shy of twenty-five. In my brief career I'd been a student, a pharmacy clerk and a shallow water sailor. I wasn't sure what to do with the rest of my life, but I knew I wasn't going back to a tobacco field or to Swift's IGA.

My grandmother met me at the airport with a broad smile and tears streaming down her face. She seemed smaller than I remembered. I did my best not to limp as I ran to her and pulled her into my arms. I drove her back to Monrovia and carried my sea bag to my room. Throughout the trip her only comment was, "Thank God! You're home."

This was a very different homecoming from my dad's. There was no parade, no mayoral proclamation, and no cheering crowds. People I'd known all my life simply stopped and stared. Guys my age were wearing their hair longer now. With my crew cut I must've looked like an alien.

Friends and neighbors told me how glad they were that I'd come home safely, but none of them asked about the war or the things I did over there, which was just fine with me. I didn't want to talk about it anyway. Still, it would have been nice if, after I'd spent two years watching friends die in a foreign land, after I'd nearly lost my life, supposedly in the defense of our country, just one person had walked up and said, "Thanks."

Instead, they went on with their self-centered lives as though Vietnam were just another television show, a survivalist holiday, summer camp with live ammunition. I saw freaks on TV who wouldn't have lasted an hour in 'Nam calling me and my shipmates "baby killers." It made me sick to think that these were the same folks I almost died for.

The only ones who made me madder were the guys who said they supported the war while they hid out on college campuses, protected by their 2S deferments. To them the war was fine, so long as some other poor son-of-a-bitch did the fighting and dying.

I thought a lot about Jenny. It would've been nice to go by and see her, but I heard she was living in Atlanta now. I avoided the rest of my high school friends. At this point I really didn't care if I never saw them again. Instead, I began, as my father had done, putting my life back together and making up the time I'd lost.

For as long as I could remember, I'd wanted to be a reporter. At the university I wrote for the school newspaper. I kept a diary when I was in Vietnam and took pictures whenever possible. At this point in my life, I had nothing to lose.

My grandmother mentioned Pug Donovan, a fraternity brother of my dad's, who went to work for a newspaper in Tampa and covered the war in Europe. When my dad and his friends returned from the Pacific, Donovan came to Monrovia to cover their celebration. In 1953 he wrote another story, about the accident that claimed my parents' lives.

Pug was now editor of the *Tampa Sentinel*. I called him to see if I could get a job interview. He answered the phone as though I'd interrupted him in the middle of something. When he demanded to know who I was and why I was calling, I almost hung up.

Instead, I introduced myself and said I wanted to write for his paper. He paused for a moment and then agreed to an interview.

***

So, on a bright, blue August morning I packed some clothes in my grandfather's old leather suitcase. I put it in the back of my now decrepit Chevy Bellaire along with my Olivetti portable typewriter and drove to Tampa. With me I brought file boxes of stories I'd written in school and in Vietnam and a stack of black-and-white photos I'd taken while out on patrol.

I'd been to Tampa only once in my life. The drive down Highway 98 from Monrovia takes four hours on most days, but in that short distance the terrain and the culture change dramatically.

My first impression of this city was that I'd ventured into some foreign port. Palm trees lined its broad streets. Multi-colored stucco houses gleamed in the harsh sunshine. With its Latin population and its Spanish colonial homes it was the most colorful place I'd ever seen.

It was nine a.m. when I arrived at *The Sentinel*, an aging three-story structure on the south side of downtown. Its worn plank floors reminded me of a tobacco packing house. The old-fashioned caged elevator gave a loud screech as it slowly ascended to the top floor. I found myself wishing I'd taken the stairs.

I stepped out into an open newsroom that took up most of the third floor. A pall of cigarette smoke hung from the high ceiling, which had probably been white at some time but by now had turned a nicotine yellowish brown. I almost gagged.

The room reverberated to a cacophony of teletype machines, ringing phones, and yelling reporters and editors. One of them, a tall, fat balding man typed frantically as he listened to a phone receiver cradled on his shoulder. A cigarette perched precariously on his lips. The trash can beside him overflowed with newsprint and piles of punched tape. A single hot ash flicked in the wrong direction would have burned down the entire building.

I found Donovan in his glassed-in corner office reading copy for the afternoon paper. Seated behind a gray metal desk that looked like it had been through the war with him, he ignored me as I walked into the room. His office looked like the aftermath of a tornado in a dumpster. Papers littered every square inch of his desk. Others stood a foot deep on the tops of his filing cabinets. I could barely make out the tip of a spindle through a pile of pink message slips. I marveled that he could find anything in this mess.

Glossy black-and-white photos of Donovan with famous people filled the walls. There were autographed pictures of him with Senator George Smathers and former Governor Leroy Collins. Another showed a much younger Donovan standing with George Patton in front of a tank at Anzio. Just beneath it was an older one of Donovan with several other young men on the steps of the KA house at Florida, among them George Martin, Bill Emmett, and my dad.

When I started to introduce myself, he extended an open palm across his desk without looking up.

"What you got?" he asked.

I stared, dumbfounded, for a moment, then handed him the manila folder with my stories and photos.

He pulled them out, studied them for several minutes without a word or a change of expression, and then handed them back to me. Finally, he looked up. He had the swollen nose and red cheeks of a man who spent

88

too much time on a barstool. His dark blue eyes seemed to bore right through me. "You really Sam Williams' son?"

"Yes sir"

"Okay… When can you start?"

Thinking he was hiring me just because I was Sam Williams' son, I started to walk out then reconsidered. "I guess I can start right away."

"Good," he said. He made some notes on a scrap of paper. "Go out there and find the nearest empty desk. Put your things down and get back in here as fast as you can. I have somebody I want you to go see."

***

My first assignment was a background story on a city council candidate. I almost panicked. I was in a town where I didn't know anyone and needed a map to find my way around. This was my first real reporting job, and I knew nothing about Tampa or its politics.

Then I remembered I needed a haircut, and if Tampa was anything like Monrovia there was no better place to pick up gossip than a barber shop. I located one on Howard Avenue and soon found myself in a high swivel chair with a sheet up to my neck.

The barber was a Korean War vet named Jack. He had a steel-gray flattop and a tightly trimmed mustache. He took his time with my hair as he filled me in on local politics, who'd married into which family, who was important and who was not. When I left, my hair was the shortest it'd been since Vietnam, but I had a much better idea who I needed to keep up with and who I might as well avoid.

I also discovered that the candidate I was covering was as inexperienced as I was. He'd recently moved to Tampa from Philadelphia, where he'd worked as a traffic cop. I figured Pug was testing me to see how well I did with a politician who had no chance of winning.

His opponent was a three-term incumbent from an old Bay Area family. In the course of my research, I discovered that the challenger's employer and primary contributor was a real estate developer in Sulfur Springs who'd lost a rezoning battle, thanks largely to the efforts of the incumbent. In my story I gave as complete a picture of the candidate as I could without making him appear either a major contender or a complete buffoon.

That afternoon I drove around in search of a place to live. I had just enough cash to last until payday. I found a run-down furnished apartment on Azeele Street above a garage. It reeked of mildew and mothballs. The outside stairway leaned away from the building and the steps shook and swayed under my feet.

The floors inside sagged in the middle, and a spider's web of cracks covered the walls and ceilings. The living room air conditioner made rattling noises but did little else. It was perfect.

This was the first place I could ever call my own. It wasn't much, but as busy as I'd be, all I needed was a place to sleep and shower. Besides, it was only temporary until I could afford something nicer. I rented it on a month-to-month basis and could move out with as little as thirty days' notice.

***

Pug must have liked my story. My next assignment was local attorney Langford Styles, candidate for a vacant Congressional seat. Styles, who portrayed himself as a defender of the working man against big, mean-spirited corporations, came from a blueblood Tampa family, had amassed a fortune as a partner in his firm and had had the good taste to marry into another wealthy family. His stylish clothes and movie-star looks made him a shoe-in.

Pug wangled me an invitation to a cocktail party in Styles' honor at a Spanish Colonial mansion on Davis Island. It seemed that members of the Fourth Estate were about as welcome at this soiree as were the poor people the aspiring congressman claimed to represent. Instead, I was to pose as a realtor and Styles supporter, my mission, to gather details about the people who were backing him and the things they said when they had a few drinks in them.

By the time I arrived, the circular driveway had filled with expensive foreign cars. I parked the old Chevy on a side street so the host wouldn't have it towed by mistake.

Wandering through colorful, brightly lit rooms and semi-tropical gardens, I must've looked as out of place as a Bolshevik at a country club. In one corner a string ensemble played selections from Vivaldi and Brahms. Three elderly Black gentlemen and a young Latino plied the overdressed partiers with silver trays of liver pate', steamed shrimp, fried calamari, and flutes of champagne. The host of the party owned a large pipeline company with operations all over the Southeast.

He and Mr. and Mrs. Styles greeted guests at the door. Styles sported a black tuxedo while his matronly wife wore a cream-colored dress straight out of the 1950s. When she smiled I noticed that one of her eyes crossed. Not knowing which one to look at, I quickly moved on to our host, Ron Aronson, who wore a tuxedo identical to Styles' but seemed far less comfortable inside it.

I made a beeline for the open bar a few feet away, where I ordered a gin and tonic. From this strategic position I surveyed the arriving guests.

A brunette, about twenty, came in wearing an ankle-length, form-fitting dress in red silk. It had a slit on one side that ran halfway up her thigh. The way it clung to her body suggested she was wearing nothing beneath it. She had an oval face and olive complexion with long, straight hair parted on one side. She brushed against Styles as they shook hands with and gave him a coquettish smile. He turned his head and eyed her as she shook hands with our host.

A young man in a silk suit, ruffled satin shirt and black patent leather shoes stepped up behind Styles and whispered into his ear. His shoulder-length hair swept back in a pompadour held in place by generous amounts of gel.

As I turned to the bar a fortyish blonde sidled up and ordered a martini. From the way she swayed I could tell this wasn't her first drink of the evening. She leaned toward me, placed a hand on my shoulder for support and smiled.

"Hi," she said in a low voice as her eyes moved up and down my frame. "I haven't seen *you* here before." Her face hovered so close I nearly passed out from the aroma of gin and vermouth.

"I just got here," I said.

I introduced myself as Tom Spivey, real estate agent. I guessed she'd been reasonably attractive once, perhaps beautiful, a faded prom queen, but at close range I saw crow's feet and laugh lines beneath her heavy makeup.

"I'm Beth Fernandez."

I'd recognized her the moment I saw her, the twice divorced city council member who, according to rumor, planned a run for the mayor's office. "Maybe you'd like to show me some of your real estate."

It had been so long since I'd been with a woman that, for a moment, I considered her offer. Then another woman joined us, a redhead much closer to my age. "There you are," she said, taking my arm. "I've been looking *all over* for you."

I had never seen her before and was about to say so, when she turned to Fernandez with a tight smile. "I see you've met our councilwoman. Hi, Beth."

Fernandez smiled back, gave me another look-over, and melted into the crowd.

"Thanks," I said.

"Don't mention it. I just saved you from a fate worse than death. By the way, what brings you here?"

"My name's Tom Spivey. I moved here recently. My boss got me an invitation."

"What kind of work do you do, Tom Spivey?"

"I'm a real estate agent."

"Commercial or residential?"

"Commercial." As soon as I said it, I knew I'd screwed up.

"Oh yeah, and what did you think about the sale of the Carlton Building last week?"

I fumbled for something to say, but she cut me off.

"There was no deal on the Carlton Building. Don't worry, Tom, I'm just messing with you. I'm Lisa Wolff, and I'm in ad sales at the paper. I recognized you when you walked in the door." She scanned the room. "I wouldn't worry though. Nobody here's going to notice a reporter. They're much too busy trying to impress each other."

"What are you doing here?"

"That guy over there..." She pointed to the young man with the pompadour, "is my date, of sorts. I'm just here for appearances."

"What do you mean?"

"He's actually gay."

"Gay?"

She looked at me and laughed. "Boy, you are country. He's a homo-sexual."

"Oh!"

"He'll probably pick up some young stud, and then we'll go our separate ways." She shrugged her shoulders and lifted her glass as if to toast.

"And that doesn't bother you?"

"Nope. Stuart and I have been friends since we were eight. I used to beat up the other boys when they picked on him."

I stepped back and gave her a skeptical look. Lisa was maybe five-foot-two, pleasant looking, not beautiful. I could hardly picture her beating up anyone.

"I was the tallest girl in my third-grade class, I'll have you know. I stopped growing in the sixth grade. After that, Stuart had to fend for himself, which he did quite admirably thanks to judo lessons his parents provided him."

"Is he a friend of the candidate?"

"He works for him as a paralegal and is helping with the campaign. He runs errands, digs up dirt on people. You'd be surprised what someone of Stuart's, um, *persuasion* can find out."

"I can imagine."

The brunette in the red silk dress reappeared. I followed her with my eyes as she ascended a carpeted staircase partly visible from where I stood. Moments later Styles excused himself from his wife and their host. He too climbed the stairs. With admirable restraint I resisted the temptation to follow them on the pretense of looking for a bathroom.

As I turned back a voice called out, "Hey, Lisa, who's your friend?"

"Stuart, I'd like to introduce Tom Spivey. He's a residential real estate agent."

"So nice to meet you…" The words rolled off his tongue like Karo Syrup.

"Nice to meet you too, Stuart. Tell me, where might I find a bathroom?"

"There's one in that back hallway. I could show you if you'd like."

"No. No. That's quite alright. I can find it."

As I left he started to move, but Lisa caught his arm and spoke into his ear. By the time I looked again they were deep in conversation.

I stepped through the patio door and stood behind a palm tree where no one would see me. From my pocket I retrieved a small notebook and jotted down the names of people I'd met and things I'd overheard, most of it useless. I also made a detailed description of the girl in the red silk dress and Lisa's gay friend Stuart, with the gelled pompadour and the black belt in judo.

On my return I passed a couple making out in the darkness near a side door. I pretended not to notice but got a good look, in case either of them was someone important married to someone else.

Before long I grew bored with the pretentious cocktail banter and decided to get some more fresh air. I strolled past a crowded bar, flaming tiki torches and a gazebo where a steel drum band played "Jamaica Farewell."

A narrow pathway led through a tropical garden and down to a long dock overlooking Hillsborough Bay. This was a small, chance decision that would change the course of my life.

***

She stood there alone in a pool of lamplight at the end of the pier gazing at the twinkling lights on the opposite shore. There was something different about her, and the walkway led me toward her with a certain inevitability. The house, the people and the noise behind me faded until she and I were alone in the world.

95

She didn't seem to notice me as I approached. "Hi," she said, without turning around. She ran her finger slowly through the cold sweat on the outside of her empty highball glass. The ice inside made a soft clink.

"That drink's getting a bit low," I offered. "Can I get you another?"

"No thanks, I have a court appearance tomorrow, and it wouldn't look good for me to show up with a hangover." She wobbled as she turned and gazed up at me for the first time with a sly smile. Her lips parted to reveal a row of dazzling white teeth.

"So… How about you? What will you be doing tomorrow when you go back to your real life?"

She barely came up to my chest. She had a small, rounded face and turned-up nose, like a cherub in a Renaissance painting, a Raphael perhaps. She wore a sapphire minidress with white stockings and blue pumps. Strawberry blonde hair tumbled over her shoulders and halfway down her chest. A stray lock fell across her right eyebrow. I reached out and gently brushed it back into place. The dim light revealed a scatter of freckles across her nose and cheeks.

Beneath the steady salt breeze, she gave off the faint, but unmistakable aroma of sexual desire. She spoke with a Boston Irish accent and looked at me in a way that made me want her right there.

"I'm afraid this is my real life," I said, coming back to my senses. "I'm a writer for the *Sentinel*." So much for the real estate crap.

"And so, you've come here to see if you could pick up something juicy."

"Not likely! Everybody in there is just trying to impress everyone else. I wouldn't trust anything they said. As drunk as they are they'd still make me for a reporter." I stopped when I read the look on her face.

"That's not what I meant," she said.

For a moment I studied her. Then I got her meaning. Not sure what to say, I fumbled for a reply. "My name's Tom Williams. And you are …?"

"Colleen Gentry, attorney at law."

"Well, Colleen Gentry, attorney at law, would you like to escape to somewhere else?"

"Sure. We could go to my place."

I was thankful she hadn't invited herself to mine.

"Sure"

***

Colleen lived in a second-floor garden apartment off Hillsborough Avenue near Armenia. It had a single bedroom and bath. A marble-topped counter separated the kitchenette from the living and dining area.

She flipped a switch as we walked in. Low level lights bathed the corners of the room in a warm glow. She closed the door behind us and was on me in a flash, biting my lower lip and pushing me backward as she unbuttoned my shirt.

A queen-sized waterbed engulfed the small bedroom. She whipped back the velvet comforter, pushed me onto the bed and jumped on top. I thrust as hard as I could as she leaned over and placed a firm nipple in my mouth.

"Bite it," she gasped.

At length, she rolled off and curled up beside me.

"Where'd you learn to fuck like that, country boy?"

I wasn't sure if this was a compliment or ridicule. For a moment, I lay there seeing the face of Dana Padgett as clearly as if she were the woman beside me.

"It's a long story."

Colleen came up on an elbow in a flash and grabbed the hair on the back of my head. "Tell me you're not married," she said, her voice cold and malevolent in my ear.

"I'm not married," I yelled, "and never have been. Stop pulling my hair."

"Good!" she said, her voice softening as if it had been a casual question.

She ran her hands gently down my body. I stared at the ceiling but felt her eyes boring into me. She expected an explanation.

I took a deep breath and slowly told of my affair with Dana, her murder and the lynching of Jimmie Lee Johnson.

She lay there, speechless, for a time. "Holy shit!" she whispered. "This sounds like something out of *Mandingo*. You poor baby! It's a wonder you're not totally twisted."

"You don't know me yet."

"Would you like to spend the night?"

"I'd love to, but I have to be at work by nine, and my apartment's on the other side of Dale Mabry."

"No problem. I'll set the alarm for five-thirty. That way we'll have time for a quickie and a shower before you leave. I might even cook you one of my world-famous omelets."

"Okay."

On the wall beside her mirror hung a picture of a man standing with John and Bobby Kennedy. It appeared to have come from the late fifties or early sixties. Bobby still had his flattop. "Who's that with the Kennedys?"

"That's my dad. He's known them since they were little."

"Wow! Do you think Bobby will run for President?"

"How the fuck would I know? It's not like he's gonna call and ask my advice. I hope he does, though. Somebody needs to get us out of this fucking war."

Another picture showed a much younger Colleen beside a girl with black hair and darker complexion. They wore identical uniforms, white starched blouses, green plaid skirts, white knee socks and black patent leather shoes. Behind them stood the entrance to a high school with a sign that read, "St. Agnes."

Colleen followed my gaze. "That's me with my best friend, Isabella. We went through twelve years of Catholic school together. She still lives in Boston. We call and write each other all the time."

I stared at the picture for several minutes. "Do you still have that uniform?"

"I'm sure my mother kept it. She never throws anything away. Why?"

"I was just thinking maybe she could send it to you... you could wear it for me sometime..."

She slapped my stomach so hard it stung. "You pervert!"

She ran her hand up between my legs and stroked me back to life. When we finished, we were again too exhausted to speak.

That night, as I lay there watching her sleep, I felt something I hadn't experienced since that summer in Monrovia and the evenings and afternoons I'd spent with Dana.

We began dating, always returning to her apartment. I was too embarrassed to take her back to mine. As soon as I had some money put aside I rented a much nicer place on Bayshore.

Colleen's father was a federal judge in Boston. The middle child of seven, she was the only one who followed his footsteps and became a lawyer. She was unlike any woman I've ever known. Quick-tempered, passionate, and courageous, she could be elegant and crude at the same time.

Time and again I came close to asking her the question, the big one, only to retreat for fear she might say no. We came from such different worlds. Her casual attitudes about sex gave the impression she didn't want a long-term relationship, but already I knew better. Like me she was a stranger in a strange land, desperate for someone she could hold onto.

Chapter Thirteen

I continued to cover elections, political appointments and city council meetings. Tampa and Hillsborough County were mostly Democrat, while Pinellas County, across the bay, was solidly Republican. Over the years this area had seen more than its share of pirates, crooked politicians, and ne'er-do-wells. I never lacked material.

My sources included a night club owner, a wealthy matron and a life insurance agent who'd worked for several campaigns. Since all of them were off-the-record, I had to get independent verification. Anonymous sources, for some reason, often lie.

By far my most colorful contact was a junkie named Freddy Martinez. Freddy did odd jobs and dealt dope on the side to pay for his habit. We met on a sidewalk one afternoon as I was leaving work. He tried to sell me a dime bag of marijuana. I told him I wasn't interested and kept walking.

"Hey, you're the reporter who wrote about the congressional race, aren't you?"

I should've known not to ask, but curiosity got the best of me. "How'd you know that?"

He gave me a smug look. "I make it my business to know stuff like that."

Freddy stood about five-foot-eight, weighed less than a hundred and twenty pounds and looked like a skeleton wrapped in pock-marked skin. Thin, greasy hair fell about his shoulders, and he trembled and scratched his arms as he spoke.

"Oh yeah? Good for you!" I tried again to escape. I was in no mood to humor this guy.

"I can tell you a lot more things you'll want to know. Why don't you buy me a beer and I'll tell you a thing or two about Langford Styles?"

I stopped and thought about it. I'd finished for the day and had nothing else to do. Colleen was working late on a big case. "Okay, but we'll have to make it quick."

The bar next to the newspaper office was little more than a nondescript storefront with darkened windows. From appearances it had once been a deli or an Italian restaurant. We stepped inside and slid into a cramped booth in the far corner.

The place was almost empty. A man in a rumpled brown suit sat quietly at the bar with his back to us nursing a cocktail.

In another booth across the room sat an older man with a young woman who was obviously a prostitute. He was telling her some story I couldn't have followed if I'd wanted, but he obviously found it quite funny because he couldn't stop laughing. The hooker laughed, stared into his eyes and stroked his thigh. Nobody noticed us but the bartender, who eventually came over to take our orders.

"Listen," Freddy said once the bartender was out of earshot, "I've got some background on your congressional candidate, the up-and-coming Mr. Styles." He paused to light a cigarette, took a deep drag and let out a long curl of smoke. He leaned across the table and said in a conspiratorial tone. "He has the financial backing of Rico Salazar."

"Who?"

Freddy looked at me as though I'd asked him who the pope was. "He's the biggest heroin supplier in South Florida… He operates out of Miami."

"And you know he's backing Styles because …"

"I saw them walking into a little bar together out on Spruce Street. Salazar stood right there and handed our would-be congressman a briefcase full of money."

"Come on. You've got to do better than that."

"You're dating that pretty young lawyer, right? I believe her name is Colleen Gentry. She works for Styles' firm." His hand shook violently as he took another pull from his cigarette.

"Dude, you're starting to scare me."

"You oughta be scared. You have no idea what's going on here. Just ask Miss Gentry to check out these corporations." He pulled a yellowed packing slip from his jeans and slid it across the table. It was a list of names in a barely legible scrawl. "They're all owned by Salazar or members of his family, and Styles and his law firm serve as corporate counsel for each and every one of them."

"Okay." I took the paper and glanced at it. "So why are you telling me this? I mean, if Salazar is the kingpin you say he is, aren't you afraid he'll hear about our conversation, and you'll wind up out in there the bay wearing concrete flippers?"

He gazed at the bar and stubbed his cigarette in an ashtray. "I'm a dead man already. One of Salazar's men was my main supplier. He ripped me off a couple of weeks ago. Last night he got busted. He thinks I set him up. He made bail a few hours ago, and now he's looking for me."

"Why don't you go to the police?"

"Take a look at me. You think the police are gonna believe me? Besides, Salazar owns half the police here."

"You could leave town."

"And go where? I don't have a car or a license, and I'm pretty sure they've got the bus station covered. There's not a place in this world where Rico's people won't find me. I'm telling you these guys don't fuck around. I figure if I tell you, then maybe you can do something with this information after I'm gone."

"That's civic-minded of you." My instincts told me this guy was full of shit. I took out my notebook and began to write, more to humor him than anything else. "So, where does this Mr. Salazar get his stuff?"

"He flies it in from California."

"They're growing poppy in California now?"

"No. He gets it from the CIA."

Now I knew he was bullshitting me.

"Air America is a front for the CIA. They're flying the stuff out of Laos to raise money for covert operations, the kind of operations they don't dare tell Congress about. They even hide some of it in caskets of dead soldiers coming back from Vietnam. They sell it to major wholesalers like Salazar. Salazar has CIA connections going all the way back to the Bay of Pigs fiasco and the Kennedy assassination. He's tied in with Santo Trafficante right here in Tampa. Trafficante helped organize the Kennedy assassination with Carlos Marcello and Sam Giancana."

"Hold on! Hold on! The Kennedy assassination...?"

"Salazar lost a brother and an uncle at the Bay of Pigs. He blamed Kennedy because Kennedy pulled out the Air Force at the last minute and left the Cuban guerillas on the beach alone. The mob was pissed off at Kennedy because they wanted to overthrow Castro and retake control of their casinos."

"So, Salazar killed Kennedy?"

"No, goddamit! You're not listening. Now pay attention." Across the room the old man and the hooker looked up then went back to their drinks. "Johnson, the CIA and the Mafia killed Kennedy, because he was going to pull our troops out of Vietnam. The Mafia and CIA were going to lose the heroin trade. They set up Oswald as a fall guy and had Ruby kill Oswald to shut him up. Ruby knew he was dying of cancer. They promised him money and threatened to kill his family if he didn't pop Oswald."

"So now President Johnson is both a drug dealer and a murderer."

"Johnson has a long record of killing people who get in his way. He had a radio announcer killed once just because he dug up a story about Johnson and his cronies fixing a Senate race."

Why, I wondered, *do I waste my time with guys like this?* "So, I'm supposed to believe that the CIA murdered the President of the United States and got away with it."

"They got away with killing Diem and his brother, didn't they?"

He had a point, but it still sounded crazy.

"Wow! That's an interesting story, Freddy. Tell me something. You ever been to Vietnam? *I* was there about a year ago, and I never heard any of this shit. How do you know all this?"

"Before I got into junk I read a lot about Southeast Asia. I know some guys who've been there more recently than you..."

I glanced at my watch again. "Ah, Jeez, I've got to go, Freddy. Look, this has been fascinating. I appreciate your sharing it with me. I really do. I'll definitely look into it." I folded the paper he'd given me and shoved it into my pocket. I rose from the table, walked to the bar, paid the tab and left.

***

Two days later the Hillsborough County Sheriff's Department pulled the body of Freddy Martinez out of Tampa Bay. A passing boat spotted him floating near the surface despite the concrete block chained to his legs. There were two small caliber holes in the back of his head.

I got this from a reporter named Dick Willis who came by my desk with a stack of photos. He took great pleasure in giving me all the morbid details.

When he finally left I got up and walked nonchalantly to our library, which in those days we referred to as the "morgue." It reeked of musty old newspaper clippings and had the sharp tang of developing solution from the darkroom next door. The walls were a snot green that hadn't seen fresh paint in years. Along one side stood a row of steel gray filing cabinets, and on a table in the center sat a card catalog with names and story subjects going back fifty years.

After nearly an hour I found an old picture of Rico Salazar, listed as "Enrico Salazar." The grainy image taken from some distance showed him standing in front of an unidentified building talking to two other men. He wore a traditional white linen shirt, a narrow-brimmed hat with a dark band, and sunglasses with thick, black frames. I slipped it into a stack of papers and borrowed it. This would be a good person to recognize if I ever saw him coming. I filed the photo in a pasteboard box I carried in the trunk of my car, along with the yellow packing slip Freddy had given me listing Salazar's corporations.

I soon forgot about Freddy and Salazar. In April I received the assignment of my young career, to cover the funeral of Dr. Martin Luther King. The next time I saw that photo was on my return trip from Atlanta.

I had a great job and a beautiful girlfriend. Life was good. There'd been a time when I believed I'd never live like this. I left Monrovia determined to put the deaths of my parents and friends behind me and become a famous journalist.

***

But on Wednesday, April 10, 1968, returning from Atlanta on a lonely stretch of highway, I found myself drawn back to my past by the story I'd written of Dr, King's funeral. Like a swallow returning to Capistrano, I returned to the place where I'd lost most of the people I'd ever loved.

Book Two

The Return

Chapter Fourteen

Monrovia, Florida (April 10, 1968)

I pulled into the Sinclair station that fine spring morning to find that little had changed in the eight years since I left for college. Located on the southeast corner of Broad Street and Third Avenue West, the small red brick building with its arched doorway once belonged to Jerry Morgan, a friend of my dad's. When Morgan died years earlier his family sold out to a man from Perry who let it go to ruin.

It still had the tall cylindrical pumps topped by white globes and the green dinosaur logo. A cobwebbed cardboard sign in the window read "Closed."

Blackened grease stains spattered the cracked concrete, sprinkled with kitty litter in a vain effort to absorb the sludge. As I studied the little mounds of grey and tan I pictured a cat strolling by later and making better use of the stuff.

Gone now was the stout red Coke machine with its silver lever that dispensed the small, six-cent bottles. The new owner had replaced it with a new one holding eight different flavors. This was his idea of progress, no doubt, but somehow the ten-ounce drink never quite tasted the same.

On the side of the building were three doors. The first read "Women" in crisp, blue letters on a white background. The second read "Men." The third had a recent coat of white paint, but through it I could still make out the imprinted letters, "Colored." As a small child, I once asked my dad what color that restroom was. He found that hysterical.

The men's and women's rooms were locked. I checked the third door and found it open. The stench washed over me like a wave on the beach. I felt along the wall for a light switch but found none. As I stepped into the gloom and reached for a pull chain, water splashed beneath my feet. I could only wonder what else I was stepping in.

I held my breath but could still feel the toxins seeping into my pores. As I wiped gathering tears from my eyes and waited for them to adjust to the meager light, I was sure I heard something rustle in the corner.

Gradually the dark outline of a toilet emerged. Loath to venture any further, I took careful aim, relieved myself and beat a hasty retreat.

As I leaned against my car, gasping, it occurred to me that somewhere in that darkness, no doubt, a condom machine hung on the wall, though for the life of me I couldn't imagine why. *How such a place could put anyone in the mood for sex is one of those great mysteries of life.*

Surveying the community, I once called home, I descried the Monrovia State Bank and Swift's IGA, where I worked as a teenager. High in the east a feathery white spray of clouds caught the morning sun's fire as it rose over the treetops. From there the bright turquoise blended to a deep indigo still lingering in the west.

Across the street a mockingbird gathered insects from the newly mowed lawn of the First Methodist Church while her mate fed their brood in a nearby cabbage palm. A light breeze stirred the Spanish moss in surrounding oaks. This was a dawn that promised peace and tranquility. It was a dawn that lied.

***

It was six a.m., and I was hungry. Early as it was, I didn't want to show up at my grandmother's unexpected, so I drove over to Sandy's, the only business open at that hour. It sat on a corner opposite the courthouse, its white-painted front facing the intersection at an angle.

Through lace curtains its broad windows afforded an expansive view of what passed for downtown.

Glancing about as I entered, the only people I recognized were Sandy and her waitress, June. From the back Sandy's brother Otto yelled to June over the crackling of bacon and sausage, "Order up". Sandy, who never trusted anyone with her money, worked the cash register.

High on the wall above the counter hung a row of black-and-white clocks fashioned to resemble cats. Their tails swung like pendulums as their black eyes darted back and forth. A discriminating purchaser could have one of these fine pieces of Americana for the paltry sum of nine dollars and ninety-five cents.

"Tom, Honey…!" Sandy yelled. Her smile conveyed something more than mere friendliness. "Where you been keeping yourself?"

"I live in Tampa now."

"How long you been down there?"

"Ever since I got back from 'Nam."

"Oh, yeah, I heard about that." As she sauntered over, threw her arms around me and proffered a kiss that barely missed my lips, I caught the cloying scent of Chanel Number Five.

"What kind of work you doing?"

"I'm writing for a newspaper, the *Sentinel*."

"I always knew you'd go places, darling." She patted me on the chest, letting her hand rest there a moment. "Look at you with that long hair. Hey, June, look who's here."

June Skinner glanced up from the table she was cleaning and managed a wan smile. She'd worked for Sandy for as long as I could remember. The hair piled atop her head had aged to a uniform shade of Popsicle yellow, and her makeup had taken on new layers as she spackled the fine wrinkles spreading over her face like a spiderweb fracture on a windshield. She wore the tired look of someone serving her time in hell for some long forgotten but particularly egregious offense.

"Hey, Tom" she uttered unenthusiastically as she returned to her work.

"You got you a wife or girlfriend down there in Tampa?" asked Sandy.

"Yeah, I'm dating somebody."

"Well, if she don't treat you right, darling, you just come on back here. Ol' Sandy'll take good care of you."

With a force of will I exorcized that fleeting image. "Thanks, Sandy. I'll remember that."

Sandy, though she stood a good six inches shorter, had at least fifty pounds on me and was undoubtedly more woman than I could handle. Besides, I figured, even at this early hour, she'd no doubt made similar offers to other men. Sandy was something of a pioneer in customer relations.

"You sure turned out to be one handsome young man," she drawled. "You know you look just like your daddy."

"Thanks."

I took a stool at the far end of the counter with a view of the entire establishment and ordered two scrambled eggs, grits, bacon, toast and coffee. As I took my first bite, the front door swung open, ushering in a warm breeze and the sound of growing traffic. An old man shuffled in and carefully seated himself at a booth. When he set his broad-brimmed felt hat on the table, I knew him immediately.

Max Brabson's hair, what was left of it, had turned completely white since I saw him last. His stooped shoulders gave the appearance of a man slowly folding in on himself, the hooked nose grown closer to his pointed chin, fine snowy tufts sprouting from his ears. He seemed to be contemplating a tiny spot on the Formica tabletop in front of him.

As I walked over I called out in a loud voice, "Mr. Brabson, how are you doing?" not sure he could hear me.

He had to turn his head sideways to see me, but his eyes still had a spark as they peered through drooping brows. "I'm doing just fine, son. How about you?"

"I'm doing great!" Not knowing if he recognized me, I added, "I'm Tom Williams, Mr. Brabson. I used to work for you out on your farm."

"Oh, yeah…" He smiled and thought for a moment. "Your granddaddy and I were good friends. He was a fine man." He paused and then chuckled. "I remember that time I caught you and that little colored boy. You were sitting up there in the tobacco field playing cards instead of working."

"Yes sir, I remember that. Gin rummy as I recall. I'd just won when I heard you yell at us."

"You know, I should have fired your asses right there on the spot," he cackled.

A vague expression clouded his face. "That colored boy was the one they hung out there on that tree, wasn't he?" He raised a palsied hand and crooked a finger toward the window as if it had happened just outside, rather than behind the courthouse.

"Yes sir… Do you mind if I join you?"

"No, no. Come on. Sit down."

I returned to the counter, grabbed my plate in one hand and coffee cup in the other and slid into the booth, sinking deep into its cracked red vinyl.

"What are you doing these days, Mr. Brabson?"

I knew he wasn't farming. He had to be in his seventies, and nobody raised tobacco in Jasper County anymore.

"Mostly I just come down here to visit, read the newspaper, work the crossword puzzle, see what's going on." A folded copy of the *Florida*

Times-Union lay on the table. "You know how this place is. Nothing ever happens, but when it does people talk about it for the next hundred years like it was yesterday. The farming's gone now, and the phosphate company's taken just about all they're gonna get from that mine out there near your grandaddy's old place."

"That's right. I remember. Bill Emmett sold his mineral rights to a big phosphate company down in Bartow a few years back. You still living out on your farm?"

"Lord, no! I sold it to Emmett and those boys from down in Miami… about four or five years ago. I'm living in town now, in an apartment, not far from your grandmama."

"What do you suppose Bill's gonna do with all that land?"

"He's been talking some nonsense about building a resort and retirement community out there."

I almost choked on my eggs. "Resort?"

"Yeah, some deal he and his friends cooked up. I don't pay much attention to that kind of stuff."

"When you say, 'his friends', do you mean the 'boys from Miami?'"

"Yeah, that's right." He studied me for a moment, his eyes narrowed, but his next thought, whatever it was, must have escaped him or he'd simply decided to let it pass.

"You don't happen to remember the names of those boys, do you?"

He thought for second. "Nope, I don't suppose I do."

"When I see Bill, maybe I'll ask him." I couldn't imagine why anyone would want to retire or vacation in Jasper County, but for as long as I'd known Bill he'd had one grand scheme or another.

Brabson started talking about his daughter, Ann, married now and living in Jacksonville with a couple of kids. I recalled that his wife had died when Ann was about fifteen and understood why he spent his days sitting in Sandy's reading newspapers and chatting with whoever wandered in.

I settled my one-dollar tab and left a twenty-cent tip for June. As I left I stopped at a *Times-Union* machine and bought a copy.

From down the street came the piercing wail of a siren. An ambulance turned onto Florida Avenue on its way to Jasper Memorial Hospital a few blocks away. For some reason the sight of it disturbed me, though I couldn't imagine why. Ambulances were so commonplace in front of my apartment on Bayshore that I'd long ago learned to ignore them.

The shopkeeper next door looked up and smiled as he opened for the day. I waved, though I didn't recognize him, climbed back into my car and headed toward my grandmother's. By now it was after seven, and I knew she'd be awake.

***

Monrovia, Florida had roughly two thousand people. Broad Street, its main drag, ran for about two miles from the city limit sign on Tallahassee Highway eastward to a dead end at the now deserted Simpson Brothers Tobacco Company. Brick and stucco storefronts crowded the sidewalk on either side.

It was a typical Norman Rockwell town with an insurance agency, a propane gas distributor, and a hardware store with pine floors and a tin plate ceiling. Above the treetops rose the competing spires of the First Baptist, First Methodist and First Presbyterian churches.

Monrovia had once seemed eternal to me, the center of the universe, my ancestors living and dying here since primordial times. Even after I lost both parents in a tragic accident and my grandfather passed away, I never imagined wanting to live anywhere else. All that changed in the summer of 1958, when I saw, as in a lightning flash, a very different side of this place, one that forever changed my view of the world.

***

When I arrived, Ida met me at the front door. I assumed my grandmother was back in the kitchen.

"Hey, Ida…" I reached out to hug her, but her worried look brought me up short. Something was wrong. She couldn't look me in the eye as she struggled to speak.

"Thank the Lord you're here, Tom. Your grandmama's done gone to the hospital. She just left out of here, not twenty minutes ago."

"Oh my God! What's the matter?"

"I don't know. I got here this morning, and I knocked on the back door, but she wouldn't answer, so I came around and knocked on the front. Finally, I just walked in and called to her, but she still didn't answer. I found her lying in the bed. She could barely talk. She told me she didn't feel good. She looked bad, Tom, so I called the ambulance, and they came and got her."

That must have been the one I saw outside Sandy's, I thought. *If I'd gone straight to the house when I got to town, maybe I could have done something. At the very least I could've ridden to the hospital with her.*

***

Overcome with guilt, I jumped into my car and in minutes was walking into tiny Jasper Memorial, a three-story brown-brick relic of the Hill-Burton Plan, a 1950s federal program that sprinkled such institutions in small towns across America.

When I got to her room I found her lying in bed, apparently asleep. Homer Green stood in the doorway, somehow still working at his age.

"Your grandmama gave us a scare, but she's resting now."

"What was it? Is she going to be okay?"

"It looks like congestive heart failure. I'll have a better idea by this afternoon."

I almost fainted. "What does that mean?"

"It's probably not as bad as it sounds. It's a long-term condition. She won't be as active as she once was, but with plenty of rest she could be around for a long time. The problem is she's working herself too hard for a woman her age. She's going to need more help around the house, for a while at least, and I'm not sure Ida can manage by herself."

"How long will she need to stay here?"

"She can probably go home in a couple of days, but she'll have to stay off her feet when she does."

"Is it okay if I sit here a while?"

"I guess so, but she won't be much for conversation. I gave her a sedative to help her sleep."

"Tom?" The weak voice seemed to come from another room.

"I'm right here Grandmama." I struggled to remain calm as I leaned over the steel railing and kissed her forehead. She'd left her glasses at home and stared vaguely in my direction.

"Don't stay too long," said the doctor. "We've gotta give that medicine some time to work."

"Okay."

I'd never seen her like this, her breath shallow, her long hair flowing over the starched pillowcase. Over the years it had gone from steel grey to Q-Tip white. During the day she wore it in a tight braid on the back of her head, but in the evening she let it down. When I was little I'd sit atop an old trunk in the corner of her bedroom watching as she brushed it in front of her mirror.

"What happened, Grandmama?" I asked.

"Well, I woke up this morning later than usual." She paused to catch her breath. "When I tried to sit up the room started spinning. I was too weak to get out of bed, so I just laid back and waited for Ida to get there." She managed a smile and tried to make it sound like a minor nuisance.

"Did this just start? Have you ever felt this way before?"

"Lord, Tom, you sound like Homer, with all these questions... I guess it's been coming on for years now. Homer says I have congestive heart failure, but it's not as bad as all that. My mama had congestive heart failure. There's not a thing you can do about it. You have it for ten sometimes twenty years. And when you die, they say that's what killed you. I just need to get home and into my own bed and I'll be alright."

"You're going to have to stay here a couple of days, Grandmama. Then you can go home. And I want you to do what Doc Green says."

I knew this wasn't what she wanted to hear. I held her hand and spoke quietly. "Ida and I can take care of the house. I'll stay here with you until you get better. The only thing you need to do right now is rest."

"I hear you," she said, gazing out the window. When she looked back she brightened. "Oh, Tom, it sure is good to see you." She patted my hand. "What a pleasant surprise! Tell me all about your trip to Atlanta."

Her eyes glistened as I described Dr. King's funeral and the story I'd written. I told her about Colleen but didn't mention that I'd proposed. Before long, her eyelids drooped, and she drifted away. "I'm going back to the house, now, Grandmama. You get some rest. I love you."

At first, I didn't think she'd heard me, but then she whispered, "Can't you stay a bit longer?"

"Sure."

When, at last, she surrendered to sleep, I wandered out of the hospital and sat on a wrought iron bench at the entrance. My head pounded, and I felt sick. A cloud of guilt descended on me as I recalled how I'd decided only reluctantly, at the last moment, to come here on my way back to Tampa.

All I wanted now was to sit in that room a while longer with my grandmother, but the doctor was right. She needed rest.

I remained a long time, watching people come and go, absorbed in their own concerns. Then I remembered Ida.

As I drove home I felt like an actor in a movie about somebody else's life. I'd lost both parents, my grandfather, Dana and Jimmie. How could this be happening again? My grandmother was all the family I had left.

I pulled into the driveway to see Ida staring out the window, her face expressionless. Glancing at my watch, I realized she'd been alone there for more than an hour with no word on my grandmother.

"Is she gone be alright?" she asked.

"I believe so."

"Lord, I been praying for her the whole time you been gone. I said 'Lord, please don't take Miss Edna away from me.' I just kept praying and praying."

"Thank you, Ida. That's all we can do right now."

There was no reason for her to stay. I could finish what little cleaning remained. Ida didn't own a car. She rode to work every morning with her cousin, Albert, who worked at a lumber yard over in Mabry. I knew he couldn't leave his job in the middle of the day to come get her, so I told her I'd take her home.

"Ida, why don't you take a couple of days off? I'll pay you for the rest of the week, and I'll come get you when Grandmama's ready to come home. I'll need your help then."

She started to protest, but I assured her there was no point in coming to work while my grandmother was in the hospital. Ida didn't have a phone, but I could drop by and keep her updated.

As we walked to the car she stopped suddenly, bemused, and stared at the Mustang with its top down. This gave me the first laugh I'd had all day. Though she wasn't a large woman, she was trying to figure out how she'd fit into the cramped back seat.

"Ida, what are you doing? Get in the front seat."

"Now you know I can't do that, Tom."

"Sure, you can. Why not?"

"But what …"

"What are folks gonna think? Screw 'em. Hop in the front seat."

"Oh Lord, Tom!" A hint of a smile crossed her face as she settled into the bucket seat beside me.

"Ida, I can't tell you how much I appreciate you taking care of Grandmama. I have no idea what would've happened if you hadn't been here."

"Well, I gotta work, Tom, and, besides, you and your grandmama are like family to me. You probably don't know this, but before the last election I'd never voted in my life. I was scared to. Even after they went and passed that Voting Rights Act up in Washington I still wasn't sure I could do it. The thought of going up to that courthouse by myself about scared me to death. Well, I got to work one morning, and your grandmama came in the kitchen all dressed up and said, 'Come on Ida. You gone register to vote.' She said it just like that, like we was going to the store. I said, 'Yes ma'am,' and we went uptown to the courthouse. You shoulda seen the looks we got from all them white folks," she cackled.

"You know, I'm gone vote this time too. I sure wish I could vote for Mr. Johnson again. He's such a nice man. I guess I'll vote for Senator Kennedy instead."

"That's wonderful, Ida." I wondered what she'd think if she heard what Freddy Martinez had to say about that nice Mr. Johnson.

Of Ida's six children, the only one still at home was Ruby. The others, besides Jimmie, had grown up and moved away, mostly to northern cities, seeking a better life. Ruby worked nights at the hospital as a nurse's aide. Between her meager income and Ida's, they somehow made ends meet.

"Don't worry about a thing, Ida. I'll come by to see you tomorrow. Right now, you need to rest up too. When Grandmama gets home, we're going to need your help."

She nodded and managed a smile between the tears.

Chapter Fifteen

Ida and Ruby lived in a leaky tarpaper shack on a dirt track off Second Street. It sat about fifteen feet from the road, perched on concrete blocks that had shifted over time. A scrawny rooster scratched in the barren yard, looking for something to eat. Palmettos and blackberry bushes encroached from all directions. I hadn't been here since right after Jimmie died.

As I pulled to a stop, a cloud of dust enveloped my car, settling over Ida and me and onto the upholstery. Ruby studied us through the rusted screen door.

"You're early," she said to Ida without looking at me.

"Miss Edna's done gone to the hospital. She's gone be okay, but Tom brought me home. Wasn't nothing for me to do there anyhow."

Ruby's expression changed. "Tom, I am so sorry. What did the doctor say was the matter?"

"Congestive heart failure. She tired herself out working around the house and needs some rest."

"I see. Well, I'll check on her when I go to work this evening. Why don't you come inside? I just made some lemonade."

I crossed the threshold into a darkened living room. It took several minutes for my eyes to adjust. When they did, I saw a black-and-white photo of Jimmie above the couch, smiling, forever ten years old. Beside it hung pictures of the Kennedys and Martin Luther King. There was a recent color photo, Lance Corporal Walter Evans in dress blues, his steady gaze fixed somewhere beyond the scrub pines of North Florida.

Born in 1949 to Ida's younger sister, Walter grew up in the Johnson household after his single mom moved to Jacksonville in search of work. In 1967 he graduated high school and enlisted in the Marine Corps. In

February I got a letter from my grandmother saying he'd died in a mortar barrage near the Vietnamese city of Hue, in a series of battles later known as the Tet Offensive.

Ruby pulled a pitcher from the small icebox and set it on the table with three glasses. The kitchen was nothing more than a corner of the living room with a scrap of linoleum retrieved from a nearby home demolished years earlier. Its furnishings included a small aluminum table somebody had thrown out and a wood–burning stove that was the sole source of heat in winter months.

The tiny back porch held a white cotton clothesline and a hand-cranked washing machine. Clothes and linens danced in the wind as though inhabited by ghosts of Johnsons past. The pull-chain light fixture contained a bare yellow bulb, meant to keep away mosquitoes and other flying bugs.

I settled in beside Ruby on the threadbare couch, squirming to avoid a sharp spring poking through the cushion. As I sipped lemonade, a brown chameleon ran across the floor.

Ruby followed my gaze. "The lizards take care of the bugs." She smiled as she smoothed her pale blue cotton dress across her knees and stretched out her bare feet.

"I'm sure you'd rather have lizards than snakes."

She laughed. "You wait long enough you just might see a snake."

"You know, Ruby, this lemonade tastes like heaven."

"Thank you, Tom."

I thought again of Jimmie and the crazy things we did. For some reason Pleasant Springs came to mind. "Ruby, what do you know about this resort Bill Emmett's promoting?"

"All I know is what I hear, mostly from folks who know less than I do. Sounds like a bunch of crazy talk to me." Her mood soured. "You know that place was beautiful once. Then they made all them folks move

122

out. The bank came, took away their property and paid them practically nothing for it. Most of them had to move into those housing projects up in Tallahassee. The phosphate company dug a big mine hole on the other side of the springs. They're done with it now and it just sits there full of nasty yellow water that spills into the Pelahatchie. It's one big mess… and Bill Emmett wants to build a resort out there! Who's gonna stay in a place like that?"

What she said made perfect sense, so I went to check it out.

***

Pleasant Springs had been an all-Black community, settled in 1868 by freed slaves. It had been part of a tobacco plantation foreclosed during Reconstruction. For generations the little community grew and flourished, until the summer of 1939, when some hunters found the body of a white man, victim of an apparent gunshot wound. His wife said he'd left home a week earlier to buy a hog from a Black man at Pleasant Springs. Nobody there remembered seeing him, and none of them had sold hogs that day.

A week later white men wearing robes and hoods set fire to the town. In the ensuing gun battle eleven whites and more than thirty Black people died. The rest of the community moved away.

For years it sat vacant. The few remaining structures fell into ruin. During World War II former residents began moving back. They cleared brush where their homes had been and rebuilt their church in a large open area near the main spring, a large sinkhole surrounded by trees. In 1965 it fell prey to Bill Emmett and his investors.

The drive leading back to the springs was now a boulevard paved in brick and blocked by a pair of wrought iron gates hung from stone pillars. A chain link fence topped with barbed wire stretched into the woods in either direction. Thick trees and shrubs obscured what lay beyond the bend in the road. A large sign read:

Future Home of Arcadia Springs
Resort and Golfing Community
Arcadia Development Company, Inc.
Financing by Monrovia State Bank
NO TRESPASSING

Bill didn't even have the decency to keep the name of the community. Below the announcement a Xanadu-like image envisioned a hotel with fountains, swimming pools, tennis courts, and a golf course. A flock of birds flew overhead, silhouetted against a sunset behind a tranquil lake.

The landscaping, what little I could see, appeared new, but there were no signs of construction. I pulled closer for a better view. A pickup appeared at the other side of the fence. A chiseled man with a flattop and wrap-around sunglasses stepped out with a sawed-off double-barreled shotgun cradled in his arms. His T shirt stretched over bronzed biceps bigger around than my legs.

I waved, but he continued staring. I cranked the Mustang, put it in gear, and drove away.

Farther down the road near the Pelahatchie I stopped at another driveway, this one unpaved. Stretched across its entrance was a heavy logging chain, padlocked to crossties buried deep in the sandy soil. A rusted metal sign read, "Little River Hunting Club – Members Only."

Then it hit me, a torrent of childhood nightmares that began about a year after I moved in with my grandparents. For a moment I thought I'd puke.

Jimmie and I were twelve years old. I'd seen this sign for as long as I could remember but knew nothing of the Little River Hunting Club. When I asked my granddaddy, all he would say was that its members were a bunch of idiots, and I should stay the hell away from them. This stoked my curiosity all the more.

Late one night, while my grandparents lay asleep, I climbed out my bedroom window to where Jimmie stood waiting. We rode our bikes to a spot near the club, hid them and picked our way through briars and prickly pear using flashlights. We stumbled upon a clearing in front of a small unpainted building. We shut off our flashlights and hid behind a tree.

Gathered there were about ten men wearing cloth sacks over their heads. The night was cool, and they'd built a bonfire from packing crates. They stood around joking and drinking, staring at something just beyond our line of sight. Over their laughter we heard a woman crying.

We slid around the edge of the woods until we saw her, hands tied above her head with a rope hanging from a tree limb. She was about eighteen, naked and scared. Closing my eyes now, I could see her as clearly as I did that night, the rope cutting into her wrists, blood flowing down her arms.

We watched the men, one after another, open their trousers and take their turns with her. Her plaintive sobs turned into a long gasping wail.

"Shit!" Jimmie whispered. "What we gone do?"

"I don't know. Do you recognize her?"

"Nope."

One of the men shouted, "Alright, boys, that's enough. Get rid of her."

"No suh… no suh. Please don't." She let out a cry, as they cut the rope and let her down. "Please suh…Please turn me loose."

I closed my eyes and hid my face in the dirt, praying this was a bad dream. I had to get away, but my arms and legs wouldn't move.

As the men dragged her toward the swamp she broke free and ran.

"Get her," one of them yelled. "Put the dogs on her."

From the distance came the baying of bloodhounds. Then all went quiet, but for the crickets and bullfrogs.

Jimmie and I ran as fast as we could, briars and twigs tearing at our clothes, to the place where we'd hidden our bikes.

"We have to tell somebody." I said, struggling to catch my breath.

"Who we gone tell? That damn sheriff? He won't believe us. We don't even know who those crackers are. Hell, sheriff might be one of them. They'll find us and kill us, just like they did that girl."

"Why would they do something like that? They can't get away with it!"

"You don't know half what goes on in this town, Tom. There ain't nothing you can do about it."

We rode home as fast as our bikes would carry us. I climbed back through my window, praying my grandparents hadn't awakened while I was gone, and slipped out of my filthy clothes. I crept into the bathroom, not daring to turn on the light. In the moonlight through the window, I studied my reflection in the mirror. I turned on a thin stream of water and wiped off my bleeding arms and legs as best I could, thankful there were no cuts on my face.

I realize now that my twelve-year-old brain couldn't process all this. For a long time, I couldn't sleep. I lay in bed, sobbing and shaking, unable to make sense out of what I'd seen.

When I saw Jimmie again, more than a week later, I didn't know what to say.

"Somebody's gotta do something," I blurted out.

"Somebody already did," said Jimmie. He stared at the ground and turned away. "Forget about it, Tom. Okay?"

We never discussed it again. Later I heard there'd been a fire out at Little River. A building burned taking several acres of pines with it. Over time I convinced myself that night never happened, that it was just another vivid nightmare, one of many that would haunt my sleep for years to come.

Now, as I gazed at that little sign, a murderous rage boiled inside me. Someone had rebuilt the place. All my unfocused anger now had a target. I considered getting out and investigating it but decided to come back after dark.

Chapter Sixteen

The sun set amid gathering clouds as the Evening Star made its appearance in the west. It was suppertime at the hospital. From inside my grandmother's room, I heard the voice of Bill Emmett.

"Miss Edna, I sure am glad you're on the mend." He looked up as I walked in. "Tom, how ya been?" He jumped out of his seat, rounded the bed and pumped my hand like he was milking a cow. "It's been a long time," he grinned. "You know, you've gotta get home more often."

"I guess you're right," I said, gazing at my grandmother.

She was sitting up on her own, looking better than she had that morning, but her appetite hadn't returned. The standard hospital supper, ham, peas and orange Jell-O, sat barely touched on the rolling table beside her.

"How are you feeling, Grandmama?"

"I'll feel better when I can go home."

"What you been up to, Tom?" Bill asked.

I told him about my job in Tampa and my trip to Atlanta. From the look on his face, I'd have almost believed he cared. I didn't mention my visit to Pleasant Springs or the Little River Hunting Club.

"That's great, son. I always knew you'd make something of yourself. Your mama and daddy'd be mighty proud. Look, I've got to head out. I know I'm leaving your grandmama in good hands. Come on by and see me while you're here."

"I'll do that, Bill." I thought for a moment and added, "Will you be in your office tomorrow morning?"

He gave me a puzzled look. "Sure."

"How early do you get there?"

"About eight o'clock."

"I'll see you then."

"You know, Tom," my grandmother said when Bill had left, "We sure are blessed to have friends like Bill.. I don't know what I'd have done when your granddaddy died if it hadn't been for him and George Martin."

"Yeah. I'm sure."

She gave me a penetrating look. "You and I certainly couldn't have run that farm by ourselves. Bill gave me a good price for it and set you up a trust fund with the money we got from selling your mama and daddy's house. He and George even added some of their own money."

"Yeah... I heard the old farm's gonna be part of a big resort Bill and his friends from Miami are developing." I tried to keep the sarcasm from my voice.

"All I know is you were able to finish college thanks to Bill. Now you have a nice job and a girlfriend, and, if I live long enough, maybe I'll see some great-grandchildren."

I smiled and changed the subject. We talked about people I hadn't seen since I left Monrovia. We watched Channel 6 News on a small black-and-white TV. Then I sat there until she dozed off, kissed her on the forehead and left.

As I stepped into the hall, I nearly bumped into an old man in a faded blue bath robe and white pajamas pushing an aluminum walker with padded feet. Bent over so far all I could see was the crown of his head, he didn't seem to notice me at first. Then he stopped and turned, the gleam in his watery blue eyes totally out of character with his stooped shoulders, halting gait and parchment complexion.

"He's coming, you know." His voice was so low and dry I wasn't sure I'd heard it.

"What...?" I wanted to ask what he meant but bit off the question in mid-sentence. He was probably senile and had no idea what he'd said.

He turned and continued his slow trek. His white hair, what was left of it, formed a thin halo, a green, fluorescent glow reflecting from his scalp. He had to be well past eighty.

"He's coming," the man repeated. He glanced back again with a grin.

I smiled back and waved. I reached the end of the corridor and turned. As he shuffled past the nursing station no one looked up. He must've been there so long he was just a part of the aging furniture.

Chapter Seventeen

By the time I left the hospital darkness had descended on the town. I returned to a roadside spot near the Little River Hunting Club and parked beneath a shady tree. Pulling a flashlight from my glove compartment, I walked along the road and stepped over the chain.

A short distance down the drive I came to a broad clearing. There stood a log cabin with a tin roof and small front porch about a foot above the ground. It looked to be in better condition than the one Jimmie had torched.

The lights were off inside, and there were no cars in sight. A chorus of crickets and frogs serenaded me accompanied by an owl hooting in the distance. The tire tracks in the soft sand didn't appear fresh, but I had no doubt that the people who'd lynched Jimmie were back in business.

For a moment I thought of going back to town for a can of gasoline, but I soon came to my senses. The more important thing was to find out who was backing Emmett's Arcadia development and what connection they might have to the hunting club. The fire could wait.

On the way home exhaustion wrapped around me like a soft, warm blanket. I nearly drove off the road.

I retrieved my box of research files from the trunk, grabbed my suitcase with my free hand and carried them inside. As I sank into my bed I considered calling Colleen but decided I could wait until morning.

***

Awake at 6 a.m., I dressed and went for a quick run out past the water plant. Though I'd long ago recovered use of my right leg, I'd never again run as fast as I did in high school. The Vietcong slug had taken nearly an inch of muscle, and all the exercise in the world wouldn't put it back.

Returning home sweaty and exhausted, I fried up some eggs and bacon and downed them with a glass of milk. The refrigerator was almost empty, and I made a note to pick up groceries at the IGA.

After showering, I called the newspaper and told Pug about my grandmother. He gave me a couple of days off, said he liked my story about Dr. King's funeral and asked me to tell my grandmother hello.

I called Colleen's office. Her secretary said she'd be in court all morning, so I left a message telling her about my grandmother and promised to call her at home that night.

It was too early to go to the hospital. Visiting hours began at 9, so I went to see Bill Emmett.

Bill inherited Monrovia State Bank, an imposing red brick and stucco structure built in 1919 by his grandfather. It perched on a corner near the square like an aging dowager and was the most impressive building in town besides the courthouse. Always the promoter, Bill's grandfather talked his customers and friends, including my grandfather, into purchasing shares of Coca Cola. I owe part of my college education to a carbonated drink that once contained cocaine and the rest to tobacco, a leading cause of heart disease and lung cancer.

Bill's corner office, on the third floor, commanded a sweeping view of downtown. Facing each other from opposite walls portraits of his father and grandfather kept watch over their progeny.

Seated behind an antique mahogany desk that filled most of the room, Bill was poring over a letter and didn't notice me at first. In his right hand he held the unlit stub of a cigar.

I gave a light cough. He looked up, dropping the stogie into an ash tray, and practically vaulted over the desk to shake my hand, no small feat for a man of his age and girth.

"Hey, Tom, can I get you a Coca Cola?"

"Sure. Thanks." I tried not to stare at his hairline, or lack of one. Since I'd last seen him, Bill had begun wearing a toupee. Matched perfectly to his natural hair, it swept across his broad forehead.

"It's been a long time," he said. He opened a small refrigerator and pulled out a dark brown, six-ounce bottle.

"Yes, it has. Not much has changed, but I did notice one thing. I drove out Pleasant Springs Road yesterday... It has a new blacktop."

His face registered no reaction.

"I also saw the sign for Arcadia Springs. It says the bank's funding it. What can you tell me about it?"

His eyes lowered for a moment as he drew himself up like a carnival barker. "Let me tell you, son. This'll be the greatest thing ever happened to this town. Some folks from down in Miami bought up all that land out there where those colored folks used to live and several of the surrounding tobacco farms."

With his right hand he made an expansive gesture as though he were Moses parting the Red Sea. "They're gonna build the biggest resort and retirement community in the whole state of Florida. It'll have a five-star hotel with over two hundred rooms, a country club with twelve lighted tennis courts and a thirty-six-hole championship golf course. Come here and take a look."

He ushered me to a large drawing table in an adjacent room. Scattered across it lay several blueprints, one of which he unfurled. "This here's the site plan. What you saw yesterday was the privacy gate at the entrance. The hotel will overlook the lake, which we've renamed Arcadia Springs. There'll be a magnolia-lined avenue running all the way up to here, just like at the Augusta National.

"On the other side of the lake will be the country club and tennis courts. The golf course starts here and winds all through the development. Most of the houses will back up to the fairways so folks can walk right out their back doors and onto the course. These cul-de-sacs off the main road will have separate gated communities with homes starting at $250,000."

He pointed to a large lot with a private lake. "This'll be my place, right across from the hotel. I should be moving in in about seven months. George Martin's already built his place over here next to the main spring near the clubhouse. It's the only one out there so far."

"If his is the only one there, why does he need a locked gate and a guard?"

Bill gave me a cautious look. "I guess he wants to keep the riffraff out." Returning to his visual tour, he added "Now, circling around the outside will be a tree-lined boulevard." He traced the circumference road, which bore the name "Sam Williams Drive." "We named it after your daddy. I hope you don't mind."

"Why should I mind?"

"Well, I talked to your grandmama about it, and she gave it her blessing."

I looked back at the map. "How much of this have you built so far?"

"Just the entrance and George's place."

As I studied the drawing I noticed something odd. "I didn't recall another lake back here." I pointed at an area east of the development.

"That's the mine hole left by the phosphate company. We're gonna fill in part of it for the golf course and leave the rest of it natural."

"Are they done with it?"

"Pretty much… They'll finish up in a couple of months."

"Who's going to clean up their mess?"

"The mining company… My investors have worked out a deal with them."

He walked behind his desk, reached into the mahogany credenza, and pulled out a can of Tom's peanuts. "Want some?" He leaned his head back and tossed a handful into his mouth.

"No thanks. Tell me something, Bill. Who in their right mind's going to pay a quarter million dollars to live out here in the middle of nowhere? We don't even have a decent road from Highway 98."

"Don't you worry. I've got some folks up in Tallahassee taking care of that. We're gonna have a four-lane divided parkway running straight out there and on through Mabry, all the way to I-75." He traced a route across the map with his left index finger.

"You're going to run a four-lane highway through the middle of Mabry? Have you talked to the folks who live over there?"

"There won't be a damned thing they can do about it, son. It's the price of progress." He chuckled to himself, "Hell, when the DOT's done there won't be anything left of Mabry. 'Good riddance,' I say."

"I still don't get it."

"Well fortunately a lot of people *do* get it. This is the first glimmer of hope they've had since we stopped raising tobacco. It'll be a revival for the whole county. Folks are buying up stock certificates as fast as we can print them. It's almost fully subscribed, but I can still get you some shares if you like."

"I'm afraid I'm short on cash at the moment, Bill." I didn't have the heart to tell him I didn't want any part of him and his land scheme. It sounded too good to be true.

"You don't have to come up with the money right now, Tom. You know your credit's good with me."

"I appreciate your generosity, Bill, but I'll have to pass."

"You're missing out on a gravy train." He beamed down at the drawings as if he were holding his newborn son.

"I see. Tell me something else, Bill, what about all those people who used to live out there? Are they gonna ride the gravy train, too?" I regretted the question as soon as it left my lips.

For a moment I saw a flicker of anger. "You mean all those colored people?" He was incredulous. To him the thought of them participating in his bounty was preposterous.

"It was their land last time I was here."

"Yes, it was, and we bought it fair and square. They took their money and left town."

I half expected him to say 'good riddance' again.

"Well," I sighed. "I hope this is as big a deal as you say. Monrovia could sure use the money and the jobs. By the way, I didn't see the names of your investors from Miami on that sign out there. Who did you say they were?"

Caught off guard, he quickly recovered. "I didn't."

"I see. Somebody put up a new sign in front of the Little River Hunting Club, with a chain across the drive." I didn't mention my late-night visit. "Didn't that place burn down a few years back?"

Bill stared at me as though I'd resurrected the memory of a prostitute somewhere back in his family tree. "I wouldn't know anything about that. Besides, who cares what a bunch of white trash do, as long as they aren't bothering anybody?"

"Well... as long as they aren't bothering anybody."

"You thinking of writing a newspaper story about this?"

"Maybe."

"Well just hold off. When we have our grand opening, I'll give you an exclusive. You can tour the grounds, play a round of golf and get some pictures."

136

I forced a quick smile. "Sounds like a great idea, Bill. Like I said, I was just curious." I rose from my chair. "I've gotta get over to the hospital. It's been great seeing you again."

"Same here… I mean what I said. Come by and see my new house when it's built. Your grandmama should be better by then. Sarah and I would love to have you two out for supper."

"Sounds good. I'll be in town a few more days. Maybe I'll come back by before I leave. Tell Sarah I said hello."

"You're welcome anytime. I'll come see your grandmama as soon as she gets home."

"Thanks. That'll mean a lot to her."

"And let her know we're praying for her."

"I'll do that, Bill."

I smiled, shook his hand and left.

Chapter Eighteen

I arrived at the hospital to find my grandmother in a foul mood. It mattered little to her that visiting hours had just begun, and I couldn't have come earlier. She *again* said she wanted to go home, and I *again* explained that she needed to stay a few more days.

A nurse came in and offered to take her for a short walk. Though tentative at first, she regained her strength and confidence with every step.

In a room at the end of the hall lay eighteen-year-old David Crichton, unconscious. His left leg, encased in plaster, hung from a pulley above the bed. A large bandage covered his forehead. His mom, an old friend of my grandmother's, kept vigil.

David had wiped out on his motorcycle while racing around the parking lot of an abandoned packing house, but the doctor predicted a full recovery. My grandmother brightened as the conversation drifted to other topics. When the opportunity arose, I made my excuses and eased out, seemingly unnoticed.

In the hall I again passed the old man on the walker.

"He's coming," he said.

I smiled and ignored him, stopping at the nursing station to let them know I was again leaving my grandmother in their care.

***

Instead of going home, I turned right onto Mabry Road. A half mile down, I pulled into a shady lane that led to a sunlit glade.

The last time I visited New Hope Baptist Church I was a freshman at Florida. Nothing had changed. Throughout the turmoil of the late sixties, it remained a defiant monument to the past, its white clapboard siding gleaming in the sunshine, its tall grey steeple reaching heavenward, pointing the way home for the saved. A missionary from eastern Tennessee founded it in 1843, with two of my ancestors among his earliest followers.

The new-mown lawn, fragrant in morning dew, reached out from the fresh-painted concrete steps to the tree line of the cemetery. Live oaks, sweet gums and magnolias stood like ancient sentinels, beards of Spanish moss swaying in the gathering breeze. Among those resting here were the wealthy and the poor, the famous and infamous, all entombed in the ultimate equality of death. Our family plot lay in a thickly wooded area. Beams of light like pencils penetrated the leafy canopy and danced across the speckled, sandy ground.

Azaleas, camellias and gardenias, planted over the years by the ladies of the church, encircled the graves of my parents, resplendent in their springtime glory. Chameleons darted beneath thick foliage and a brown thrasher trotted by proudly displaying a fat grub he'd found for his young.

I came here often when I was in high school to get away from the noise. Nearby stood a stump where I'd sit for hours, thinking and writing. By now it had rotted, its jagged top covered in ferns. I found a clear patch of ground and leaned back against a tree, carefully avoiding sandspurs and a rather large ant bed.

For a long time, I stared at the flat granite rectangles bearing the names of Samuel Dickson Williams, Jean Spivey Williams and David Clarence Williams. Beside my grandfather's plot lay a conspicuously empty space where one day I would bury my grandmother... if I lived that long.

The marble spires of my ancestors' tombs, in stark contrast, were almost as tall as I was. I never knew these folks, but their mere presence told me I was part of a chain of humanity stretching all the way back to

Adam and Eve and rolling forward into the unforeseeable future. I wondered, as I surveyed this tableau, who else might come here, sixty or a hundred years hence, and gaze down at my grave with the same thoughts.

A shadow fell over me.

"Well, Tom, it's good to have you back home." The syrupy voice startled me.

Pastor Don Fullerton studied me through dark eyes pinched tightly beneath bushy, gray brows. Though the day was still cool, he'd already shed his plaid sports coat and clip-on tie and had opened the top button of his white, short-sleeved shirt.

"You know, I used to see you out here all the time back when you were in school. You'd sit there on that old stump for hours, writing in your little notebook." He took a deep breath and gazed around. "This certainly is a fine place to sit and meditate."

"Yeah, I guess it is." I fought the temptation to remind him that what made this such a great place to sit alone was *being left alone*. The thought of this sanctimonious asshole staring out a window at me made me nauseous.

"You know, Tom, when I heard you were back, I thought what a blessing it was that the Lord should guide your footsteps home in your grandmama's hour of need. I tell you there are no accidents."

"It's a miracle alright." I stared at my parents' markers and wondered. Had their accidental deaths been part of God's plan?

The preacher paused for a moment, hooked his thumbs in his armpits, and contemplated the tassels on his brown loafers. "Tom, I sure hope you'll devote your brief time here to comforting your grandmama rather than going around asking questions and stirring up bad memories."

Amazed at how quickly he cut to the chase, I fought back the temptation to tell him what I really thought. Instead, I gazed up at him.

"Don, doesn't it bother you even a little, as a *spiritual leader* in this fine community, that Jimmie and Dana could be murdered on the same day, and nobody cared enough to find out why. All these years later we still don't know. Everyone just wants to forget, as if it never happened."

"What do you expect to find out, Tom, that your friend was innocent and somebody else murdered Mrs. Padgett? It's terrible they hanged him like that and didn't give him a fair trial... but they did catch him with her necklace in his pocket."

"It sounds to me like you tried him and convicted him yourself, Don, just like everybody else. Would you make the same assumption if Jimmie had come from a nice *white* family?"

"Well..."

"Of course not. You'd assume he was innocent, there was some mistake, an accident perhaps. But all you needed to know was that the accused was Black and the victim a white female, and you immediately took the word of a corrupt sheriff who *says* Jimmie had the necklace."

"Now wait a minute..."

"No, no. I'm sick of this."

I rose, stalked back to my car and left. Looking back at him in my rear-view mirror I felt like a heel. Smarmy as he was, the man probably meant well. I had no reason to unload my anger on him. Now my grandmother would hear about it, and she'd be mortified. To her he was a saint.

***

It was almost noon, and I was hungry. I stopped at Sandy's for a club sandwich and a Coke. I pulled out a ballpoint pen and my small, wire-bound notebook and began to write. Occasionally I'd glance around to see who else was there and whether they noticed me. Customers drifted in and out, accompanied by the outside symphony of traffic and passers-by.

In the short time I'd been here I'd made several startling, seemingly disconnected discoveries. On an empty page I constructed a simple list of names, places and events, hoping they'd connect into a narrative.

I began with "Arcadia Development Company." Beside it I wrote "Bill Emmett" and connected the two with a dotted line.

I added "Pleasant Springs", "phosphate mine", "Little River Hunting Club", "new highway", "Jimmie Lee Johnson" and "Dana Padgett." My gut told me the last two had something to do with the others.

I stopped and stared at the page, convinced there was something I wasn't seeing.

"Whatcha doin'?"

Startled, I nearly dove under the table, spilling my Coke. Just in time I retrieved the notebook.

June Skinner stood over me, my bill in her outstretched hand.

"Oh nothing...," I said. "Just making some notes." I flipped the notebook shut, hoping she hadn't read it, caught my breath and willed my heart to slow. "You startled me. That's all."

"You might wanna switch to Sprite, Tom. That caffeine's making you jumpy." She gave me one of her rare smiles and handed me the check.

When she'd left, I returned to my notes. Beside Emmett's name I wrote "boys from Miami." What the hell did all this mean?

As I gazed at the courthouse a thought occurred to me. Perhaps part of my answer lay in the county records office. I decided to visit there the next day and research land transactions in the vicinity of Pleasant Springs.

I stared at the page a few seconds longer and slipped the notebook into my pocket. As I approached the counter to pay my bill I realized I was the last of the lunch customers. Sandy and June had waited patiently for me to leave so they could close.

***

Ignoring the yellow pollen haze enveloping the town, I drove aimlessly with my top down scanning the dial for something besides country music. I found a station playing "Mrs. Robinson." An image of Dana came to mind. I didn't know whether to smile or cry.

As I passed Monrovia Elementary and High School, I glanced at my watch. It was just past four. I'd spent twelve years there, back when they were all-white schools. The complex, comprised of six red brick buildings built in the 1930s, spanned an area the length of two city blocks, with football and baseball fields in the back. I circled around behind for a closer look.

The last yellow school bus was just pulling out. On a barren, dusty practice field the baseball team worked out in the hot sun. At first it seemed nothing had changed in the nine years since I graduated, but as I slowed for a closer look I saw one major difference. Nearly half the players running bases, taking batting practice and fielding pop flies were Black.

Four years earlier, following passage of the Civil Rights Act, the State of Florida finally began integrating its schools. A reluctant and controversial move, it put Florida well ahead of most Southern states. Maybe Monrovia was creeping into the twentieth century after all... maybe not. Either way, it was running from its past as fast as it could.

As I contemplated my last two years here, I thought of Clara O'Connor. I couldn't pass through town without stopping to see her.

Besides my grandmother, she'd been the biggest influence on my life. I hadn't seen her since I moved to Tampa. I figured she was still teaching, though by now she would be well into her sixties. I couldn't imagine her doing anything else.

I pulled my car into the small faculty lot and went inside on the off chance she was still there. The pale blue walls were just as I remembered, only dingier, and many of the lockers no longer had doors. But the place still had the familiar smells of a public school, that combination of body odor, Pine Sol and musty old textbooks.

Clara sat at her desk in the same classroom where she'd taught me Senior English. At first she didn't notice me standing quietly in the doorway. She regarded a stack of essays with an obvious look of disgust. Her cloud of white hair appeared to have done battle with a comb, and the comb lost. She had the same pale complexion and ruddy cheeks, but the overhead fluorescents highlighted fine lines around her eyes and mouth.

She wore no discernible makeup yet looked younger than her sixty-odd years. Her duties as girls' physical ed teacher had kept her in excellent condition despite her cigarette habit. Unlike most PE coaches, she ran laps with her students. After school, whenever possible, she spent time with them on the basketball court shooting hoops.

I cleared my throat. When she looked up, it took her a moment to register.

"Tom Williams! Well, I'll be! I'd never have recognized you with that long hair. What brings you here?"

"You don't think I'd come into town without paying a visit to my favorite teacher? I was on my way home from the hospital and thought I'd stop by."

"Oh yes! I heard about your grandmother. I hope she's doing better."

"She is. You know her. She's already trying to escape the place. The hardest thing will be making her rest and relax when she gets home."

"Well, bless her heart. I'll have to go by and see her. This *is* a special pleasure, Tom. It's been such a long time. A good friend of mine in Tampa sends me copies of the *Sentinel*, just so I can read your stories. I'm so glad you decided to keep up your writing."

"Thanks. I see you're still teaching."

"You know me. I'll keep doing this until the day they drag me out of here."

"Are you still teaching girls' PE?"

"Of course, and you won't believe this. We finally have a girls' varsity basketball team. We start playing a regular schedule next year, and I'm going to be the coach. I have twelve young women ready to play."

"That's great, Clara. Monrovia's never had a girls' athletic program."

"Not until now"

"I guess things *are* changing."

"I read the piece you wrote about the Martin Luther King funeral. It was excellent. Your parents would be so proud."

"Thanks."

Scanning the classroom, I noticed a black-and-white photo of Clara, smiling and holding a plaque. For once, she wore makeup, and what appeared to be a white dress offset by a beautiful necklace.

Clara rose from her chair and came around the desk. "What are you working on next, Tom?"

"I don't know, perhaps a story about Monrovia, girls' basketball, school desegregation and that resort Bill Emmett's building."

She paused for a moment and gazed out the window. "That would make an interesting story, one focused on the future of this community instead of its past."

"What do you mean?" I knew exactly what she meant.

"So many tragic things have happened here. A good many of them involved you personally, but they're all in the past and there's nothing we can do now to make them right. All we can do is put them behind us and move on. Our schools are finally desegregating, and Bill's promising an economic rebirth in Monrovia."

"You mean Arcadia Springs?"

"I do. Bill's worked hard on that project. He's pulled together the funding, and I understand he's already lined up the builders. I think it has a very good chance of success."

"I hope so, Clara. We need something. The phosphate mine hasn't done much for us, and from what I hear they're about through with it."

"Yeah, so what's going on with you? Are you married yet?"

"Not yet. I am dating someone, a lawyer I met in Tampa. She comes from a large family in Boston."

"That's fantastic. I'm so glad to see women finally breaking into professions like law and medicine and accounting."

I told her about Tampa and some of the locals I'd met. She filled me in on other changes in Monrovia, mostly businesses that had closed and people who'd died or moved away.

I was about to say goodbye when, for some reason, I remembered something Clara told me years earlier. "You once said, back when I was high school, that I should move away from Monrovia when I graduated."

"And you did. You've already seen more of the world than most people will."

"If you want to call Vietnam 'seeing the world'... You also mentioned that you planned to retire and move to Sanibel with a friend. Whatever happened to those plans?"

Her face darkened for a moment, and she looked away. "That was a long time ago, Tom. It was just one of those things that didn't work out."

146

I could see this was a sore subject, so I dropped it. "Look, I'm sorry. I didn't mean to pry. I guess it's an occupational hazard." I forced a smile. "Listen, I have to go. It's been great seeing you. I'll try to stop by again before I leave."

"Please do. Maybe you and your grandmother can come by the house one evening. We could sit on the porch and talk, just like old times."

"That'd be great."

Chapter Nineteen

I arrived home to find the living room lamp still on from that morning. It stood silently between two recliners we brought with us years ago from the farm. The headrest on my grandfather's chair had a worn spot where he leaned back as he sat. After all these years it still smelled of stale cigar smoke. In the fireplace stood a tiny space heater with white ceramic grates that turned bright orange on cold winter days.

The wood-framed, shotgun house, built in 1905, had three bedrooms and a bath on the right side, the living room, dining room, and kitchen on the left. I'd lived here little more than a year before I graduated from high school, but it was as much a home as the farm had ever been.

The dining room was so small I had to detour around its large table to get to the kitchen, where, with me gone, my grandmother now took her meals, except on those occasions when I came home.

The only phone in the house had an old-fashioned rotary dial. It sat on a lace cloth atop a small table in the hallway. As I tried again to reach Colleen, I contemplated how far back in time I'd traveled in the past forty-eight hours.

"Hello." Her voice sounded a million miles away.

I sank into a nearby chair, rubbed my eyes and yawned. "Hey, baby."

"Tom! Where are you calling from? I got the message. How's your grandmother?"

"Getting better. She had some supper, and she's starting to get her color back. The doctor told her to rest. Whether she will or not I don't know."

"That's good. How about you? You sound tired. Get some rest, yourself."

"Sure. Sure." Colleen was right. I still hadn't caught up from my overnight drive. I closed my eyes and pictured her in my mind, blonde curls tumbling over her shoulders. "I'm getting ready to turn in. I just wanted to hear your voice. What are you doing?"

"Just poring over some briefs. I have an arraignment in the morning."

"Is it a murderer this time or a rapist?"

"That would be 'alleged murderer' or 'alleged rapist.' As a journalist you ought to know better. Besides, it's neither. It's Frankie Tavares. The police pulled him over last night on Kennedy for a broken taillight. They claimed they found two ounces of marijuana in his car and busted him as a dealer. Frankie says it's totally bogus. The cops planted it."

"Don't you just hate it when they do that?"

"Alright, smartass!"

"Wait a minute! Are we talking about Frank Tavares the state representative?"

"His son, Frank Junior"

"And you're going to get him off."

"Of course. The police set him up. I'm telling you, it's all bullshit. The DA's a political enemy of Frank Senior, and he's just trying to embarrass him."

"Okay. Well, if I ever need a lawyer, I'll know who to call."

"You bet your sweet ass you will. Listen, I've got to finish this up and you need to get some sleep. Call me tomorrow night. I'll have more time"

"Sure. Before I go though, I was wondering if you could do me a favor."

"Is it billable?"

"You told me once you had friends in the Florida Secretary of State's office."

"Yeah, a couple of guys from law school."

"See what they can find out about a corporation called 'Arcadia Development Company.' It's buying up land around here, supposedly for a golf resort and a bunch of luxury homes. Something about it doesn't smell right."

She nearly choked. "They're building a resort in Monrovia?"

"I know. It sounds like a load of crap. The banker financing it is Bill Emmett, an old friend of the family. He tells me some investors from Miami are behind it, but he won't say who they are."

"Baby, what are you getting yourself into?"

"Not sure, but I'll let you know when I find out. I'll be here a couple of days, at least until my grandmother gets back on her feet and Ida can take care of her. This'll give me something to do so I don't go stir crazy."

"Okay. I'll let you know what I find out. Just take care of yourself."

"Thanks. I'll call you tomorrow night."

"I love you, Tom Williams, ace reporter."

"I love you too, baby."

Returning to the kitchen, my gaze fell on the file box I'd left on the table the previous night. Sticking out was a tab that read, "Martinez, Freddy." I recalled the addict's crazy stories, especially the one about Rico Salazar and the Bay of Pigs.

I laid the file on the table and quickly thumbed through it, pausing at the photo of Salazar. Behind it was the yellow packing slip Freddy gave me with the list of corporations. About halfway down I saw "Arcadia Holdings, Inc." Was this a coincidence? Was there a connection between Arcadia Holdings and Arcadia Development?

I thought about calling Colleen back but decided against it. Instead, I put the file in the box and pulled out my notebook. Beside "Arcadia Development" I wrote "Arcadia Holdings?"

Looking back through my notes I thought again about the murder of Dana Padgett. If Jimmie didn't kill her, who did? I'd probably never know. From what little I remembered the sheriff and his nephews hadn't gathered any evidence at the crime scene. They were too busy gawking at Dana's naked body. As far as they were concerned, they solved the case the moment they arrested Jimmie. Given my experiences with them, I sure as hell wasn't going to call them with questions.

Then it occurred to me that Doc Green would have autopsied both Dana and Jimmie. At his age and with the passing of years, he might not remember anything useful, but I could ask him when I saw him next. I wrote his name beside Dana's and Jimmie's and connected them with dotted lines.

Exhausted from my trip, I showered, brushed my teeth and went to bed. Tired as I was, I lay there listening to the mantle clock in the living room chiming at the top of every hour. I startled more than once, thinking I heard voices, before remembering they were the sounds of the house settling.

A glow of headlights from the street outside drifted across the ceiling, floated down the wall like an apparition and faded into the darkened hallway. I rolled and tossed on the iron-framed bed disturbed by half-dreams of my parents and my grandfather in their coffins. Again, I saw the empty space beside them in the cemetery. I thought of my grandmother lying in the hospital, wanting to come home and began to sob, more alone in that moment than I'd ever been.

***

At six a.m. I awoke and went for another run, struggling to sort out the things I'd discovered about Pleasant Springs. No matter how I looked at it, Emmett's story made no sense.

With the break in my work schedule, I'd lost track of the days and had to think back to my arrival from Atlanta. That had been Wednesday, so today was Friday.

The sky clouded over. A moist breeze blew in from the southeast. Before leaving home I caught the tail-end of a news report, a storm system building in the mid-Atlantic. With hurricane season still more than a month away, it was probably little more than a squall. The weatherman predicted it would come ashore sometime early next week.

When I got back I showered again and dressed. On my way to the hospital, I stopped at the courthouse to see what I could find out about Arcadia Development. The three-storied yellow and white brick structure dated to the late nineteenth century. Around it lay a park filled with live oaks and magnolias draped in Spanish moss where there had once been a broad lawn.

Among those trees lay the spot where three returning World War II heroes addressed their neighbors from a red, white and blue bunting-draped bandstand. Now a granite marker stood there, about three feet high, its bronze plaque grown green with age. It read:

Dedicated to the memory of our fallen brother,
Samuel Dickson Williams
(September 8, 1918 – May 16, 1953)
Courageous American, loving husband and father, untiring
servant of this community
Semper Fi.

For years I thought the county had paid for that stone. Later I learned that Bill Emmett and George Martin obtained permission to place it there.

In my childhood memories the courthouse loomed solid and time-less. Now, with its marble steps worn by the feet of countless citizens, cornices fading and paint peeling, it seemed to have diminished.

The ground floor, commonly known as the basement, held the drivers' license bureau and the tag and title offices. It was here that Jasper County residents could obtain, among other things, liquor licenses, marriage licenses and gun permits. Its long-time guardian, Eunice Wilson, was the one person in Jasper County most able to help me in my investigation. I found her seated at her desk in the cramped confines of the title office.

"Hey, Miss Eunice, I'm Tom Williams. I don't know if you remember me."

"Oh yeah, I remember you, Tom. How you been?" Her voice was soft and cordial, but she never smiled as she peered over reading glasses suspended by a long cord around her neck. The pile of white curls atop her head was immaculate. A spot of pink rouge on each cheek offset an alabaster complexion, remarkably smooth given her age. She wore a shade of red lipstick that would have made Dracula thirsty, and her dress, a relic from the fifties, was as clean and crisp as the day she'd bought it.

She pursed her lips as if remembering something. "You're Edna Williams' grandson, aren't you?"

"Yes ma'am."

"I heard she was in the hospital. How's she doing?"

"She's gonna be alright. She should be coming home soon."

"That's good. How can I help you?"

Despite her smile, something said she neither cared how I was, nor how my grandmother was, nor whether she could help me. She was simply being polite the way people in the South customarily are. No doubt she was intent on returning to her paperback romance novel lying on her desk. Eunice was either close to retirement or had already retired and still came in to collect a paycheck. It's hard to tell sometimes.

"I need to look at title information for a property off of Pleasant Springs Road."

"Are you looking to buy a home out there?"

"No ma'am. I'm doing some research."

She waited quietly, as though expecting further explanation, and then replied, "I see. Well, you'll find all the land transactions from the past five years in those filing cabinets over there against the wall. Everything older than that is going to be up on the third floor in the records archive."

My first step was to locate the Arcadia property in the county plat book using the land and lot number I'd memorized from Emmett's site plans. Then I looked up surrounding locations. I didn't know yet what I was looking for, other than purchase dates and names of previous owners.

I glanced back and saw that Eunice had returned to reading her paperback, seemingly oblivious to my presence.

According to title records, Arcadia Development had purchased several tracts over the past five years, not only in the immediate area of the springs, but for nearly a mile in every direction. They included, as Ruby had mentioned, the soon-to-be-abandoned phosphate mine. I took out my notebook and scribbled down the names of former property owners and the attorneys who handled the transfers.

Eventually I discovered a 1967 sale of a property referred to as The Little River Hunting Club. Focusing on the Little River Hunting Club property, I found that Arcadia had bought it in 1967 from a Lester Suggs, whose name sounded vaguely familiar. I jotted it down beside the hunting club and drew a solid line between them.

I drew another line from Arcadia Development Company to the Little River Hunting Club and wondered what connection a Miami drug dealer like Enrico Salazar would have with a bunch of ersatz Klansmen in Jasper County. Maybe there was none, other than the transaction, but I've never put much stock in coincidence. This was my first tentative link between Arcadia and the people I believed murdered Jimmie.

Before long I exhausted the information available in the filing cabinets, put my notebook back in my pocket and asked Eunice where I could find the earlier records on the third floor.

She looked up from her book and managed a patronizing smile. "I'll need to take you up there myself. The judge is very particular about who goes poking around in those archives."

"I understand," I said.

As she came around the counter and led me toward the door, I gazed down into her cloud of white hair. "By the way," she asked without turning, "what was it you said you were doing these days?"

"I write for the *Tampa Sentinel*."

She froze in her tracks, and I nearly stumbled into her. For a moment I thought she'd collapse onto the floor. She turned and focused a penetrating stare at me above her glasses. "You'd better not be writing about Jasper County."

"I don't think so, Miss Eunice. Is there something going on here I should be writing about?" I smiled at her as though I were joking.

"Certainly not! Not anything those people down in Tampa need to read about."

"Don't worry about it then. I'm just curious about this Arcadia project. Bill Emmett tells me it's a great investment and I should get in on it, but I'd like to do a little research first."

This seemed to placate her. "Yes. People all over town are investing with Bill, folks with more money than sense. I've never heard such foolishness in all my life. Who in the world wants to retire in the middle of nowhere?"

"That's a good question, Miss Eunice. I'm sure old Bill knows what he's doing."

"Well, he'd better. I'd hate to see folks lose what little they have left."

I followed her to the end of a narrow hallway and up two flights of stairs. For a woman her age she climbed it with very little effort, from years of practice no doubt.

The archives took up most of the third floor and consisted of a single large room behind a locked door. From the layers of dust on the cardboard boxes and manila folders, I was the first person to venture up here in years. Makeshift shelves, built from raw pine boards, lined the walls, bearing pasteboard boxes marked by year, land lot and parcel numbers.

"The most recent years are over here on the right," Eunice explained. "You probably saw 1963 to 1968 downstairs. We haven't moved them up here, yet. These boxes over here end in 1962. You can work your way back from there. When you finish, please lock the door and bring me back the keys. I need to get back to my work."

In one corner stood an old roll top desk with a peeling veneer. The only other furniture was a cane-backed chair with the remains of a woven seat. I sat in it carefully, half expecting to wind up on the floor. Above the desk hung a bare light bulb suspended from the ceiling with a pull chain.

One-by-one I pulled down boxes, opened them and chose files with land lot numbers along Pleasant Springs Road. As I read through them I found names of people I knew and a good many I didn't. By now many had relocated to plots four feet wide, eight feet long and six feet deep.

I went as far back as 1952. Before that there were only a handful of transactions, most involving small tracts purchased by farmers in the area.

I was about to call it quits when one of them caught my eye. It was the transfer of the Little River property to Lester Suggs from a couple whose names I didn't recognize. I gazed at the date for several moments, not sure of its significance. I put it back in the box, then pulled it out again and stared at it... May 19, 1953, three days after the death of my parents. I noted the date beside Little River Hunting Club and in parentheses the date of my parents' accident.

The dark and dusty room became claustrophobic despite its size. There were no windows, yet I could sense gathering clouds outside, as though the barometer were falling and a gloom descending over the town.

This Lester Suggs, whoever he was, was owner of record for the Little River Hunting Club on that night, years ago, when Jimmie and I witnessed the gang rape and murder of a young Black woman by white men in hoods. *He'd bought the property right after my parents died.*

Later he sold it to Arcadia Development, owned by mob boss and drug smuggler Rico Salazar, *but the hunting club was still there.* Salazar was in partnership with Bill Emmett. I heard the faint click of a puzzle piece slipping into place. I had to find out more about this Suggs.

Glancing at my watch, I saw it was already past ten, and my grandmother would be wondering where I was. Frantically I shoved the folders back into the box and returned it to the shelf. I locked the door behind me, ran down the two flights of stairs and tossed the keys onto the counter.

"Thanks again, Miss Eunice. I have to go see my grandmother now."

She stared at me solemnly above her glasses. "You're welcome," she said softly. There was something strange in her voice, fear perhaps.

Outside a dark cloud had indeed descended on the town. Lightning flashed, accompanied by echoing thunder, as the skies unloaded. It seemed that never in my life did I have an umbrella when I needed one.

Chapter Twenty

Drenched and out of breath, I arrived at the hospital to find my grandmother propped up in bed, entertaining two visitors, Ms. Hattie Lovejoy and another lady I didn't recognize.

They wore matching pink hats. Their white-gloved hands lay neatly folded in the laps of their flower-print dresses. I grabbed a stack of paper towels from a nearby table and dried myself as best I could, mopping up what had dripped onto the linoleum.

"Tom," said my grandmother, "you remember Ms. Lovejoy. This is her sister Mrs. Wright from Mabry. Hattie, this is my grandson, who seems to have gone swimming in his clothes."

Hattie Lovejoy was the official Good Samaritan of New Hope Baptist Church and unofficial town gossip. I said "hello" and sat in one of the vinyl upholstered chairs. A spinster not much older than my mother, Ms. Lovejoy lived three streets over from us.

"Ms. Lovejoy and Mrs. Wright have been kind enough to come see me here in the hospital," my grandmother added. "You know, it means so much to have visitors when you're stuck here all day staring at these four walls."

I ignored her obvious play on my guilt.

"I'm going to leave you with your grandson, Edna," said Ms. Lovejoy. "I'll come by and see you when you get home."

When they were safely out of earshot, my grandmother scowled, "Tom, where have you been?"

"I'm sorry. I was at the courthouse, looking into some things."

"What in the world would you need to *look into* at the courthouse?"

I immediately regretted my answer but decided to find out how much she knew. "Grandmama, tell me about this resort Bill's promoting."

"Oh that! It's supposed to be a big deal. He wanted me to put some money into something called a *limited partnership*. I don't know anything about that stuff. I told him to talk to you while you were here."

"Well, he did. In fact, I dropped by to see him yesterday at the bank. He showed me a site plan for the development, but I came away with more questions than answers. Did he mention anything to you about his business partners?"

"No. I just heard they were some big, rich folks from down in Miami."

"That's more than I could get out of him. What do you know about the Little River Hunting Club?"

She looked at me as though I'd slapped her face. This was obviously not a topic for polite conversation. "I can assure you I know *nothing* about those people." She obviously knew *something* but didn't want to talk about it. Realizing I'd get no further with that, I changed the subject. "Tell me how my parents died."

Her face darkened. "I can't imagine what I haven't told you already. Your granddaddy, God rest his soul, woke up one morning to find Win Stevens knocking on our front door. Win was one of your daddy's deputies. You'd spent the night with us, and your mama and daddy had gone to Tallahassee for dinner, only they never made it there... Win found their car in the Pelahatchie River... with them in it."

Her voice choked. I could have kicked myself for bringing this up, even after all these years, with her lying here in the hospital, but the reporter in me took over, and I knew there had to be more to this story than the explanation she'd given.

"How did he say the accident happened?"

"He said they hit a deer and then crashed into the bridge."

"Is that all?"

"What do you mean *is that all*?"

"It just seems like a strange coincidence." For years I'd heard stories of how my dad and his deputies went after the moonshiners of Jasper County. "That deer did a mighty big favor for a lot of crooks around here. Did Stevens say anything else?"

"No, but he acted kind of strange after that. I remember he left the funeral early, with the other deputy, the one from Tallahassee. I think his name was Watson. He was such a nice young man. We asked them to come out to the house, but they made some excuse about needing to go check on something."

"Where did they go?"

"He didn't say. He just apologized and left."

"Where would I find this Win Stevens?"

"I have no idea. I haven't heard of him or even thought about him in years. When Sheriff Willingham took over he fired Win right away. The last I heard he'd taken to drinking and was living down by the river. The Watson boy moved back to Tallahassee, as I recall."

"Thanks, Grandmama."

"Why do you want to know all this stuff?"

"I'm just curious. That's all."

"Well, don't you go sticking your nose where it doesn't belong. There's no need to stir up old troubles with all your questions. I don't want you getting hurt again and me having to come see *you* in the hospital."

"Don't worry, Grandmama. Has Doc Green been by to see you yet?"

"No, but I sure hope he gets here soon. I want to know when I can get out of this place."

As if on cue, the doctor appeared in the doorway.

"Good morning Edna… Tom. Edna, how you feeling this morning?" He picked up her chart as he spoke and pored over it.

"I feel like getting out of here, Homer. That's how I feel."

161

He pulled on his stethoscope and placed the flat metal disk discretely above the top of her gown. He listened for a moment and said, "Well, if everything goes well tonight I should be able to discharge you in the morning.

"Not a minute too soon. I'm sure my house is a mess."

"No, it's not, Grandmama. Ida and I will have it spotless by the time you get there. All you need right now is some rest."

A nurse came by with a tray of medications and a shot. Doc Green and I stepped outside while she administered it. The hall was empty, and I took the opportunity to ask him about Dana and Jimmie.

"Doc, you did the autopsy on Dana Padgett. Did you see anything about the murder to indicate what sort of person did it?"

He blinked in surprise. "Tom, why in the world would you bring up something like that now, after all these years?"

"I'm sorry. It's just that I was there when they found her, and, as you know, Jimmie Lee Johnson was a good friend of mine.'

He regarded me for a moment. "So, what you're really asking is, do I think Jimmie did it?"

"Well … yes."

"Hell no, he didn't do it, and I told that idiot Willingham he didn't."

He turned as if to leave and then stopped. "It was a Saturday when they found her, and I wasn't particularly busy. I finished early that afternoon and went by the jail to give the sheriff my report. His deputies already had Jimmie there in handcuffs. The way they paraded him in the front door you'd have thought they'd caught John Dillinger. I took one look at that boy's hands, and I knew he didn't do it. The cause of death was manual strangulation. I tried to explain to Willingham that Jimmie's hands were too big."

The doctor held up his own hand, fingers outstretched, as an illustration. "His fingers were too long to have left a bruise pattern like the one

162

I found on Mrs. Padgett's neck. Whoever did it had strong hands but shorter fingers."

An image came to me in a flash, Jimmie grinning and holding out a basketball in the palm of one hand. Before I could grab it he'd snatch it away.

"What did the sheriff say?" I asked.

"He said they'd picked up Jimmie near the crime scene and that he had a necklace belonging to Mrs. Padgett. I didn't think to ask him how he knew the necklace was hers. They just went ahead and locked him up. I left there and went home. That night I got a frantic call from your grandmama. A mob had lynched Jimmie and somehow you'd gotten caught up in the middle of it. When I got back to the jail you were lying on a cot with a goose egg on the back of your head."

I couldn't bring myself to speak. All these years I'd known Jimmie couldn't have murdered anybody. Now I knew it beyond any doubt. Joy, anger and relief washed over me. I stifled it all and asked, "Do you know if Dana was strangled there where we found her body?"

"She was not. She had scratches on the backs of her heels with dirt in them and some bruises on her legs and elbows, like you'd get from thrashing around in a confined space. For that, and other reasons I won't go into, I concluded she'd been brought to the golf course in some vehicle and dragged into the woods."

"That's right," I said, my excitement growing. "Her car wasn't there... Were there any other signs of a struggle?"

His thick eyebrows knitted in a perplexed look. "No, not really... She had a couple of small bruises on her arms and legs, but not much for a woman who'd been strangled."

"One more thing, Doc ... was there any evidence she'd been raped?"

"No. But it seemed she'd had sex shortly beforehand." He paused and blushed a bit. "She was active sexually, but I'm pretty sure she wasn't raped."

He stared at the floor for a moment and in a quiet voice added, "Listen, I'm not supposed to be telling you any of this, especially with you being a newspaper reporter. You're not writing anything about it are you?"

"Don't worry, Doc, I don't think so, and if I do I won't name you as a source."

"Yeah. I'd appreciate that."

We stood in awkward silence until my grandmother called. Unnoticed by either of us, the nurse had left, and Grandmama was by herself.

"Thanks a lot, Doc."

"Don't mention it … I guess I'll see you tomorrow."

I sat and talked with my grandmother until she dozed off. As I left, I pulled out my notebook and jotted down what the doctor had told me. Even a dumbass like Willingham had to know Dana didn't walk to the country club alone and naked. Somebody drove her there. It couldn't have been Jimmie, who didn't own a car, and, to my knowledge, had never driven one. With so little evidence of a struggle, Dana's murderer had to be someone she knew.

A sickening feeling came over me. *If she wasn't raped, why was she nude when we found her?* According to the doctor she'd had sex recently. Mike Padgett was out of town, and the last time I saw her was more than twenty-four hours earlier. *Dana was out that night with somebody else.*

I looked at my watch. It was almost two, and I hadn't eaten since that morning. I wasn't hungry, but I needed something on my stomach, so I stopped at the hospital cafeteria to see if they were still serving lunch.

The only other person there was a woman behind the food counter who was well past sixty. She wore a white pants suit and matching crepe-soled shoes. She'd stuffed most of her graying locks into a black hair net, with stray wisps peeping out around her face. She was closing up when I walked in and didn't appear thrilled to see me. Without the hair net I might have mistaken her for a nurse, until she opened her mouth and revealed perhaps three upper teeth.

"What can I get you, sugar?"

I eyed the special of the day, or what was left of it, on the steam table, unable to identify it. Maybe she was a nurse, after all, and these were leftover body parts from the operating room. The white plastic letters on the blackboard read "Meet Loaf and 2 Veggies $1.25." The vegetable choices were fried okra, now dried to the color and texture of an iguana, English peas, and some watery squash. The dessert of the day was orange Jell-O. *What a surprise!*

Not wanting to become a patient myself, I ordered a grilled cheese sandwich and a Coke. I paid the lady and choked down my meal, as best I could, given the smells emanating from the kitchen and the antiseptic aroma from the hall.

As I left, I almost bumped into the old man on the walker. He seemed to have materialized in the doorway.

He snickered as I made my way around him and rolled his eyes.

"Blow the trumpet on Zion," he bellowed. "Shout a warning on my holy mountain. Let all the people who live in the land shake with fear. The Lord's special day is coming; it is near."

As I fled down the hallway his voice trailed behind me.

"Cry havoc," he shouted, "and let slip the dogs of war... The sack men are coming."

When I was little, before my parents died, Ida would babysit me. She told me stories, late at night, to frighten me into behaving. Her favorites were tales about a "sack man" who traveled the countryside, snatching up children and dragging them into the depths of the nearby swamps.

When I told my parents, they laughed and said there was no sack man, that the worst things in those woods were alligators and water moccasins, which I'd better have the good sense to avoid.

One night, right after their deaths, I awoke screaming. I'd seen the sack man waiting for my parents beneath the Pelahatchie Bridge. I saw his face clearly, and it seemed familiar. It took my grandmother hours to calm me down. She gave me ice water and held me close. *It was just a bad dream*, she kept saying... *There is no such thing as the sack man.*

I chased that memory from my mind as I drove to Ida's place to tell her my grandmother was coming home the next day and I needed help cleaning the house. In my rear-view mirror I saw a yellow El Camino. When I reached Second Street, he was still there.

As I turned onto the dirt road to Ida's house he slowed, as though contemplating whether to turn into the small Black neighborhood. Instead, he sped down Pleasant Springs Road. I told myself I was just being paranoid, that it was probably someone who'd been at the hospital visiting a friend or relative.

A purple Lincoln Continental with gold trim filled Ida's tiny front yard. I parked on the narrow shoulder hoping nobody ran into my car.

Seated on the porch in his white, three-piece suit and brown wingtips was the Reverend Doctor Clarence Mays. The cane-backed chair fitted with a thick quilted cushion was one Ida reserved for her most honored guests. It barely accommodated the good reverend's ample girth, his butt sagging on either side.

He held a tall glass of lemonade in one hand and used the other to fan himself with his white, broad-brimmed hat. Despite all the fanning, a thick row of sweat droplets gathered on his brow, and stains darkened the armpits of his suit. As I approached he regarded me and ran the cold glass across his forehead.

Ruby sat on the steps at his feet. She jumped up as I came into the yard. "Hey, Tom, how's your grandmama today?"

"She's getting better."

"Good afternoon," offered Reverend Mays with a half-smile, continuing to fan himself. His tight white curls glistened in the bright sunshine.

"Reverend Mays," I smiled. Turning back to Ruby, I asked "Is your mama home?"

"Sure." She called to Ida through the screen door.

"What brings you out this way?" asked Reverend Mays, with more than a trace of suspicion. I'd seen him here a couple of times, but he didn't seem to recognize me.

"Reverend Mays, I'm Tom Williams. Miss Ida works for my grandmother, who's been in the hospital. My grandmother's coming home tomorrow and I came to ask Miss Ida to come over and help me clean up." This was already more explanation than he deserved, seeing as this wasn't his home.

"Boy, I didn't even recognize you. I don't think I've seen you since right after the murder." Only for a moment did I wonder which of the two murders he meant.

"It's been a long time, Reverend."

"Seems like yesterday to me."

"Tom's the one who tried to save Jimmie's life, Reverend," said Ruby.

"Yes, I guess he is." The preacher gazed heavenward as though seeking inspiration. "The only thing is… Jimmie Lee's still dead. Isn't he?"

"Yes sir. I guess he is." I never took my eyes off the man, wondering to myself if he would have risked his life to save Jimmie, or anybody else. Try as I may, I couldn't quite conjure up an image of the good

167

reverend, big as he was, sprinting down the hallway of the jail with a ring of keys in his hand.

"And now you come around here 'cause you want his mama to come over and clean yo house." He carefully annunciated the last three words.

I didn't answer him. Reverend or not, the self-righteous bastard was beginning to piss me off. Ida appeared in the doorway, rescuing me from any further conversation with him. "Hey, Tom, how's Ms. Edna doing?"

"She's coming home tomorrow, and I was wondering if you could come by and help me get ready for her."

"Sure. I'll be there at six."

"Thanks."

As I turned to leave the reverend called out, "It's good to see you again Mister Tom. You come back any time."

I bit my tongue. There was no use embarrassing Ida and Ruby, who were apparently quite fond of him.

He kept talking as I walked toward my car. "I understand you're some kind of reporter now, down there in that *big city* of Tampa. Maybe you can help find out who had that white Cadillac over at your country club the night that white lady was killed. After all this time, I reckon it'd be good to know who *the real murderer* was."

I wheeled in my tracks and stared at him.

"Now, Reverend Mays," said Ruby, "you be nice to Tom. He's an old friend of ours."

"Tell me about the white Cadillac, Reverend," I said.

A look of exquisite satisfaction spread like sunrise across his broad face. He paused for effect and continued to fan until I almost turned around and left. "It seems there was a white Cadillac up at your country club that night. Didn't any of *your rich, white friends* tell you about it? Now, I don't know anybody around here who owns a white Cadillac, or owned one back then, but I heard it was a *brand new* one. Still had the dealer tag on it."

"Who told you this?"

"Benny Stillman, the caddy over there at your country club. He said he told the sheriff about it, and the sheriff told him to shut up and mind his own business."

For a moment I wondered why Benny never told me this. Then I realized that, despite our friendship, he had no reason to trust me any more than he trusted the sheriff. Besides, I was a teenager at the time, and there was nothing I could have done with that information.

Things had changed, however, and tonight I would pay Benny a visit.

"Thanks, Reverend. I'm glad you told me that."

"Any time, son, any time"

With some effort, I turned my car around and headed back toward Pelahatchie Road. The earlier rain had left a large mud puddle beside the reverend's purple and gold Lincoln. As I drove past I splashed mud all down the driver's side. *Oops!*

Chapter Twenty-One

As twilight descended, I arrived at the Monrovia Country Club to find the dance hall ablaze with lights. Cars arrived with teenagers and their parents decked out in tuxedos and evening gowns with corsages. This happened, by chance, to be the night of the annual Cotillion Ball honoring the sixteen-year-old debutantes. I took one of the few remaining parking spaces in a distant corner of the lot hoping no one would notice.

The last golfers were gone for the day. As I came around the building Benny Stillman was locking up the clubhouse. He squinted at me for a moment, before recognition set in. "Mister Tom," he smiled, "is that you?" He seemed shorter than I remembered, and what was left of his hair had gone completely white.

"Hey, Benny"

"Where you stay at now, Mister Tom?"

"Tampa... I'm writing for a newspaper down there."

"You married yet?'

"No, but I'm working on that too."

He chuckled. "Well good for you. Good for you." He paused a moment and gazed out across the fairway toward the second hole. His smile faded. "You know I haven't seen you since the morning we found that white lady."

"Yeah, well, actually that's what I came to ask you about. Somebody told me you saw a white Cadillac here the previous night. What can you tell me about it?"

He stared at the ground for few seconds before he replied. "You know, these days I try not to think too much about that stuff. It ain't gone do nobody no good." He paused again. "But the one thing I do remember is that white car. I remember it like it was yesterday."

"Where was it, Benny?"

"It's like I tried to tell the sheriff. It was sitting right over there. It didn't have no business here. It was after midnight, and I'd already closed up. There wasn't no dance or *nothing* that night. I saw it from my house over there." He pointed to a small, green, plywood-paneled building, not far from the first tee.

From inside the hall a cheer went up as the band played an old R&B standard.

"Did you get a good look at the car, Benny?"

"Well, sir, the back part was sticking out from under the shadows of that tree. It was a bright moon out that night, and I could see it was a Caddy. Brand new one too. Still had one of them paper license plates on it, like it just come off the lot."

"Do you remember the dealership?"

"No suh. I always reckoned it was one of Mr. Martin's. He's got the only GM dealership in town."

"Did you see anyone in or around the car?"

"No suh. I seen lots of crazy things over the years, but this was something, that brand new car out here in the middle of the night, parked over there where it could get all scratched up."

He paused, staring at the ground, as though recalling what followed. "Then that lady turned up dead that next morning," he said quietly. "You think there's a connection?"

"There might be, and there might not, but it's worth looking into. You say the sheriff didn't want to hear about it."

"No, suh, and he told me not to tell nobody else neither."

"I'm sure he did, Benny. Don't worry. I won't mention we talked."

"Thank you, Mister Tom. I sure appreciate that. You're alright."

171

"Thanks. I just want to know what really happened."

He nodded, turned and walked the short distance to his home. As I watched him I wondered how long he'd lived by himself in that little camouflaged cabin. He must have had a family at one time. Maybe he'd had dreams and aspirations. But here he was, alone and slowly wasting away, invisible to everyone around him.

As I returned to my car I peered through an open window. The scene before me, in the context of a highly segregated society like Monrovia's, was positively surreal. Amid the multicolored streamers and balloons a mob of teenagers in formal dress gyrated to the sounds of a popular soul group, the Debonairs.

Decked out in matching blue velvet suits, the group sang their only hit, a song titled "Ooh But She Do." The debutantes and their dates, drunk by now, struggled through the suggestive lyrics, most of them singing off key. Their parents sat or stood in the back of the room amid the streamers and looked on. Some smiled uncomfortably, while others seemed amused.

I glanced behind me just in time to see a blue Pontiac station wagon back out of a parking spot and pull around the corner of the building toward the pro shop. I continued to listen to the band as they did a cover of "Be Young, Be Foolish, Be Happy," by the Tams. Then it occurred to me that there was no exit at that end of the building.

I hung close to the wall so no one could see me and nonchalantly strolled to the edge. The vehicle seemed to have disappeared. For a moment I thought it had come back around the building and left while I wasn't looking.

Then I noticed a tiny reflection barely visible through the trees at the opening of the path, the corner of a chrome bumper.

There was no one around, and the only light was a dim glow spilling from the ballroom's rear window. Kneeling, I crab-walked to the car, so

172

close I could touch it, listening carefully, hearing nothing over the music and the crowd. This was the exact spot where Benny had seen the white Cadillac.

When I peeped through the window all I saw at first was a pair of legs and bare feet extending from a prom dress. Then, pressed against the other side of the glass, inches from my face, was a big, hairy butt.

What began as a low moan gathered intensity as the family station wagon rode up and down on its squeaking suspension. From deep inside the cargo hold a female voice exclaimed, "Oh, God! Hold on, Bubba. Not yet."

I dropped to the ground, praying neither of them had seen me. The muffled groan that followed sounded like an injured beast giving up its last breath.

"I told you to hold on!" she yelled.

I retired discretely to my car and was about to leave when I noticed a small piece of paper neatly folded and inserted beneath my windshield wiper. It turned out to be a torn piece of stationery with neat, unmistakably feminine handwriting.

"Leave it alone, Tom. Nothing good can come from this," it read.

I looked around, but there was no one in sight.

My next stop would be George Martin's Chevy dealership, where I hoped to find out more about the white Cadillac, but that could wait until morning… after I picked up my grandmother from the hospital.

***

I arrived home and went through the refrigerator, finding nothing to eat. The loneliness of the empty house washed over me.

173

I had to speak to Colleen. Her phone rang several times before I gave up. Perhaps, I figured, she was out with her girlfriends. Restless, I decided to go get a hamburger.

As I pulled onto Broad Street, a pair of headlights loomed in my rear-view mirror. I hadn't seen them when I left the house. This was not good. Even in Monrovia there couldn't be two yellow, ragged-out El Caminos.

I made a couple of turns to see if I could shake him, but he hung onto my tail like a hound after a rabbit. When the lights of The Burger Shack came into view, I swerved into the parking lot.

This had been a popular hangout when I was in high school and, judging from the number of cars in the lot, it remained so. I took the last empty spot, near the front door. The El Camino slowed as it passed, then sped on. Through its tinted windows I could just make out the driver's silhouette.

I walked inside, ordered a hamburger and Coke and found an empty booth. I'd just finished when in stumbled a man a couple of years older than me, looking out of place in a teenage dive. He bumped into an undersized kid and nearly knocked him off his feet. As he took a stool at the counter a couple quietly moved to a nearby table.

It had been ten years I last saw him, and he'd aged, but I recognized him by the way he carried himself. Behind the sagging jowls and drooping eyelids still lurked the menacing scowl of a schoolyard bully.

The zenith of Denny Tompkins' life was his brief career as quarterback for the Monrovia High Lions. He'd had athletic skills and agility, despite childhood injuries, but, as many were quick to point out, he was no Sam Williams. How often he'd heard that, I had no idea, but it went a long way in explaining why he detested me.

Denny had a metal plate in the top of his head from a fall he'd taken as a kid, and his skull never grew back completely. Whether it was bad wiring or lack of parental attention, he'd grown into a mean kid. As big as he was, he learned at a young age not to pick on guys his own size. Instead, he found deeper satisfaction pounding on younger and smaller kids.

One afternoon in my sophomore year, as I left school, Denny intercepted me in the empty hall. He was a senior and had at least four inches and sixty pounds on me. As I tried to slip past, he threw me against the wall. Knowing I would take a beating anyway, I pushed away and brought my knee up into his groin. As his expression changed from shock to pain, I knew I'd struck pay dirt.

I tried to escape, but he grabbed the back of my collar and slammed me to the floor. When he'd finally spent his fury, he left. I picked myself up and got out as fast as I could. Too groggy to balance on my bike, I walked it home. Fortunately, none of his punches had landed on my face.

My grandmother looked up from her chair as I walked in and gasped. "Are you alright?"

"I fell off my bike. I'll be okay." I retired to my room to avoid any further conversation.

I never forgot that afternoon. I swore that someday, when Denny was no longer bigger than me, I'd catch him somewhere and beat the crap out of him. Tonight, though, I had more important concerns. As I paid my bill, I couldn't resist cutting a glance in his direction.

He glared at me. "What are you looking at?"

"I'm looking at a piece of shit that grew legs and learned to walk."

The crowd around us quietly moved away. I turned toward the exit but could see his reflection in the glass. His face turned a deep crimson as he rose from his stool.

I stepped outside and placed my back against the wall beside the door. As he rushed past, I grabbed the back of his hair and tripped him over my left heel. His face crashed into the bumper of an orange Camaro conveniently parked in front of the door, and he sank to the ground where he lay unconscious, blood pouring from his nose.

As stupid as this was, I had to admit it felt good. I glanced around, relieved to see there were no witnesses.

A crowd poured out. Someone helped Denny off the pavement and took him inside.

As I reached for my keys a voice called out. "Tom Williams! I knew that was you. Man, you kicked old Denny's ass!" I turned to see Buddy Cole.

Long and rangy, Buddy was a year behind me in school, and though we weren't close friends, we'd grown up together.

"Looked to me like he tripped," I said.

"Yeah! Right!"

Someone yelled, "Tom, you'd better get out of here, the manager's calling an ambulance for Denny, and the sheriff will be right behind them."

"We're gonna pick up some PBRs and head over to the junk yard," said Buddy. "You wanna join us?"

A short, attractive redhead walked up, took his arm and gave me a coy smile.

"You remember my girlfriend Kay," Buddy said. We're getting married in September."

As much as I liked these guys, I'd never imagined myself sitting around, chugging beer and reminiscing with them. Most of my old times were ones I preferred not to remember.

"I don't know, Buddy, it's been a long day, and I was heading home. I have to pick up my grandmother from the hospital tomorrow."

Then I saw the El Camino, reflected in the picture window of the John Deere dealership across the street. He'd circled back and parked in a darkened alley beside the Burger Shack. I could just make out his bumper and hood.

"On second thought," I said, "why don't you guys come over to my grandmother's house? I've got the place to myself. We can sit on the front steps for a while and have a few drinks."

"Great! We'll meet you at Brad's."

Brad Barber ran a bait and tackle shop on the edge of town. Since Jasper County was still dry, it mattered little to Brad if his customers were adults or minors, so long as they could get their noses above the countertop and paid him in cash.

"Wait a minute, guys," I said. "I need to pee, and I definitely don't want to go back inside."

I stepped out of sight of the El Camino and ran around the opposite side of the building. The Burger Shack had recently undergone renovations, and behind it in a dumpster lay several discarded two-by-fours. I picked out one about four feet long with framing nails poking out of both ends.

The El Camino sat in the alley, facing away from me. In the faint light I could make out its "Wallace for President" and "Impeach Earl Warren" bumper stickers.

At that moment the ambulance arrived, lights flashing. As predicted, a sheriff's deputy pulled in behind him. I waited for them to go inside for Denny, then knelt and crawled into the alley with the board resting across my forearms, hoping the driver hadn't noticed me. Carefully, I laid it on the ground with the nails about six inches in front of his back tires, then crouched and ran back behind the building.

When I returned to my car four other people had joined Buddy and Kay.

"You must have had to pee pretty bad," said Buddy.

"Yeah. Let's go."

As I pulled out, with Buddy and the others following in their cars, I glanced in my rear-view mirror to see Denny, leaning against the ambulance with what appeared to be a bloody washcloth over his nose.

The El Camino's headlights blazed as he pulled out. Suddenly there were two loud bangs like gunshots. Two of the onlookers dropped to the pavement. Others ducked behind cars as the deputy ran out of the restaurant with his pistol drawn. When we got to Brad's those who had followed us were still laughing.

Chapter Twenty-Two

When we arrived at the house, Buddy and his friends parked on the street. Already drunk, one of them tripped getting out of his car. Sprawled on the pavement, he laughed hysterically. Worried that a neighbor might complain to my grandmother, I managed to quiet everybody down.

Buddy had played baseball in high school, but he couldn't pitch well enough to earn a scholarship, and he was never much of a student. His parents couldn't afford college so, he joined the army and wound up in Vietnam. He looked like he'd lost twenty pounds and aged fifteen years. It didn't take long for me to figure out why.

In February 1968 Buddy and his company came under attack while on patrol in Quang Tri province. One of three survivors, Buddy took a round in his right shoulder yet managed to carry another G.I. to safety. For all that he received a purple heart. He'd been home less than a month following surgery and rehab. He would never pitch again.

"Buddy," I said, "it's great having you back."

"Thanks."

"What'd you do over there?" asked one of the guys we met at Brad's.

"Mostly… I just tried to stay alive."

Like so many vets, Buddy didn't want to talk about Vietnam.

"Tom, I heard you were over there too," someone said. "When did you get back?"

"About a year ago"

We sat for a while, drinking our beers. Buddy lit up a joint, took a toke and passed it. I started to object but figured *what the hell*. My grandmother wasn't home and nobody on the street would notice.

At length, the beer and pot loosened Buddy's tongue. He gazed at me bleary-eyed. "You know, man, things have changed over there in the past year. There's a lot more dope and a *lot* more dying."

"No shit!" I said. "From what I see on the news it's getting rough."

"The worst part was the idiots we had for junior officers. Our lieutenant at Quang Tri couldn't find his ass with both hands." He shuddered as he took another toke, held it and let it out slowly. "First time he took us out on patrol, the son-of-a-bitch was the first one hit." He choked, then continued, "There was another officer tried to lead his platoon into a village full of VC with no way out. His own men fragged his ass … They said Charlie did it."

"Damn, Buddy! You don't hear *that* on the news."

"There's a lot of stuff you don't hear about." He took another swig and scratched his arm. "You know… I grew up thinking everything our country did was right. We were always the good guys. That's what they taught us in school, and that's what we saw in the movies. That's why we won every war we ever fought ..." He raised a clinched fist. "… *cause God is on our side.*"

He shook his head. "I tell you, what we're doing over there…it ain't right, and me and most of my buddies, we knew it. What's more, we're losing this war. I guess that's why so many of us started using."

Suddenly a thought hit me. "Buddy, what do you know about the CIA and the Mafia smuggling heroin out of there?"

"Going on all the time… Stuff's coming out of Vietnam and out of Laos, a place called the Plain of Jars. They've got this shit called *Double U-O Globe*, Grade 4 smack. *It'll kick your ass.*"

In the western sky the moon burst through a torn fabric of clouds. Out on the street, the El Camino cruised slowly past. Somehow he'd fixed both flats. He hesitated, perhaps counting the eight people sitting with me.

Buddy followed my gaze.

I waved at the driver and smiled. He reached out his window and flipped me a bird.

"Somebody you know?" Buddy asked casually as he took another toke.

"Beats hell out of me"

As the car eased away I caught his license plate in the streetlight and committed it to memory. I excused myself, went inside and wrote it down in my notebook. In the morning, I'd call Colleen and ask her to have her friend in Tallahassee run the number.

Buddy and the others soon forgot about the El Camino. They went back to smoking, drinking and swapping stories about high school. They updated me on what this person or that was doing. I let them stay a little longer, though several times I had to ask them to pipe down so they wouldn't wake the neighbors.

Kay asked if I was still dating Jenny. I said we'd broke up a year before graduation and that the last I heard she was living in Atlanta. Apparently she hadn't stayed in touch with these people either, despite her promises at graduation.

I told them about Colleen. No one mentioned Dana or Jimmie.

"I hear you're a newspaper writer down in Tampa," said Buddy.

"Yep"

A Sheriff's Department vehicle stopped at the end of the driveway, and the beer cans disappeared. From the corner of my eye, I saw Buddy drop the joint into the flower bed beside the steps.

I stood and walked over to the deputy. The last thing I wanted was for him to get out and talk to these guys in their condition.

Behind the wheel sat Bubba Jeter, one of Willingham's nephews. Coming up to the passenger side so he wouldn't smell the pot on my clothes, I said, "Evening, Bubba, what can I do for you?"

"I heard you were over at the Burger Shack. You wanna tell me what happened to Denny Tompkins?"

"Well, as I was leaving, he stumbled out the door behind me. He must have been drunk. He tripped on something and hit his face on the bumper of a Camaro. He looked pretty bad. I yelled for somebody to call an ambulance. I sure hope he's okay." I put on my sincerest face.

Bubba stared at me for what seemed an eternity. It was then that I realized no one had seen what happened. Either Denny didn't recognized me, or he kept his mouth shut hoping to even the score later.

Bubba called out to my guests, "What you folks doing out here so late?"

"We're just sitting here talking," I said. "You want me to tell them to go home?"

"You boys ain't been drinking have you?" He was reaching for his door handle when a squawk came over the radio. He grabbed the handset. "Yeah, whaddya want?"

The voice on the radio sounded like his brother, Sonny. I couldn't tell what he was saying.

"Alright," said Bubba. He glared at me. "I've gotta go. I'll be back in a few minutes, and I want them folks gone. You hear?"

"Sure thing, Bubba"

He sped away as I walked back to the steps.

"Man, that was close," said Buddy. "Hey, you guys remember that time we put sugar in Sheriff Willingham's gas tank?"

I wondered if the story were true or simply for my benefit. My dislike for the sheriff had never been a secret. I was about to ask them to leave when a thought came to me. "Do any of you remember a former deputy named Win Stevens?"

"I know Win Stevens," said Buddy. "He lives up on the river, off Talbot Road. He fixes outboard motors every now and then when he ain't drunk. My dad and me took ours up there to him about a week ago."

I pulled out my notebook and he gave me directions.

"Thanks a lot, guys. It's great seeing y'all, but I've gotta turn in. I have to get my grandmother from the hospital in the morning." It was late and I knew I'd feel like shit on a couple of hours of sleep.

When they'd left I went inside, passed out on my bed, and began to dream.

I was back at the hospital, walking down a long corridor to my grandmother's room. From behind me came the sound of slippers shuffling on linoleum. I turned to see the old man on the walker. He moved as if each step would be his last, yet somehow he gained on me.

I was again taken by the sharpness in his eyes. "He's coming."

Unnerved by his icy stare I gave him a weak smile. "Sure," I said, "Maybe he's coming for you today."

"No, Tommy," he answered in a long, drawn-out rasp. "He's coming for you." His face morphed into that of my grandfather, much older than I remembered.

"Who is?" I whispered.

"The sack man"

I awoke, startled by a soft, scraping sound. I sat up and strained to hear it. I came again... from the back door, not fifteen feet away.

Quietly, I rose and listened. I needed a weapon. I thought about my dad's .45 automatic, packed away in a box in the attic. I padded softly to my open closet and reached into the darkness. In the back corner stood my golf bag, which I hadn't used since I was in high school. My hand caressed the heavy face of the sand wedge.

As I slid it from the bag, the backdoor hinges squeaked. From the hallway came the momentary flicker of a flashlight.

A hand extended slowly into the bedroom holding a pistol. As I lifted the club over my head I silently prayed he was alone. Before his eyes could adjust to the darkness I brought it down as hard as I could across his forearm.

His scream almost drowned the sound of crunching bone. He dropped the gun and stumbled backward. I didn't think to pick up the pistol but instead chased after him with the sand wedge.

He was a big man, well over six feet with what appeared to be a crew cut. For his size he was remarkably quick, bounding out the door before I could hit him again. He vaulted the porch railing and grunted in pain as he landed. Still clutching his shattered arm, he sprinted around the corner of the house.

By the time I got outside he was climbing into the passenger side of the El Camino. Tires squealed as they sped away. Crazed with anger I ran into the street, clad in nothing but my boxer shorts.

A neighbor's porch light came on. My only thought was how to explain this to my grandmother.

I went back inside, pausing to examine the old-fashioned lock. It was still intact but had taken little effort to pick. First chance I got I'd go to the hardware store and get two deadbolts.

The kitchen clock read 4:30. Even if I could've gone back to sleep, I had no idea when the El Camino might return. I dressed and turned on all the lights, hoping to discourage them.

In the hall a stairway led to the attic, where my grandmother and I put all our unused stuff when we moved here from the farm. There I located a box of my dad's things she'd kept for me. Inside, wrapped in oil cloth, was the .45 and a couple of full magazines. In the bottom were two cases of cartridges.

I hadn't been up here in years. Dust-covered boxes loomed amid cobweb-laced rafters. In the front gable a slatted vent allowed meager ventilation. The hardware cloth behind it had come loose in one corner, and on the floor lay the desiccated remains of a bat. From scattered droppings I knew he hadn't been alone.

My grandfather's double-barreled 12-gauge stood in another corner. Beside it lay a case of Remington double-aught shells.

As I started to close the lid my eyes fell on a wire-bound notebook with my dad's handwriting on the cover. Beneath it were two pairs of handcuffs he'd carried as sheriff. Thinking they might come in handy I put them back in the box, which I carried downstairs along with the shotgun and shells.

I recalled the sickening sound the intruder's arm made when I hit it with the sand wedge and the way he screamed. He wasn't likely find a doctor who'd set a compound fracture at this time of night. The only place he could've gone was the emergency room at Jasper Memorial.

I shoved a loaded magazine into the .45, jacked a round into the chamber, and put it in a paper bag I found under the kitchen sink. It still reeked of gun oil after all these years and seemed to be in good firing condition. Its grip felt rough and cold in my hand. The last time I held one of these was on the pistol range at Cape May.

In the bedroom I picked up the .357 magnum my visitor had dropped and placed it in the box, which I placed on the floor of my closet and covered with an old blanket hoping Ida wouldn't see it while cleaning.

The Mustang would be too conspicuous by now, so I drove my grandmother's Buick to the hospital instead. Before I left I grabbed a flashlight and scoured the garden beside the front steps for the remainder of the joint Buddy had dropped. I rolled it carefully in Saran Wrap and placed it in my shirt pocket.

Parking in a darkened corner of the emergency room lot, I located the El Camino near the entrance. Through the doorway I saw two men who appeared to be in their late fifties talking to a nurse. The taller one clutched his arm, wincing in pain. Even from that distance, I could make out a broken radius poking through torn flesh. I studied his face and that of the short, stoop-shouldered man who limped down the hallway behind him.

In their haste they'd left their car unlocked. Checking that no one saw me, I climbed inside and found the ash tray full of cigarette butts. I removed the joint from the Saran Wrap and pushed it down among them, hoping it wouldn't be too obvious.

I was about to leave when another idea struck me. Up under the rear bumper I found wires leading to the passenger side taillight. With a swift jerk I disconnected them, hopped back into the Buick and drove home.

Careful not to reveal myself in the kitchen window I took out my dad's notebook and opened it on the Formica-topped table. The lined pages contained lists of names. At the top of each was a date. It covered the months of January through May 1953. The only name I recognized was Lester Suggs. Beneath it was a Larry Suggs. These could be the two men I saw at the hospital. They'd be about the right age.

I added Larry's name to my notebook beside Lester's and tried in vain to make some sense of it all. Giving up, I put a coffee pot on the stove and awaited the sunrise.

Chapter Twenty-Three

Albert dropped Ida off at six a.m. The hospital wouldn't release my grandmother until nine, so in the meantime I helped Ida clean the house.

When the time came, I took the Buick, since the three of us wouldn't fit in the Mustang. Ida started to get in the back seat, which I reminded her she didn't need to do.

Stores hadn't opened yet, and traffic around the square was light. Passersby stopped and stared at Ida sitting beside me.

In the time I'd been back, I'd noticed fewer shoppers than in years past. A thrift store had replaced the establishment where, when I was little, my mom bought me clothes. Back then the streets and sidewalks teemed with people. Those who ventured out now seemed desperate in their struggle against the tides of change. Many were older and living on retirement. Others subsisted on food stamps and welfare.

At length I asked, "Ida, how well did you know my parents?"

"I guess I knew them pretty good," she said. "Your daddy was a mighty brave man. When he and your mama died I reckoned it was the moonshiners did it."

"Did what?"

She paused as if searching for words. "There was talk going round. Folks said somebody ran your mama and daddy off the bridge and made it look like they hit a deer."

I stopped the car. "Ida, where did you hear this?"

"I don't rightly know. It was just something people were saying."

I grew up believing my parents died in an accident. If, in fact, moonshiners murdered them, then they were probably among the criminals in my dad's notebook, perhaps the Suggs brothers. Figuring all this out would be hard enough if their deaths tied to Dana's, and damned-near impossible if they didn't, especially after all these years.

Why was the sheriff so quick to blame Jimmie for Dana's murder, even after Doc Green told him Jimmie couldn't have done it? Was it, as Jimmie believed, that the sheriff was out to get him? Why?

More likely Cuz needed to make a quick arrest, and Jimmie was a convenient fall guy. *Did he know who the real murderer was? Did he decide it would be better to blame a Black kid with a criminal record? Did he have any idea there'd be a lynching, or did things simply spin out of control?*

My head throbbed. I needed to find out who owned that white Cadillac.

I stopped at Farmer's Hardware and bought a pair of deadbolts while Ida waited in the car.

"What you gone do with them things?" she asked when I returned.

"This morning I was looking at our outside doors. It'd be easy for somebody to break in when we're not there. These will help prevent that."

She gave me a skeptical look but said nothing.

I arrived at Jasper Memorial to find my grandmother, already dressed, sitting in a chair gazing out the window. Doc Green came in and gave her strict instructions not to do any housekeeping or traveling for the next two weeks, nothing but rest. He handed me a prescription and said to bring her by his office on Monday. A nurse helped her into a wheelchair and rolled her to the car.

Back at the house, I helped her up the back steps and down the hall to her bedroom, while Ida made her some iced tea. I told them I was going to the drug store to get the prescription filled.

***

188

Griffin's Pharmacy sat in the middle of the block on the west side of the square. As a kid I'd go there every Wednesday, after school, when the new Marvel and DC Comics arrived. I'd order a Cherry Coke, as an excuse to hang out, and read X-Men, Superman, Batman, and Green Lantern until old man Griffin came out from behind the counter and told me to either buy them or put them back. "This is not a library, son," he'd say.

My parents and grandparents considered comics a waste of time and money. One year for Christmas my aunt sent me a box of them she'd saved, one of the few childhood presents I still recall. By the time I could buy them myself I'd lost interest. To this day, though, when I pass a small-town pharmacy I think of them and smell the sweet aroma of Cherry Coke.

Mr. Griffin stood behind the high counter, working energetically despite his advanced years. For a moment I expected him to tell me I'd have to buy the comics if I wanted to read them. Instead, he gave me a vague look of half recognition before he broke into a smile.

"Tom Williams! Well, I'll be. How you been? I hear you're working for some newspaper down in Tampa. How long are you back?"

"I'm not sure. My grandmother had a spell and had to go to the hospital."

"I heard about that. How's she doing?"

"She'll be okay. She got home a little while ago, and I have a prescription from Doc Green."

He took the paper and stepped back between the shelves of pills, tonics, and salves. Overhead fluorescents cast a sickly green glow against the glossy white surfaces. Behind the counter stood a row of tall apothecary jars filled with multi-hued liquids. As a kid I imagined them as magic potions, like the ones comic book villains concocted. Later, to my disappointment, I discovered they contained colored water.

The bell hanging from the front door tinkled. I turned to find Jenny, her dark hair longer and straighter now. Gone was that outward flip where it hit her shoulders. She'd parted it down the middle and wore wire-rim glasses with large oval frames. The effect was stunning.

"Tom Williams, is that you? I heard you were in town." She spoke with that same chirpy little voice and perpetual smile. It had been eight years since graduation, but the scene came back to me as though it were yesterday. I saw her standing at the podium delivering her valedictory and again felt the pang of having broken up with such a wonderful, not to mention attractive, young woman.

True to her plans, she'd graduated from Agnes Scott in Atlanta. I'd always pictured the place with hundreds of Jenny Maxwell clones strolling the campus in starched white blouses and dark skirts, straight black hair flipped up at the shoulder. We'd promised to stay in touch but hadn't.

"Hey, Jenny, how've you been?"

"Fabulous. I'm living in Cobb County now, outside Atlanta. I'm teaching third grade, and I am engaged to an attorney named Don Waters. He and my brother were in the same fraternity at Emory."

"That's great! I'm happy for you." I wasn't sure how happy I was, but it seemed like the thing to say.

"How about you? Are you married yet?"

"I'm also engaged to a lawyer. I'm writing for the *Tampa Sentinel*, and I was on my way back from covering the funeral of Dr. King."

"I'm so glad to hear you stuck to your plans."

"Thanks. So, when's your big day?"

"August 15th. I came down to plan the wedding with my mother. We're having it at the First Presbyterian Church, with a reception in our back yard. Why don't you give me your address? I'd love to invite you and your fiancée."

Like I really wanted to introduce Colleen to Jenny's mother. She'd faint the first time Colleen opened her mouth. Still, I wrote my address and phone number on a page from my notebook and handed it to Jenny, who gave me hers.

"Well," she said, "it looks like we both kept our promises not to move back here."

"Yep..." I paused for a moment studying her handwriting. "Tell me... did you have a good time at the Cotillion last night?"

She started to answer, then stopped in alarm. *The note on my car could only have come from her.*

"How did you know?" she asked.

"I didn't... until now."

"Well... I just don't want you getting hurt, Tom. That's all." She didn't say how she knew I was at the country club or that I was asking questions about Dana's murder. For once I didn't ask.

"I appreciate that."

I smiled and, looking up, saw Mr. Griffin, pill bottle in hand, eaves-dropping on our conversation. "Well, I have to get this prescription back to my grandmother."

"Oh, I heard she wasn't feeling well. I hope she gets better soon," Jenny said.

"Thank you. I'm sure she will."

I paid Mr. Griffin and said goodbye.

"Take care of yourself, Tom, and stay out of trouble."

"I'll try."

***

The sidewalk had grown more crowded. It brought back memories of Saturday mornings, years ago, when I'd ride my bike downtown to buy candy and drinks and hang out with other kids.

191

A station wagon pulled into a parking space. A small child jumped out and ran squealing into a store, his mother in tow.

The toy store next to Griffin's was now a record shop. A phonograph speaker in the doorway played "White Rabbit" by Jefferson Airplane. In the picture window hung a large orange sign with yellow stars, a rainbow and bright red and turquoise lettering. Silhouetted against this psychedelic background stood the slender frame of a beautiful young Black woman with an afro, looking as though she'd stepped down from a Peter Max poster.

I nearly passed Panky Carter before I recognized her. She stood holding hands with a *very large* Black man with gold chains around his neck and a massive ring on one hand. Her orange hot pants and tight maroon halter top accentuated everything I remembered about her. She gave me a sidelong look and quietly mouthed, "Hey, white boy."

I was about to say something when a menacing glance from her boyfriend stopped me. I half smiled, waved, and continued to where I'd parked.

***

It was almost eleven when I returned to my grandmother's house to find her asleep. Ida was dusting the furniture.

"Ida, these are the pills Doc Green prescribed for Grandmama. Give them to her when she wakes up, but get her to eat something first, even if it's only a little bit. She's not supposed to take them on an empty stomach."

"Okay."

"I'm going out for a little while. I won't be long."

If the Suggs brothers returned it would probably be after dark. Meanwhile, I needed to find out about the white Cadillac, and this was the best opportunity I'd have.

＊

I arrived at Martin Chevrolet just before twelve. George opened his business early on Saturdays and closed at noon. The dealership, located on Broad Street at the edge of the business district, took up an entire block. Rows of Chevys, Buicks, Oldsmobiles and the occasional Cadillac or Corvette gleamed in the bright Florida sun. The original site, owned by old man Turner, was now a vacant corner lot near the courthouse, overgrown with weeds and strewn with broken coke bottles.

George had run the same "Colossal Blow-out Sale" for as long as I'd known him. Across the front a string of brightly colored triangular flags flapped noisily in the warm breeze. A large banner proclaimed this the largest volume dealer in the Big Bend Area.

The showroom, its full-length windows plastered with signs, advertised low prices on new and used cars. From its five-bay repair shop in the rear arose a bedlam of impact wrenches, hydraulic lifts, and roaring engines.

A voice called out from behind me. "If you're looking to trade that ugly-ass Ford out there, I'm afraid I can't give you much for it." It had been seven years since I'd seen the man, but I recognized him before I turned around. He reached out and grabbed my hand.

"I thought I might park it out here for a while to give this place some class," I replied.

George ushered me into his spacious corner office. His desk backed up to a large plate glass window. He dropped into a high-backed chair, as I sat across from him, squinting into the glare of the open blinds, something I'm sure he arranged on purpose. On the corner of his desk sat a picture of his only child, a daughter, now married and living in Ocala. His wife, Jo Anne, left him not long after my parents died, and he'd lived alone ever since.

"Tom, what can I do for you?" He was a good two inches taller than me and leaned back, long legs propped on his desk like mating pythons.

"I'm in town to see my grandmother. She's been in the hospital."

"I heard. How's she doing?"

"She'll be okay. She got out this morning, and she's at home now asleep. Ida's looking after her."

"So, you decided to do a little visiting."

"You might say so."

"It's about that lynching. Isn't it?" he inquired casually.

The man never missed a thing. Somebody had spread word I was asking questions again. For a fleeting moment I wondered if he also knew what happened at the Burger Shack the night before.

"George," I said flatly, "I knew Jimmie Lee Johnson. He didn't murder Dana Padgett. He didn't even know her."

"I see…" He gazed out on the sparkling row of automobiles. "You know, you're a busy young man, Tom. Your grandmama's sick in the hospital, and you still have time to be the investigative reporter."

I ignored his implications. "There was a white Cadillac at the country club the night Dana died."

"Meaning what?"

"From what little we know, given the way Willingham and his nephews trampled the scene, Dana died sometime around midnight. Her car wasn't there when Benny found her the next day, so she must have arrived by some other means. Benny noticed the Caddy parked there sometime around midnight. That's quite a coincidence, don't you think?"

"I suppose."

"It was a brand-new one, with a dealership tag. Whose do you think that was, George, and where do you suppose it came from?"

He glanced down. We both knew he had the only GM dealership for fifty miles in any direction. For a moment I expected him to jump up and throw me out.

Instead, he took a deep breath, picked up a ballpoint pen and tapped it on his desktop. "It wasn't one of mine. You can believe that or not. I don't care. I saw it a day or so before the murder. When a new car rolls through town and it's not one of mine, well, I notice that sort of thing. It was from a dealership down in Ft. Lauderdale."

"And that dealer is …"

"Out of business… I knew the owner… good man… Jewish fellow. He shut down a couple of years ago after he had his first heart attack."

"What was his name?"

"Bernie Solomon... I understand he died a few months later."

"So, you saw the car. Did you see who was driving it?"

"Nope. It was parked in front of the bank."

"You think anybody else noticed it? It's not often you see a car like that in Monrovia."

He cracked a smile. "Not yet, but I'm working on it."

"I'll bet you are," I laughed. "Do you recall what time of day it was when you saw it?"

"It must have been early afternoon. I was on my way to the club."

"What afternoon would that have been?"

"Thursday... I close early on Thursdays, just like every other business in town"

"Including the bank?"

"Including the bank…" He gave me an incredulous look. "You don't think this involves the bank, do you?"

"Did you play golf with Bill Emmett that day?"

"Hell, I don't know who I played golf with on a particular day ten years ago."

"Do you still play golf with Bill?"

"Well, now that you mention it, I don't suppose we've played together in years. About the only time I see Bill at the club is when he's entertaining his rich Cuban friends from Miami."

"Do you happen to know the names of those friends?"

"Nope."

"Did you mention seeing the Cadillac to the sheriff?"

"Nope. By the time I heard about the car being at the club that night, it was too late. Those crackers had already lynched your friend, and, besides, Benny could have been mistaken. He's getting up in years. Everybody in town believed Jimmie Lee killed Dana... case closed. Besides, it's not like Cuz was going to reopen the investigation. Shit, those boys couldn't solve a crime if the perpetrator confessed and had photos of himself in the act."

"You're right about that." I thought for a moment and chose another tack. "Who do you think the men were who lynched Jimmie?"

"I have no idea. Hell, you were there. You tell me."

"I didn't see their faces. They wore cloth sacks over their heads. What do you know about the Little River Hunting Club?" I learned long ago the best way to control a conversation is to keep asking questions.

George shifted uncomfortably. "They're a bunch of dumbass rednecks, mostly moonshiners and other low life. I heard the Suggs brothers were mixed up in it."

"Do you think the Suggs brothers lynched Jimmie?"

He shrugged and gazed out the window. "Those boys are just about mean enough. They probably got some out-of-town help. How many of them did you say there were?"

I pictured the scene again. "It seems like there were about eight trucks with three or four men in each, maybe thirty altogether."

"I don't think they had that many members in the Hunting Club back then... not that I'd know."

"Do you think they might've had connections with the Ku Klux Klan?"

"That's hard to say. Rumors had them linked up with the Grand Knights, but I don't think even the Klan would associate with those assholes. They spend most of their time drinking, whoring and shooting up things. I always figured they were pretty harmless."

"Harmless?" I nearly choked. "Let me tell you how harmless they are. When Jimmie and I were eleven we slipped out one night and rode our bikes over there just to see what was going on. We hid in the woods and watched those animals gang rape and murder a young Black woman for the fun of it. I can still hear her screaming. I wanted to call the sheriff, but Jimmie said it would just get us both killed."

George looked genuinely shocked. All he could say was, "Holy shit!" He thought for a moment, "I'd say old Jimmie was right."

"Jimmie made me promise not to tell anybody. He said for all we knew the sheriff was one of them."

"Now I don't believe that for one minute. Cuz might be stupid and corrupt, but I can't imagine him getting tied up with that scum."

Searching for something else, I started to ask him about my parents' deaths, but decided that could wait.

"Tommy boy," he said, "your daddy was my best friend and one of the finest men I've ever known. For his sake *and yours* I'm going to give you some advice you need to hear whether you want to or not." He looked me in the eye. "*Leave this thing alone.* All you're going to do is stir up trouble asking questions and jotting down things in that little notebook of yours. Your grandmama doesn't need any more heartache."

He set his feet on the floor and leaned toward me, "And as for your little scene at the Burger Shack last night, that was pretty stupid don't you think? I'm sure Denny Tompkins deserved everything you gave him and more, but unless you think he killed Dana Padgett, that was a dumb move. Willingham would love nothing more than to throw your ass in jail on assault."

Shocked for a moment I reminded myself this was Monrovia, Florida, where nobody keeps secrets, nobody, that is, except the people who murdered Dana and lynched Jimmie. I had another question, prompted by something George said, but it escaped me.

We both knew I wouldn't drop my search for Dana's killer. I also knew he was right about the incident with Denny. I stood and extended my hand. "Thanks, George. Listen, I've got to get back to the house."

"Tell your grandmama I said hello, and when you get ready to trade in that Mustang… come see me."

"I just might do that, George."

Chapter Twenty-Four

Ida met me at the door. "Tom, where you been? Your grandmama's been asking for you."

"Sorry. I didn't think she'd be awake yet. I went to see an old friend."

"You know better than that. It's all I can do to keep her from getting up and cleaning house."

"Did she take her medicine?"

"Yeah, but she don't like taking pills. I gave her a glass of water and told her I wasn't gone leave until I saw her swallow it."

"Thanks."

From her bedroom I heard my grandmother clear her throat. I knocked at her door.

"You're back!" she whispered hoarsely. "That girlfriend of yours called. Ida talked to her. She said to call her right away."

"Thanks. How are you feeling?"

"I'm fine." She sat up with a scowl. "Where have you been?"

"I went out for a few minutes. I stopped by to see George Martin."

She made a face at me. "Tom, you know I hate taking pills."

"You've got to take them, Grandmama. You promised Doc Green... Mr. Griffin at the drugstore said to tell you 'Hello', and so did George. Now, lay back and rest."

She sipped some water. "When are you going to bring your girlfriend up here to see me?"

I smiled. "I don't know yet, but it'll be soon."

"If I didn't know better," she yawned, "I might think you were hiding her from me. Are you afraid she's gonna run off and leave you when she sees where you're from?"

"No. We just haven't had the time. She's busy at work, and I've been in Atlanta covering Dr. King's funeral."

"Yeah. I know... That was horrible. I hope they catch whoever killed him. How could somebody do that and not get caught? They have his photograph, for Pete's sake."

I shook my head. "We've seen the same thing here. You keep thinking someday the killer will get caught, but they don't."

Her eyes narrowed. "Tom, you've got to stop beating yourself up about that. It was a long time ago, and you can't do anything about it now."

"But Grandmama, there are people in this town who know Jimmie didn't kill Dana. Those people are just as guilty as whoever did it, and they're just as guilty as the animals who lynched him."

I was on a roll. Before I could stop I blurted out, "and I bet they know who murdered my parents."

I expected a look of shock. Instead, she sighed and stared at the ceiling. "I know. I know. I heard those rumors. When folks you love die like that it makes you mad. You tell yourself somebody's responsible and you want them to pay. The last thing you'll believe is that it really was an accident. When a famous person gets killed, like Martin Luther King or John Kennedy, we can't accept that it was just some kook acting alone." She leaned toward me. "That's why there's conspiracy theories."

I started to say there *was* a conspiracy behind the Kennedy assassination, the King assassination, and the Malcolm X assassination. I could have told her about my conversation with Freddy Martinez, but I didn't want to change the subject. "If somebody did murdered my parents, who do you think they'd be?"

"I don't know. I remember, right before the accident, your daddy was upset about something. I asked him what it was, but he wouldn't tell me. When he got like that you couldn't pry *anything* out of him, no

200

matter how hard you tried. All he said was that he'd found out something and was looking into it."

"Did it have to do with moonshiners?"

"I don't think so. He never had problems talking about them."

"I keep hearing about these people. Who were they?"

"How should I know? It's not like I associate with those people.
There were a bunch of them. The only names I remember were the
Suggs."

"Lester Suggs?"

"I think so."

"Who do you think would know?"

"Those deputies who worked for your daddy..."

"Maybe I ought to see if I can find them."

"*Maybe you ought to leave well enough alone*. You're all I have
now, and I don't need you running around getting yourself killed."

"There are murderers walking free in this town, and nobody seems to
care."

"And there are a lot of good people here too, Tom Williams. And
don't you forget it, folks like Bill and George."

"Yeah, and why do you suppose they've done so much for us?"

"*You've known them all your life and you don't know that?* Bill and
George were your daddy's best friends. They were in school together.
They went off to war together. They almost *died* together. When your
daddy got wounded, it was Bill Emmett who saved his life."

"I remember you telling me."

She was getting worked up, so I changed the subject.

"Oh! I meant to tell you. I ran into Mr. Brabson the other day right
after I got into town." I didn't mention that I was eating at Sandy's when
I should have come straight here. "He was the one who told me about the
resort Bill's putting together."

"Yeah… They've been talking about that for years now. It all started when you were off at the University."

"Why am I just now hearing about it?"

"Maybe because you don't keep up with your family."

I ignored this.

"Bill and his friends began buying up land," she went on. "About two years ago they created a company and folks started buying stock. He even gave me a couple of shares. He wants me to buy some more."

"I don't think that's a good idea, Grandmama."

"Oh, and you're a financial expert now, Mr. Newspaper Reporter?"

"No, but there's something about it that doesn't make sense. For one thing, why is it taking so long to get construction going? And why is Bill in business with a drug dealer from Miami?"

"How do you know they're drug dealers? Bill says they're investors. He needs to buy some more land before they can start."

"That's even more reason not to invest any money in it. It's not like you have money to burn."

"Okay! Okay!"

"Promise me you'll concentrate on taking care of yourself."

She folded her arms and tucked her chin into her chest. "Fine. I will."

I smiled and kissed her forehead.

As I left the room I glanced at my watch. It was three p.m., and I felt like shit. Sleep deprivation weighed on me. I tried to reach Colleen but got no answer. I slipped into my bedroom and stretched out. In Vietnam I learned to take short naps whenever opportunity presented. I rewound my clock, set the alarm for six and fell asleep.

***

I awoke to the clattering of pots and pans. The aroma of fried chicken filled the house. I got up, dressed, and found Ida in the kitchen singing to herself. "You gone back to taking naps now?" she asked.

"I couldn't sleep last night thinking about all the stuff I had to do today."

I set the table as Ida finished cooking. From outside I heard Albert's vintage Studebaker pull into the driveway. Its sewing machine sound made honking unnecessary.

When Ida left, I tried to help my grandmother out of bed, but she insisted she could manage on her own. A television weather alert showed the growing storm in the Atlantic drifting toward the Bahamas. The Coast Guard had small craft warnings out for beaches from Fort Lauderdale to Daytona.

Through the window I gazed westward into a golden sunset. Tree limbs and palm fronds swayed in the breeze, like a typical day at the beach. News of bad weather would upset my grandmother, so I changed the channel.

When we'd eaten, I cleaned the kitchen and she retired to her bedroom with a novel. I waited fifteen minutes, tiptoed to her door to see if she'd gone back to sleep, then reached for the phone.

Colleen picked up on the first ring. "Hey, you," she said, "why didn't you call me back?"

I replied in a low voice. "I did. You didn't answer. I was so exhausted I took a nap. We just finished supper."

"How's your grandma doing?"

"Much better... She's asleep now. She wants to know when she can meet you."

"Yeah. I'd like to come up there. But you need to bring her down here as soon as she's well. You've gotten yourself into a world of shit."

"What do you mean?"

"I mean your friend Bill Emmett's in business with some of the nastiest racketeers in the state, in particular Rico Salazar. The other night you asked me about a company named Arcadia Development. I ran a check on them. They're a wholly owned subsidiary of Arcadia Holdings and Rico is the principal shareholder. You didn't hear that from me. They're corporate counsel is one of our partners, Langford Styles, and I can't divulge anything. My friend in Tallahassee tells me they found a body Hillsborough Bay a few months back, some drug dealer who'd snitched on Rico."

"I knew him. His name was Freddy Martinez."

"How'd you know him?"

I told her about my meeting with Freddy and his crazy stories about Salazar and the CIA smuggling heroin out of Vietnam. "I ran into an old classmate last night who just returned from there. He told me the same things."

I also told her what I'd discovered about Arcadia at the courthouse.

"The state attorney general and the feds are investigating Rico, but they haven't been able to get close enough to him," she said. "That's why they're anxious to work a deal with Frankie Tavares. I'm not supposed to tell you this, and you cannot repeat it to anyone. Frankie saw Rico supervising shipments arriving at an airstrip out near Brandon. The feds have agreed to put Frankie in witness protection somewhere, in exchange for his help."

"What do you know about Salazar's background?" I asked.

"His dad was a cop in Havana under the Batista regime. He ran security on the side for Meyer Lansky and Santo Trafficante. Rico and his family escaped to Key West when Castro took over in 1959. From there he moved to Miami and went to work for the mob. Rumor has it he lost an older brother at the Bay of Pigs."

"Sounds a lot like Freddy's story. Maybe you oughta look out for *yourself*."

"Don't worry about me. I have a gun my dad gave me, and I know how to use it."

"I'll remember not to piss you off."

"Smart man."

"Is Styles going to be a problem for you representing Frankie?"

"He'd better not. He's in corporate. This is a criminal case. It's none of his fucking business. I don't care if he *is* a partner."

To help her put Frankie in a better bargaining position, I pulled out my notebook and gave her the names of other people possibly related to the Arcadia deal, including Sheriff Willingham and his nephews.

"Why would Bill Emmett get in bed with somebody like Rico Salazar?" I asked.

"Jeez, what do you think? You told me he's a banker. Maybe he's laundering money. Why don't you ask him?"

"Yeah… Look… There's something else I need to tell you."

I told her about the attempted break-in the night before.

"Tom, *get the fuck out of there*."

"I can't do that yet. My grandmama's in no shape to travel. I'll have to protect her and myself as best I can for now.

"Listen. My parents' deaths were not an accident. At the time my dad was investigating some local moonshiners, including a couple of brothers, Lester and Larry Suggs. About a year ago, Lester sold a site known as the Little River Hunting Club to Salazar. I think he and his brother were the ones who visited me last night. *And* I think they're the ones who lynched Jimmie."

"My God, Tom, this town of yours sounds like something out of *Birth of a Nation*."

I started to argue but instead told her about the white Cadillac and George Martin's claim that it came from a dealer in Fort Lauderdale. "Do you think your friend in Tallahassee could find out who bought it? The dealer's name was Bernie Solomon. He's dead now, but he would have sold it in August 1958?"

"I'll see"

She started to say goodbye, but I stopped her.

"There's something else I need help with. I have the tag number for the vehicle I saw leaving here last night. I followed it to the hospital and saw the two men, one with his arm apparently broken where I hit him with the golf club. Do you have any contacts with the Florida Highway Patrol who could find out where the Suggs brothers live and pay them a visit? Their car has a burned-out taillight on the rear passenger side, and if they look in the ash tray they'll find something very interesting."

"Don't even tell me how you know that. Even if the Highway Patrol finds these guys and busts them, they'll be out of jail in no time."

"They don't have to make the charges stick. All I need is a little breathing room to investigate them without getting shot."

"I'll see what I can do. Just don't get yourself killed. And don't go snooping around asking questions. Leave the police work to the cops."

***

That night, with my grandmother asleep, I sat out front in the shadows of an oleander with my granddaddy's loaded shotgun across my lap, in case the brothers returned.

At some point I dozed off. When I awoke the sky had paled in the east. Carefully, I sneaked back into the house, returned the shotgun to the closet and went to bed.

Chapter Twenty-Five

An hour later I was awake again. It was Sunday, which meant *one thing*.

From her bedroom I heard my grandmother dressing. As much as I tried to talk her out of it, she *was going* to church. She said if I didn't take her she'd call someone to pick her up.

We were among the last to arrive. As we eased down the aisle, every head in the sanctuary turned. Some waved at my grandmother. Others smiled. I might as well have been her chauffeur. After the service, she shook hands with Reverend Don and spoke briefly with friends at the foot of the steps, none of whom proffered me more than a polite smile. I was just as glad they didn't.

I hurried home, half expecting to find the house in flames, but found no sign anyone had been there. I helped my grandmother out of the Buick and walked her to her room. While she rested, I warmed some leftover chicken breasts smothered in cream of mushroom soup along with a can of English peas.

Ducking into the hallway, I searched our tiny phone directory for "Stephens" or "Stevens," but found nothing under "Win," "Winston," or even "W." Chancing that my grandmother might overhear me, I called the operator. She said there was a "Win Stevens" with an unlisted number. I would have to rely on Buddy Coles' directions, hoping to find Stevens at home. My next problem was how to get out of the house without leaving my grandmother alone.

The phone rang. Ms. Liddy Munroe, a family friend, wanted to know if we'd like some company that afternoon. Without asking my grandmother I said that would be wonderful.

Ms. Munroe arrived at two with her husband in tow, both still dressed for church. He stood quietly behind her, his grey felt hat in hand. Five feet tall, he'd aged since I last time saw him. I hardly noticed him behind the ample girth of his spouse. When I spoke to him he mumbled something and gave me an uncomfortable look. Clearly, his attendance had not been optional.

"Edna, bless your heart. How you feeling, darling?" Ms. Munroe asked as she bustled through the door. "I brought you a jar of my scuppernong preserves." I took them from her and retreated to the kitchen.

"Thank you, Liddy. I'm doing *much* better. Would you like Tom to get you some lemonade?"

"That would be wonderful." The Munroes sat on our old sofa with their backs to the front window. He placed his hat carefully in his lap and said nothing while his wife prattled on about the sermon that morning, the fine weather we were having and the latest medical reports on everyone she knew.

When the phone rang again I practically dove for it. It was Colleen.

"Hey, guess what!" she said.

"What?" I asked, cupping my hand so no one would hear me.

"My friend from Tallahassee just phoned. He spoke yesterday to a highway patrolman in Madison who owed him some favors. The patrolman said he knew your dad. It seems he and his partner came down to Monrovia last night and located the Suggs brothers at a honky-tonk on Tallahassee Highway. They stopped them for a taillight violation and found a joint in their ashtray. Imagine that."

"Did they bust them?"

"Yep"

"Where are they now?"

"In the Lafayette County jail in Mayo. Somehow they managed to cross a couple of county lines."

"Great! It'll take the brothers longer to make bail there than it would in Jasper County."

"Not much longer. They should be out by tomorrow. They were pretty upset about the joint, swore it wasn't theirs. The patrolmen had to subdue them. He said the big one had a cast on his forearm. What are you doing right now?"

"My grandmother has guests over."

"Well, I'll let you get back to them. Call me tonight."

"Sure thing, baby..."

I returned to the living room and sat in my grandfather's old chair.

"Who was that?" asked my grandmother.

"It was Colleen."

My grandmother explained to the Munroes that I was dating a woman in Tampa who was an attorney. Their eyes widened. Apparently they'd never contemplated the notion of a female lawyer.

I sat quietly for what I felt was a respectable amount of time. Taking advantage of one of Ms. Munroe's rare breaks for air, I stood nonchalantly and excused myself.

"I have an errand I need to run. I'll be back soon, Grandmama. Mr. and Ms. Munroe, it's been great seeing you again."

Before anyone could ask about my errand I was out the door. Ms. Munroe went back to her latest story.

***

I drove up and down sandy roads along the banks of the Pelahatchie and took several wrong turns before locating an ancient, silver Gulfstream, parked under a spreading chinaberry tree beside a wide bend in the river. Next to it sat a battered 1957 Dodge truck with its hood raised.

209

Along the riverbank ran a sandy beach, where a jon boat lay in the sun. In an open shed two outboard motors perched on wooden sawhorses. A power pole brought in overhead lines from the nearest county road. From somewhere beyond the trailer came the hum of a window unit air conditioner. The owner was nowhere in sight.

Bees buzzed about me as I knocked on the aluminum screen door. I waited for a moment and knocked again, this time louder. Still no reply. I looked around for somewhere else he could be. I was about to leave when a face peered out. A hoarse voice whispered, "What do you want?"

"Are you Win Stevens?" I asked.

"What if I am?" His face came into view as he stepped closer. He must have been fifty, the same age as my dad, but he looked closer to sixty. Years of hard drinking and outdoor work had given him a craggy face and sallow complexion. Sparse, white hair stuck out in all directions.

"Mr. Stevens, I'm Tom Williams. I was hoping I could speak with you for a few minutes."

There was a long pause. "You Sam Williams' boy?"

"Yes sir, I am."

"Well, I'll be damned." He stared at me for several beats. "Come on in."

The sour odors of sweat-stained clothes and stale cigarette smoke assaulted me as I crossed the threshold. My eyes watered as they adjusted to the darkness. Stevens knocked over something and scattered trash on the floor.

"Sit over here," he said, and pointed at what turned out to be an old barstool with a large tear in its plastic seat cover. He turned on a low wattage lamp in the corner.

"How's your grandmama doing?"

"She went to the hospital earlier this week, suffering from exhaustion, but she's home now and doing a lot better."

"I'm sorry to hear that." He squinted at me, face more rutted than the dirt road I'd come in on. "I'm glad she's better. She's a real nice lady."

"Thanks."

"I've got some Coca Colas in the ice box. Want one?"

"Sure."

He pulled two bottles from the small refrigerator, popped the tops, and handed me one.

"Mr. Stevens, I was wondering if you could tell me about my parents' accident?"

With his free hand he pulled a pack of Marlboros from his shirt pocket, shook one out, and grabbed a lighter from a coffee table. "For starters you can call me 'Win.' I didn't just work for your daddy. He was one of my best friends."

Win gazed for a moment at a spot on the wall. "Your parents didn't die in an accident. I tried to convince that bastard Willingham. Instead, he fired me and hired his idiot nephews.

"There was a blue streak on your parents' car. Lester and Larry Suggs both drove blue Chevy pickups back then. A week later I saw Larry's parked outside Shirley's, a juke joint out on Tallahassee Highway. It had a fresh coat of paint and Bondo on the right front fender."

"Where might I find these Suggs boys?"

"They moved off their old home place after your daddy and I busted up their still. The IRS came in and took the land. I don't have any idea where they're living now."

"I understand Lester, at one time, owned the Little River Hunting Club property. He sold it to some shady characters from Miami but leased it back from them. I went by the place the other night. It was deserted but looked to be in pretty good shape."

211

"They don't live there," he said. "I don't even know what they use it for. There used to be a bunch of Klan types who met there occasionally, but I don't think we've had any of that for years. You might ask about them over at Shirley's."

He paused for a moment. "Maybe we could get in touch with the Suggs brothers and have them to meet us at the Hunting Club. We need to be careful, though. Those boys are some mean motherfuckers."

"You're telling me!" I recounted my run-in with them the other night and their subsequent arrest in Lafayette County. "They'll probably be out tomorrow if they aren't already. Would you like to come with me while I pay them a visit?"

A grin blossomed across his face. "Yeah... The sheriff up in Mayo's an old buddy of mine. Why don't I give him a call and see if the brothers are still there?"

He cleared some newspapers from a rickety dinette table, dug out a black rotary phone identical to my grandmother's and dialed. A male voice answered on the other end.

"Doug, this is Win Stevens... Yep, yep, it *has* been a long time. I understand you have some old friends of mine up there in your jail, Larry and Lester Suggs... They are? ... Oh no, no rush, I was just curious... Thanks a lot. You take care."

He hung up. "They won't be out until tomorrow," he chuckled, "From what I understand they're madder'n a couple of wet tomcats. This is probably the first time either of them got hauled in for something they didn't do."

I waited outside while he washed his face, ran a comb through his hair and changed clothes. He seemed unsteady as he stepped into the bright sunlight. Not sure how good he'd be in a fight, I was still happy to have somebody on my side. When he climbed into my car he reeked of

Scope and aftershave. His red eyes peeked out through little slits above bags fatter than my middle finger.

***

Tallahassee Highway was on the other side of town. Our route took us past the country club. As we passed, a group of golfers stared across the fence at us from the ninth hole. Whether they recognized us or were just curious I wasn't sure. I avoided eye contact and hoped Win would do the same.

Along the way we stopped at the Pelahatchie Bridge and climbed down the steep embankment. Win described how he'd found my parents' car upside down in the river. He seemed uncomfortable talking about it, but I assured him I wanted to know everything he could remember.

He said he'd received an anonymous call from a woman about an accident that night. "There's no way in hell they could've seen a car down here from up there on the road in the dark."

I stood a long time watching the swirling water where my parents died then straightened and turned. "Alright. Let's go find those bastards."

I'd driven past Shirley's many times over the years but had never been inside. It wasn't the kind of place a good Southern Baptist boy frequented, certainly not one whose grandmother did her best to raise him right.

It was early afternoon and the only patrons, a man and a woman of indeterminate age, sat in a corner booth sipping beer and muttering at each other.

They glanced up in unison as Win and I walked in. On the juke box Roy Acuff sang the old gospel standard, "The Great Speckled Bird." I

213

smiled as I recalled seeing a hippie tabloid by that name at Underground Atlanta.

The woman behind the bar recognized Win and gave him a broad grin revealing widely spaced, brown-stained teeth. "Well, I'll be. Look what the cat drug in. Who's your friend?"

"This here's Tom Williams… Sam's boy."

She gawked at me as if she'd seen a ghost.

"Shirley," Win said, "we were wondering if you knew where we might find the Suggs boys."

"I haven't seen them in years." As she wrung a tattered bar towel between her hands, her eyes shifted. She was lying.

From the look he gave her, Win had seen it too but chose not to press the point. "That's what I thought. Here's my number. Let me know if you hear anything." He scrawled it on the back of a bar napkin.

On the way out I glanced at the couple in the corner just in time to see them look away and resume their conversation. Before the door closed the man's voice called out, "You start looking for the Suggs, they might come looking for you."

Which was exactly what I wanted.

As we climbed into my car I asked Win, "Do you think it was Shirley who called you the night my parents died?"

"No. I'd have recognized her voice right off. It was somebody else."

On the way back to Win's house we drove past the Little River Hunting Club. We could see the outline of the building through the trees.

"Call me if you hear from the Suggs before I do," he said as I dropped him off. He handed me a piece of paper with his number.

As I was about to pull away he yelled, "Wait a minute! I've got something for your grandmama." He disappeared into the trailer and came back carrying a porcelain wash basin with a half dozen bream. "I just caught them this morning. I had them in the ice box."

"Win, you don't need to do that."

"Shit! Take 'em. I've got a bunch more, and I can't eat 'em all by myself. Besides, if I need more I'll just go over there under that tree and throw out a hook."

"Thanks, Win. I know she'll appreciate them."

"Don't mention it. Just call me as soon as you hear from the Suggs."

"I will."

On my way home I mulled over the things I'd learned. Lester and Larry Suggs had murdered my parents to stop my father's crusade against their criminal activities. They'd once been members of a Klan-like organization, the Little River Hunting Club, which was apparently inactive, though the building and sign were still there. Moonshining by now had declined almost to the point of extinction. While Jasper County was still dry, it was easy enough to buy liquor from illegal retailers or legally in nearby counties, brand-name stuff that hadn't passed through someone's radiator.

Lester Suggs no longer owned the hunting club property. Arcadia had acquired it, along with several other tracts, supposedly for a luxury resort and retirement community in an area where most residents lived on welfare.

The story was ludicrous. It seemed Emmett and Salazar were running a money laundering scheme, but why would that require so much land?

I now had, or could obtain, evidence that Jimmie Lee hadn't murdered Dana. According to Doc Green, her autopsy photos were on file at his office, complete with a ruler showing the size of the strangulation marks. It would take an exhumation of Jimmie's remains, however, to prove that his hands were too big to have made those bruises, and Ida would never agree to that. Neither Jimmie nor Dana would benefit from such an exercise, but it might help bring the real murderer to justice.

215

The men who lynched Jimmie were, no doubt, members of the Little River Hunting Club, led by the Suggs brothers. I couldn't figure out, though, how such blind rage, driven by racial hatred, related to my parents' deaths or the criminal activities of Mr. Salazar.

I pulled to the side of the road and scribbled furiously in my notebook.

Chapter Twenty-Six

It was 5:30 when I got home, and the Munroes had left. I came in through the kitchen, put the fish in the refrigerator and found my grandmother still sitting in the living room.

She glared at me. "Tom, where have you been?"

I thought about it and decided to tell her the truth, or at least part of it. "I ran into someone the other night who told me where I could find Win Stevens, so I paid him a visit. He said to tell you 'Hello,' by the way and gave me some fresh bream for supper. They're in the refrigerator."

She shook her head, stood and followed me back to the kitchen. I cleaned the fish while she pulled out two frying pans and a can of Crisco. As I sliced green tomatoes picked from our garden, she put a pot of water on the stove. When it came to a boil I dropped in two tea bags, let them steep, then poured in a cup of sugar while the water was still hot.

"What did you and Win talk about?" she asked.

Through the open window I contemplated a brilliant coral and golden sunset. The fragrance of gardenia blossoms wafted on the breeze. From the street came the sounds of children playing, moms yelling at them to come inside for supper.

I chose my words carefully. "I asked him what he knew about my parents' deaths. He thinks the Suggs brothers ran Mama and Daddy off the road to keep Daddy from arresting them and busting up their stills. They made it look like an accident by laying a dead deer on the side of the road. Naturally, we can't prove any of that."

She placed her hands on either side of the sink, leaned against it for support, and took a deep breath. "Just what do you think you're going to do with that information, Tom, go running off to that dumb sheriff?"

"No. Colleen knows some folks in Tallahassee. I'll give them whatever information I have and see what they can do with it."

"And what will that be, after all these years?"

"I don't know, but I intend to find out."

"Tom, let it go. There's no way anybody's going to arrest those men for killing your mama and daddy."

"Grandmama, there's more. I believe they're the same men who lynched Jimmie."

"Well, the sheriff sure isn't going to arrest them for that. Everybody in this county, besides you, me, Ida and Ruby, thinks Jimmie killed her. They'll just say he got what he deserved."

"Doc Green knows Jimmie didn't kill Dana, and he tried to explain that to Willingham at the time. He told me the killer had smaller hands than Jimmie's."

"I still don't see what you think you're going to accomplish besides getting yourself killed."

I dropped the subject, not mentioning the trip to Shirley's or our expected call from the Suggs brothers once they got out of the Mayo jail.

Instead, I set the table, and we ate our supper.

Later, as we sat in the living room watching Lawrence Welk I remarked, "You know, sometimes I worry about you being here in this house all by yourself, especially at night."

She gave me an inquisitive look but said nothing.

"Yesterday, on the way to the hospital I bought new locks for the front and back door. I'll put them on first thing in the morning."

"What in the world do I need new locks for?"

"I'd just feel better knowing the house is more secure."

218

"I have locks on my doors."

"And half the time you don't lock them. Look, I've already bought them, and I'll show you how to use them."

She let out a long sigh. "Alright. Some of my friends have them. I guess it won't hurt."

She turned in early, as usual, and having nothing else to do, I went to bed as well. I slept well, thinking the Suggs brothers were still in the jail.

***

I awoke the next morning to the sound of Ida pounding on the back door. My grandmother was still fast asleep thanks to the pills Doc Green prescribed.

"Tom, you starting to worry me," Ida said as I let her in.

"Sorry, I was sound asleep. I didn't hear you knocking."

While she cooked breakfast I showered, dressed and got the morning paper.

My grandmother awoke, shuffled into the kitchen and sat in her bathrobe sipping coffee while I read her the news, most of which dealt with the election campaigns.

She gazed at me and smiled. "When you were little you used to spread the Sunday paper on the front porch floor and read the news and sports. I should've known right then what I was getting into. You must've found life in Monrovia pretty boring."

"I'm afraid life in Monrovia's been anything but boring, especially lately. Right now, I could use a little less excitement."

"Yes, but you always wanted to travel and see the world."

I laughed to think I'd once dreamed of traveling. "Yeah. I left the United States once, and all I brought back were a purple heart and a scar on my thigh."

219

She leaned forward, her smile fading. "Look, I know you aren't going to leave this business alone. You're *so* hard-headed. I'm just asking you to do two things for me. Don't get hurt, and don't hurt innocent people with the things you find out."

"I'll do my best. I'm going to stay here a while. I need to put those locks on, and maybe this afternoon I'll go back out to Win's."

"Well, okay. Just remember what I said, and try to get back before Ida leaves, so we can have supper together."

"I'll try."

She retired to the living room, while I searched for a drill and key-hole saw and set to work. Ida watched me in curious silence.

With my grandmother safely out of earshot, it was time to come clean with Ida as well.

"Ida, I need your help with something."

She looked at me bemused.

"I need to go out tonight to take care of something, and I may be late getting back. I don't want to leave Grandmama here alone."

Her eyes narrowed.

"I was wondering if you could stay here in the third bedroom."

She gave me a pensive look. "I don't know, Tom."

"I had a visit with Win Stevens yesterday. He was a friend of my daddy's and a deputy sheriff... He's the one who found my parents."

"I know him, or least I used to."

"He knows who killed them... And we're pretty sure they're the ones who hanged Jimmie. We're going after them."

The reality of what I'd just said hit me. For the first time I realized this was what it had come to. I would finally confront the people who murdered my parents and Jimmie.

Ida thought for a long time. In a soft voice she asked, "What do you want me to do?"

"I'll tell Grandmama I have to do some research on a story I'm writing. She won't believe me, but that's the truth, and it's as much as I want to tell her right now. The two of you should be safe enough here. I'm going to finish installing these locks, and I want you to keep the front and back doors deadbolted the whole time I'm gone. Understand?"

"I understand."

"There's a loaded shotgun in my closet. I got it down from the attic. Grandmama doesn't know it's there. Have you ever fired one?"

"Yes."

"I'll make sure it's ready in case you need it. If those boys come here for any reason, do you think you could use it on them?"

She looked away, her eyes glistening. "If they the ones hung my boy then, Lord help me, I'll shoot 'em without thinking about it." Large tears rolled down her face.

"Okay. I'm not going to tell Grandmama about this right now. I'll wait until after lunch."

When I finished with the locks I called Pug Donovan while Ida sat in the living room with my grandmother.

"Hey, Tom," he said, "how's your grandmama?"

"She's getting better. I didn't catch you at a bad time, did I?"

"No, no, it's okay. I was just going over this story Bright Wilson wrote about the Frankie Tavares arrest. I'm telling you this is *huge*." He paused. "By the way, isn't your girlfriend Frankie's lawyer?"

"That's her."

"Well, this case oughta make her career."

"I hope so... Look, I've stumbled onto something here in Monrovia, and I believe there's a story in it. Do you have a few minutes?"

"Sure."

"I know you were a friend of my dad's, and I'm sure you remember the circumstances of my parents' deaths."

"Yes."

"I have reason to believe they were murdered. Yesterday I talked to Win Stevens, my dad's deputy."

"Oh my God," he chuckled. "Where in the hell did you dig up Win Stevens? I thought he was dead a long time ago."

"No. It took me a while, but I found him. He lives in a trailer down by the river. He told me he found paint on my parents' car and that somebody had rammed them into the bridge. Win was investigating this when Cuz Willingham became sheriff and fired him, supposedly for drinking."

"I remember that. Old Win always had an alcohol problem. He and your daddy and I were fraternity brothers at Florida. How Win ever managed to graduate, even as a PE major, is beyond me."

"There's more to it. Before he died, my dad arrested some local moonshiners and destroyed their stills. Among them were a couple of brothers named Lester and Larry Suggs. Lester later became owner of a piece of property known as the Little River Hunting Club. The guys in this club were a bunch of Klan types, Neanderthal assholes. When I was about eleven, a friend and I saw these animals gang rape and murder a young Black woman. We wanted to go to Willingham, but we were scared. As far as we knew, he could have been one of them. They all wore cloth sacks over their heads. A few days later my friend went back and burned the place down."

"This is a pretty old story. How's it relevant now? Can you get any details from your friend?"

"No. A few years later a white woman named Dana Padgett was murdered. The sheriff arrested my friend, Jimmie Lee Johnson, who was Black, and a group of white men lynched him, presumably members of the Little River Hunting Club."

"Ah shit! I remember that. I didn't know you were involved in it."

"Yeah, I'll fill you in on the rest later. Suggs sold the hunting club property to a company out of Miami called Arcadia Development. Over the next few years Arcadia bought up other land in the area. They're supposed to be building a golf resort and retirement center. I drove by there the other day. The only house out there so far belongs to George Martin."

"I still don't see a story in this."

"Pug, the principal owner of Arcadia Development is Enrico Salazar, the drug dealer..."

"I know who Rico Salazar is."

"...and the principal force behind the project is Bill Emmett."

"Whoa! How in the hell did Bill get tied up with Rico Salazar and a bunch of Klansmen? And, no offense, but what would Salazar want with a bunch of rednecks from up in that part of the state? This whole thing doesn't make sense, Tom. Rico's got enough problems with the Feds down in Miami."

"You also need to know that the lawyer who handled the incorporation is none other than Langford Styles, the same Langford Styles who wants to be our next Congressman."

"Look, Styles is slimy, but I don't think he's stupid enough to get mixed up in this kind of crap either. Before we put anything in print you'd better be ready to back it up. I don't need him suing this paper for libel. We could claim he's a public figure now, but it would still make us look bad."

"I understand. I talked to Colleen about it. She thinks the whole Arcadia deal is a scam by Salazar to bilk these country folks out of their savings and launder his drug money through Monrovia State Bank."

"Could be... Boy, have you gotten yourself into a shit storm. And so has Bill. That dumb fuck has no idea who he's messing with. Be careful,

Tom. Guys like Salazar play for keeps, and I'm pretty sure those Suggs brothers do too. Listen…"

There was a moment of silence on the other end, and I heard a door close.

"I have a problem with you writing this story. You're too close to it. You can't write a decent piece about the people who killed your parents and your best friend. There's no way you can be objective, no matter how hard you try. If this turns out to be real, then I'll need somebody else on it, maybe Bright. You could do a follow-up, perhaps, since you witnessed it."

I winced. This was my story, and the last thing I needed was Bright Wilson or anybody else stealing it from me. "Pug, I can handle this. Besides, didn't you tell me Bright's tied up on the Tavares story?"

"Tavares is up for indictment this morning. His trial won't be for weeks, and he'll be out on bond. I can send Bright up to Monrovia this afternoon, tomorrow at the latest. I want you to call him as soon as you can and fill him in on what you already have."

He gave me the number at Bright's desk and his unlisted home number. "I'm telling you, you're too close to this, Tom. You can't write the story and be part of it at the same time. Besides, you're much better with the in-depth stuff, like the story you wrote about the King funeral. That's why I ran it behind the wire stories. Bright's good at writing the front-page stuff."

"Okay. Sure. I'll call him."

This was great! I'd probably end up writing the whole damned story, and Bright would get the byline. I began to fantasize about him getting hit by a car outside the Hillsborough County Courthouse.

In the back of my mind, though, I knew Pug was right. I was already so tied up in this I'd begun to lose sight of how the pieces fit together.

There were too many loose ends, and I was trying to tie them up in a way that suited me, instead of following the story wherever it led.

After lunch I told my grandmother I had plans for that evening and didn't know how late I'd be. I explained that Ida agreed to spend the night just in case she needed help with anything while I was out. Through the whole explanation my grandmother sat in her chair knitting and never said a word.

About mid-afternoon I drove Ida out to her house to get her things. I waited in the car while she went inside. I heard her explain the situation to Ruby. All the way there and all the way back neither of us said a word.

For the rest of the day, I hovered near the phone so my grandmother wouldn't answer it, in case Win or the Suggs brothers called. At about four I called Bright at his desk.

"Hey, Bright, it's Tom Williams."

"Hey, man, what's this I hear about you getting mixed up in some shit with the Klan and the Mafia?"

"Listen, I can't talk about it now. I just wanted to make sure you're there. Stay where you are. I'll go to a pay phone and call you back."

I made an excuse to my grandmother about going to the store to get something. Ten minutes later I was standing at a phone booth in the IGA parking lot.

"OK, here's what I have so far." I pulled out my notebook and gave him a detailed account, including the Suggs brothers' break-in and their arrest in Mayo.

"And you say they're getting out of jail today?"

"That's what I've heard."

"Damn! Well, I'd better let you go. Take care of yourself, man. I've got to wrap up this Tavares story and get some sleep. I'm dead on my feet and in no shape to drive up there this afternoon. I'll probably get there first thing in the morning."

I told him how to get to Monrovia, hung up, and started to leave before remembering I'd gone to the store to pick up something. I went inside and bought a gallon of vanilla ice cream and a bottle of chocolate syrup.

Later that afternoon, as the last of the sunset streamed through the front window, my grandmother and I sat in the living room eating our home-made sundaes.

After supper we were watching television when the phone rang. I jumped out of my chair. "I'll get that," I said. "You just relax."

The voice sounded like gravel under the tires of a truck. "Hey, boy, you wanna meet us? We'll be at the hunting club in two hours." He hung up before I could say anything.

"Who was that?" my grandmother asked.

"It was a wrong number."

I waited a half hour, then told her I needed to go out. I wanted to get to the hunting club early, in case it was a trap, which it probably was. It'd be dark by the time I got to Win's place. I told Ida to lock all the doors behind me. I felt better knowing she was there.

I stopped again at the IGA and called Win to make sure he was home and would be ready when I got there.

He was waiting on the stoop when I pulled into the yard and seemed to be in much better shape than earlier. For a moment I thought how pathetic he looked as he sat anxiously waiting. Immediately I felt ashamed. This was almost as important to him as it was to me. I worried about his ability to handle himself in a tough situation, given his age and condition.

I wondered what the hell we'd do, once we met the Suggs brothers, besides getting ourselves killed. "Win, I, uh, brought my dad's .45 automatic in case we need it."

I'd taken it from the closet when my grandmother and Ida weren't looking and put it inside my waist band, the way guys always did in the movies, covering it with my shirttail. It's an honest-to-God wonder I didn't shoot my dick off.

"Good. I was gonna tell you to bring something." He pulled a .38 from under his shirt. It looked old, and I resisted the temptation to ask him when he'd fired it last.

Chapter Twenty-Seven

At the hunting club entrance, we slowed for a quick look. Someone had removed the chain across the drive, and fresh tire tracks creased the sand. A pinprick of light shone between the trees. Whether it came from the building or from a security lamp outside neither of us could tell.

"Don't stop here," Win said. "I know a better place."

Where Pleasant Springs Road crosses the Pelahatchie lay an open area below the level of the highway, a favorite local fishing spot. I parked in the shadow of a low-hanging willow.

A heavy cloud cover obscured the moon. Instead of walking back up the road, we followed a path through the woods using flashlights Win had brought. We switched them off when we reached the edge of a clearing, about fifty feet from the clubhouse and stood for several minutes letting our eyes adjust. A bright light from the rear window cast shadows across the landscape. I'd just stepped from behind a tree when its bark exploded a foot above my head.

"Get down!" Win screamed.

Hyperventilating, I dropped into the tall grass as another bullet ripped through the brush to my right. The muffled sound of barking dogs came from somewhere on the other side of the building, two of them as best I could tell.

"Win," I whispered, "where are you?"

"Shut up!" he said, no more than three feet away.

A voice in the distance called out, "Howdy boys. Nice night for huntin', ain't it? Unless you the ones being hunted…"

It was the man I'd heard on the phone. Off to my right someone snickered, how far away I couldn't tell.

A hand grabbed my shoulder, and I almost pissed myself.

"Lester's over there in the palmettos," Win muttered in my ear, "I'm guessing about fifty yards. Probably has a deer rifle. He's waiting for us to step into the light."

"There's another one to your right."

"Yeah. That sounds like Larry."

"What do we do?"

"Our pistols are no match for a rifle at that distance. Let's make him come to us. Slide up under that thicket to your right. I'll ease back down the trail a ways. If one of them cuts across in front of me I'll pick him off. Let me get about ten yards away. Then pick up something and throw it over there." He pointed to our left. "That oughta draw Lester out. Larry won't come any closer because that'll put him in Lester's line of fire."

"What if he puts those dogs on us?"

"Then we're fucked. It sounds like they're locked up and he can't get to them without us seeing him."

"Is that you, Win Stevens?" came another voice, more nasal, apparently Larry, circling behind us, getting closer to the trail to cut off our escape.

I slid into the thicket, thorns tearing at my arm, praying I didn't come upon a rattlesnake. I gave Win a few minutes to get away, then ran my hands along the ground searching for something I could throw.

Two shots rang out behind me, the second a bit louder than the first.

Sonofabitch!" Larry wailed, closer to me now.

"Hey, you alright?" Lester called from somewhere near the perimeter of light.

"They're over here," was the reply. One of 'em shot me in the leg!"

"You get him?"

"I think so."

229

I peered in Lester's direction. As I did, my left hand brushed a short piece of rotten limb. I picked it up carefully and heaved it as hard as I could to my left.

For what seemed an eternity I waited, listening to the cicadas. A mosquito buzzed inside my ear as the dogs' barking became more frantic.

I stole a glance in Lester's direction and almost missed Larry emerging from behind a tree. I could just make out his form in the darkness, like that of a bear, moving without a sound, staring intently into the woods above my head. Slowly I drew my arm back.

Limping, he edged closer, a dark stain spreading down his right trouser leg below the knee. He held a pistol in his left hand, his right arm still suspended from a sling, and stopped not five feet from me. I brought out my gun, clutching it in both hands.

"That little pussy probably ran off into the woods," he bellowed. "Go get the dogs."

"Shut up, Larry." Lester was now closer as well.

I had a clear shot at Larry, but Lester would see my muzzle flash.

Just when I thought Larry would walk past me, another loud shot echoed behind him. A volcano of blood, bone, hair and brains erupted from the right corner of his forehead, its sticky spray hitting me in the face. I fought back the urge to puke. He made a slow pirouette, his right eye staring down at me, the other rolling back into his head. With a low gurgling sound, he hit the ground like a log.

"Larry!" Lester screamed. He crashed through the brush for several steps, then stopped and retreated before I could fire. I listened in vain for any sound from Win. Beyond the building the dogs bayed louder.

Clutching the .45 in both hands, I came up in a crouch, edging closer to the light for a better view. Suddenly Lester broke from the bushes several yards away. He carried a large rifle and, ducking low, scrambled toward the clubhouse. I brought up the pistol and, leading him by about a foot, fired two rounds.

The first went wide, but the second struck home. He stumbled, let out a yelp, and dove out of sight. For the moment I'd stopped him from getting to the dogs.

Edging closer, I saw the bushes move.

"You just wait 'til my dogs get you, boy. I'm gonna kill you just like I killed yo mama and daddy."

Time was on Lester's side. He was up and moving again, slower now. If he got to the dogs there was no way I could outrun them carrying Win. Nor could I shoot them without giving away my position.

Knee-deep in palmettos, I moved in closer and dropped to the ground. Another shot whizzed overhead. I fired two more rounds in his direction to keep him down and sprinted around the opposite end of the building.

When I got to the front Lester was in the open and running for the El Camino. I brought the pistol up and fired again, hitting the passenger side mirror. The dogs went berserk. Unable to reach them, Lester crouched low and took cover near the opening of a trail leading down to the river, the same spot where years ago I'd seen men in hoods chase a naked, screaming girl. I was close enough to catch the fetid scent of the encircling swamp.

I raised the gun and aimed at the opening to the path. When a flash of clothing appeared, I squeezed off another round. He dropped the rifle, stumbled and crawled toward the river.

I eased closer, aiming at the trail and straining for any sound of movement. I was almost upon it when I heard a limb snap deeper in the woods.

Suddenly there came a deep, rumbling croak, a primeval, reptilian growl, as though a monster from one of Ida's stories had risen from the depths. Before the word "gator" could form in my mind a piercing scream split the night. As its echo faded, I retreated to the cabin porch and rested against the door to catch my breath.

With the help of my flashlight, I located Win, seated with his back against a tree, clutching his shoulder. His eyes could barely focus as he gazed up at me. Carefully, I helped him to his feet and into the cabin.

"Let's take a look at you," I said.

He collapsed onto an old sofa while I peeled off his shirt and tore it into long strips. Larry's shot had grazed the outside of his arm, missing both artery and bone. I wrapped a piece of cloth around it and had him hold it while I searched for something better.

The place consisted of a single large room with a roll top desk, a couple of card tables, some folding chairs and a cast iron stove. In one corner an open doorway revealed a small toilet.

In a drawer I found a half-empty fifth of Ancient Age, which I used it to disinfect the wound. I folded some cheap toilet paper from the restroom into a makeshift pad and secured it with another strip.

As I worked I noticed shelves along the outside wall stacked with hate tracts showing cartoon pictures of Blacks and Jews. One bore a caricature of Pope Paul.

"We're gonna have to call the sheriff," said Win.

"But he'll think we murdered the Suggs."

"He'll sure as hell think that if we *don't* call him. This may be our only chance to explain what happened."

As I reached for the phone it suddenly rang.

Startled, I asked "What do I do?"

"Answer it, but don't let 'em know who you are."

"Yeah," I said into the receiver, trying to sound like Lester.

"Who's this?" a woman asked. The connection was poor, and I could barely hear her.

I didn't answer.

"Let me speak to Lester," she said, clearer now.

"I'm afraid Lester's indisposed."

The phone clicked.

"Who was that?" Win asked.

"I'm not sure, but she sounded familiar, and I think she knew me. She asked for Lester."

"We've gotta get out of here," Win said.

"But the sheriff said…"

"Fuck the sheriff. Whoever she was, she knows Lester's dead and she's calling Willingham right now. If we're still around when he gets here he'll shoot us both and claim we murdered the Suggs."

"Okay. I'll go get my car."

"No!" he winced. "We don't have time. Besides, that damn thing sticks out like a whore in church. Let's take Lester's truck."

In the desk I found a ring with three keys, one of them a Chevy. Inside the El Camino a pair of bluetick hounds bayed, darting from one window to the other. When I opened the door they circled, sniffing the ground, and then followed Lester's scent down the trail on their way to becoming the alligator's next course.

Win stumbled getting into the cab. My homemade bandage had soaked through.

"Take my belt," I said. "Use it as a tourniquet."

Spinning gravel, I raced onto the highway. On a long straightaway three patrol cars appeared in the distance, red lights piercing the night. I turned onto a side road and doused my headlights hoping they hadn't seen us.

When they'd passed, I turned back toward town.

"Win," I asked, "What if tonight had nothing to do with my parents' murder? What if the Suggs were working for Bill Emmett and his friends from Miami?"

"Hell. I don't know."

"Besides building a resort, what use do they have for all that land?"

"First of all, Arcadia ain't building shit," he croaked. "It may have started out that way, but now it's just a front."

"A front?"

"You ever seen what a phosphate mine looks like when they get done with it?"

"No"

"It looks like a bombing range, nothing but barren ground and big-ass holes full of nasty water. There's no way they'll ever smooth it out and plant enough trees for people to live there."

He clenched the belt between his teeth and fumbled in his pocket for a cigarette. I found the lighter and pushed it in.

"How come nobody ever asked?"

"People believe what they wanna believe. You tell them they're gonna get rich and that's what they believe. None of the workers even live there. They brought 'em all in from Dade City put them in trailers on the site. They haul the phosphate out through a back road over near my place. They made the development look real nice over there near the main entrance, but there's never gonna be a resort."

"You never told anybody this?"

I passed the glowing lighter to him without taking my eyes off the road. He lit the cigarette and took a deep drag.

"I guess I've spent the last few years minding my own business. I fix outboard motors and do a little construction work in Tallahassee or down in Tampa. Then, a couple of weeks ago, I noticed a lot of white silt in the river. I got curious and took my jon boat upstream for a look. When I

234

rounded the bend I saw just how fucked up the place was. They'll finish up soon and, when they do, it won't be fit for anything else."

"What are the investors going to do with it? Bill couldn't have gotten enough from the phosphate to repay them?"

"Well, I saw them grading out this long flat spot. It ended not far from the river. I don't know what they plan to do with it."

"What does it look like?"

"About a mile long and twenty yards wide, like a runway for a decent-sized plane." He shook his head. "With all the crop dusters out of work around here, the last thing Jasper County needs is another landing strip."

I glanced at Win. His face had turned paper white.

"Look," I said, "just take it easy, and let me get you to Doc Green."

We were almost there when the tumblers fell into place.

"Win," I said in a low voice, "I think I know somebody who could use a large runway in a remote place like this."

In my mind I again saw the photo of Rico Salazar stepping down from a plane at the airfield near Brandon.

I told Win all the things Freddy Martinez had said about Salazar and his connections to Arcadia. I repeated the stories Buddy Cole told me about Vietnam, Air America, the CIA, and the Mafia. I'm not sure how much of it he believed, but it all made sense to me. I had to call Colleen, but first I'd take care of Win.

Chapter Twenty-Eight

Doc Green lived on a dead-end street four blocks from my grandmother's house. Late as it was, the lights still shone in the back when we arrived. Still, it took two loud knocks before he answered.

"Yeah, what is it?" he called from behind the door.

"Doc, it's Tom Williams. I've got Win Stevens with me. His arm is hurt, and he needs you to patch him up."

"Alright," he said, and reluctantly opened the door. "Bring him back to the kitchen and let me take a look." He eyed my makeshift bandage suspiciously. "Careful, don't drip any blood on the rug. My wife will shoot all three of us."

He sat Win down at the table and removed the bandage. "Who made this thing?"

"Tom did. And he tore up my best damned shirt doing it," Win said in a voice so weak I could barely hear him.

"This is a gunshot wound. How did it happen?"

I knew better than to lie to the man. "Larry Suggs shot Win, and Win shot him back in self-defense."

"Well, I'll still have to call the sheriff."

"We already called him, and we're going to his office as soon as we leave here."

The doctor studied me. He knew I had no intention of going to the jail.

"I'll sew him up here, but he's gonna have to go to the hospital. He's lost a lot of blood and needs a transfusion. I'll meet you there."

This was perfect. I could call Willingham and tell him I'd rushed Win to the emergency room, afraid he might bleed out. The sheriff and his nephews would have a tough time gunning down two unarmed men in a well-lit hospital full of eyewitnesses.

The wound was ugly. Muscle tissue hung from its gaping maw, and I could see what appeared to be bone. Win gritted his teeth as the doctor applied alcohol and stitched it up with a kit he kept at home. Apparently anesthetic was not something he carried in his little black bag. He taped a large cotton pad over it and loaned Win an old shirt two sizes too small.

When he'd finished I thanked him and helped Win to his feet. "I'll take him straight there."

"No." exclaimed the doctor. "This man needs an ambulance!"

"I can get him to the hospital much quicker." I left before he could say anything else, not knowing who might arrive with that ambulance.

Our route took us past my grandmother's house. I slowed, put the .45 and Win's .38 into a brown cloth bag I'd found in the El Camino and tied it shut. Making sure no one saw us, I threw the bag out the window. It landed out of sight under an azalea. I could retrieve it later when I got home from the hospital.

***

The emergency room at Jasper Memorial was busy, as usual, with all manner of injuries and a young girl who'd gone into labor. She looked to be all of twelve.

Doc Green had called ahead, and a nurse and orderly met us at the door. Win passed out as they lowered him onto a gurney and asked for his blood type. Within minutes they'd begun a transfusion. I borrowed a phone at the nursing station and called Willingham.

When I told him what had happened he was furious. "Where the hell are you? Why didn't you wait at the hunting club?"

"Win's lost a lot of blood, Sheriff, and I had to get him down here right away."

"Don't you dare go anywhere..." I heard his teeth clench. "I mean it."

While I waited I called my grandmother. By now it was ten o'clock. I figured she was in bed and Ida would answer the phone, but I was wrong. She didn't sound groggy, which told me she'd waited up for me.

I tried to sound as casual as possible. "Hey, Grandmama, I wanted to let you know I'm going to be a little late coming in tonight, and I don't want you worrying about me."

"Where are you?"

"I am at the hospital, but I'm fine. Win's been shot, but I'm sure he'll be okay. It's a superficial wound."

She took a deep breath and let out a long sigh. "Tom, when will you learn?"

"I went back over to Win's tonight, and we went to the Little River Hunting Club to talk to the Suggs brothers about what happened to Mama and Daddy. They pulled guns on us, and Win had to shoot them. Win has a flesh wound on his arm. That's all.

"Tom, I knew it would come to this," she sobbed.

I felt like shit.

"I'm alright, Grandmama, and the men who murdered my parents are dead."

"Does that make you feel any better?"

"It makes me feel better knowing they won't kill anybody else."

"This is horrible."

"It'll be okay. Listen, I've got to go. The sheriff will have some questions for me, I'm sure. It'll be a while before I get home. Just promise me one thing."

"What?"

"I need you to call Colleen and tell her what happened. Tell her I'm at the sheriff's office and to come up here as soon as she can. I wrote her number down earlier. It's on the pad next to the phone."

"She doesn't mind me calling her at this hour?"

"Not at all."

"Okay."

"Thanks." I said goodbye and hung up. She was upset but sounded relieved that I wasn't hurt.

Wondering what I looked like after crawling around in the woods, torn by briars and bitten by bugs, I stepped into a restroom and stared at myself in the mirror. A thin scratch ran down the right side of my face through a cluster of mosquito bites. I didn't even want to see what I looked like under my shirt and inside my pants.

My hair was a mess, matted with leaves and twigs. I pulled out a comb, did my best with it, and washed the dirt off my face. There was nothing I could do about Larry Suggs' blood and brains all over my shirt but try to hold down my gorge.

Ten minutes later the sheriff stormed in, his nephews in tow. I sat directly in front of the nursing station, where I made a point of telling everyone within earshot what happened.

"You two are in a world of shit, boy," he said. "I've got one man dead up there, and you shot him. His brother's missing and it looks like you killed him too."

"Win shot Larry in self-defense, Sheriff. They both pulled guns on us. Lester was wounded and I think a gator got him. I didn't kill anybody."

"A gator got him? You're gonna tell me a gator got him. What were you boys doing up there at the hunting club in the middle of the night anyhow?"

239

"We went there to talk to the Suggs brothers about the murders of my parents. I just wanted to ask them some questions. Lester called and told me to meet him there."

"You always carry a gun when you interview people? Is that how you reporters work nowadays?"

"The Suggs brothers murdered my parents, Sheriff. Lester admitted as much before he died."

"Yeah, yeah …" He turned and bellowed, "Where's Win Stevens?"

"He's in one of the treatment rooms, Sheriff," a nurse said from behind the counter.

He started in that direction.

"You can't go back there, Sheriff," she called out, chasing him down the hall.

He ignored her.

I looked at the two deputies, standing in the entrance like a pair of Dobermans, blocking my escape.

A moment later Willingham came back, still fuming. "He's asleep, and they say I can't wake him up." He pointed at Sonny. "You stay here, right outside his door. When he comes to, you call me." He jabbed a finger in my direction and said, "You're coming with me. Bubba, search him for weapons."

I was glad he'd ordered the search in the middle of the waiting room. Everybody there would see I was unarmed.

"He ain't got no weapons, Uncle Howard," said Bubba. He resembled his uncle, only taller and thinner. His flattop made his little head look like a clinched fist sitting atop a long, skinny neck, and his Adam's apple bobbed up and down like a yoyo when he spoke.

"What'd you do with that gun, boy?" asked Willingham.

"Win must have dropped it in the woods."

Lester and Larry had dropped their own guns, and I knew the sheriff hadn't had time to find them.

"We're going back out there and look for them as soon as the sun comes up. You'd better be telling me the truth."

His face was no more than six inches from me. Spit flew from his jowls, and I could barely make out the black eyes between his folded lids. As he turned I realized that, for all his bluster, he was as scared as I was, if not more. The Suggs brothers were dead, and he must have dreaded the call to Rico.

He handcuffed me and put me in the back of his patrol car. He and Bubba climbed into the front. "You better appreciate all I've done for you, boy. As I recall, I saved your life once."

I didn't know which sickened me worse, having him slobber on me or listening to his bullshit.

When we got to the jail, Willingham and Bubba dragged me out of the backseat. They frog-marched me in and threw me into an empty cell. As Bubba locked the door behind me, Cuz placed a small stool outside the bars and began questioning me. As far as he was concerned, Miranda was just another Latin dancer wearing bananas on her head.

"Now you just tell me what happened, and everything'll be alright." He had the look of a man trying to get his temper under control and I wasn't about to help him do that.

"Sheriff, I'd like to call my lawyer now." I had no idea whether my grandmother had gotten through to Colleen.

"You'll do what I fucking tell you to," he screamed.

I made no reply.

"You don't get a lawyer until I arrest you, and I haven't arrested you yet."

"Does that mean I'm free to go?" I loved messing with this idiot.

He took a deep breath and struggled to regain his composure. "No. You are *not* free to go. Now *I'm* going to ask the questions, and *you're* going to answer them. Why did you go up to the hunting club tonight?"

"We can skip that question, since I already answered it."

"Just answer the damned question!"

"Sheriff, I'm not answering questions until I talk to my lawyer."

"What if me and my deputy came in there and kicked your ass?"

"Then my lawyer will have some interesting photos to show the judge… and the voters."

"You think just 'cause you're Sam Williams' son I'm gonna treat you different from anybody else."

"I think the sooner I have my lawyer here, the sooner I can explain everything to you, and you can get this whole mess cleared up."

"Yeah, well you better think again, boy, because you ain't going nowhere or talking to nobody until I get some answers. You can just sit there 'til you're ready to talk." With that he left.

My thoughts returned to the last time I was here, and I tried to remember which cell I was in. I wondered how Win was doing at the hospital. I worried what my grandmother would think when she awoke and discovered I hadn't come home. Still, I knew better than to try to talk my way out of this with a sheriff who wanted to arrest me and didn't care what the facts were.

I must have dozed off just before dawn. When I awoke sunlight poured through the bars. There was a loud conversation at the other end of the hall and what sounded like a woman cursing.

"Mr. Williams has already explained to you and the sheriff that Mr. Stevens shot Larry Suggs in self-defense, and that an alligator killed his brother, Lester. We both know that Mr. Stevens will corroborate Tom's story when he regains consciousness. My client did not kill anybody. He acted properly in taking Mr. Stevens to the hospital, and if he's not under arrest, then you can *god-damned well* release him now."

"Now, ma'am, the sheriff ain't here yet, and I can't release the prisoner without his permission."

"You will release him now, or I'll go get a court order requiring you to."

"Ma'am, I have my orders."

"Fine. First, let me see him." Moments later I gazed through the bars into the face of Colleen Gentry.

I choked when I saw her. "My God, you're a sight for sore eyes. When did you get here?"

"About five minutes ago. I drove through the night after your grandmother called. I thought I'd never find this place. It has got to be the worst shithole in the state of Florida!" She gave me a look that could have boiled water.

"Baby, I didn't mean to drag you into this."

A wicked smile played across her face as her tone softened. "That's alright, sweet thing. You owe me big. I don't seem to be getting anywhere with this redneck deputy, so I'm going to see the judge and get a court order releasing you. I'll be back in a few minutes. In the meantime, don't say anything to anybody."

When she'd left I heard the deputy say, "Boy, I ain't never seen a lady lawyer, and I ain't never heard one talk like that. Where you reckon she's from?"

Chapter Twenty-Nine

At long last, the sheriff and Colleen returned. He quietly opened the door and stood out of my way. As I left he yelled to me from the end of the hall, "Don't you even think about leaving town, boy." An inmate glanced at me, forlorn, as I passed.

"And don't you think about hauling him in here again unless you're going to press charges," Colleen shouted back at him.

Outside she turned and whispered to me, "You *have* to remain in town, at least until the sheriff has a chance to talk to Win. I'm afraid that's a condition of your release."

"Okay. Right now, all I want to do is go home, take a shower, and get some rest."

"Good idea." She pulled me close and nibbled on my ear. "Do you think your grandma would mind if I got in the shower with you?"

"Probably... How'd you get Judge Adams to sign my release?"

"He took some convincing, especially with the sheriff whining the whole time about how this would mess up his murder investigation."

"There was no murder last night."

"I know that, and I'm sure the judge knows it. I'm just not sure he cares. I made a convincing legal argument, and I smiled and batted my eyes at him."

"Yeah, I can see how that would work."

"It was about as much as I could stomach. If he'd called me 'Little Lady' one more time I'd probably be in jail myself."

When we got to her car she grabbed me by the shoulders and kissed me hard on the lips.

"Let's go," I said. "You can meet my grandmother and Ida, and we can get some breakfast. First you'll need to drop me off where I left my car last night. You can follow me home from there."

"Sounds good... I'm afraid I'll have to leave right away though. I'm on my way up to Tallahassee."

"Why?"

"Frankie Tavares and I are going to meet with some people from the state attorney general's office. We're discussing a deal for clemency, or at least reduced charges, in exchange for information on Rico Salazar. My original plan was to ride up there with Frankie myself... but I had to come here and take care of another client," she said with a tight smile.

"What kind of information?"

"Seems there's a large heroin shipment coming in by plane. Frankie thinks he knows where it's landing but isn't telling anyone until we work out a deal. That's his only insurance."

"Why can't the Tallahassee people come to Tampa?"

"I don't trust the authorities in Tampa. We think Salazar has some of them on his payroll. They're probably waiting to get Frankie outside so they can have him killed. Frankie's dad was able to pull some strings and get him a separate cell under the watchful eye of a deputy who's a family friend. There's no telling how long that'll last. Frank Senior called in a favor from the AG to get this meeting in Tallahassee. A man from the FBI will be there as well."

"I have some more information that might help. But first I need to get home and see my grandmother."

When we arrived at the house, I introduced Coleen to my grandmother and explained, as gently as possible, what happened the previous night.

She stared back at me eyes welling in tears. "Tom, you know what the scriptures tell us about vengeance."

"This wasn't vengeance, Grandmama. For too long those men have terrorized the people of this county. We had to stop them. Win and I did what we had to do."

She buried her face in her hands and began to sob. I put my arms around her.

"All these years I've known it was no accident, that somebody murdered my boy and his wife. Lord, forgive me, but I'm glad those animals are dead. They got what they deserved, and now they can burn in hell."

I left Colleen with my grandmother and went to the kitchen to help Ida make sandwiches for lunch. I placed an extra one in a bag with an apple for Colleen.

When we'd eaten, I walked Colleen to her car. "How do I get from here to Tallahassee?" she asked.

"If you have a map I'll show you."

I pulled a pen from my pocket and marked the roads she needed to follow. She seemed distracted. I kissed her and held her close. "Are you gonna be okay?"

"I'm just worried about Frankie. He's under heavy guard now, and the FBI has promised to relocate him, but Rico could have someone waiting to ambush him on his way to Tallahassee."

"Frankie's a brave man. Baby, you've done all you can do for him."

A thought came to me. "Listen, last night, Win said something about the Arcadia property. The phosphate company's no longer mining it, and Arcadia's grading out a long flat area, like a landing strip, big enough for a small cargo plane."

"That could be the place Frankie told me about," Colleen said. "And I'm sure your buddy Emmett's in this all the way up to his ass."

"I don't know about that. As shady as Bill can be, I can't picture him as a drug smuggler. For one thing, he wouldn't have the balls for it."

"We'll see. Just don't mention this to anybody. If it turns out to be the spot Frankie told me about, I'll need that information in the plea bargaining. It doesn't do us any good if the authorities already know about it."

"Who the hell am I gonna tell, the sheriff?"

"Just be careful."

I kissed her on the lips, knowing full well my grandmother and Ida stood watching us from separate windows.

When I returned to the living room the interrogation began. "She seems like a nice girl. How did you meet her?" my grandmother asked.

"We met at a party for a political candidate in Tampa."

She went straight to the point. "When are you getting married?"

Ida suddenly decided the dining room needed dusting. From there she could hear every word we said.

"We haven't set a date. I just asked her about a week ago."

"She has an unusual accent. Where's she from?"

"Boston."

"Oh. I hope she comes from a nice family."

"Absolutely! Her father's a prominent judge and a personal friend of the Kennedy's."

"How wonderful!" Then came the inevitable question. "What church does she go to?"

"Roman Catholic"

There was a long pause. "Oh."

This, at least, took her mind off the murders and my run-ins with the sheriff.

I decided to leave before the conversation went any further. In the bathroom I stripped out of my clothes and stepped into our old claw foot tub, to which I'd added a curtain ring and shower head. I set the temperature as hot as I could stand it and stood for what must have been ten minutes.

When I'd finished and dried off I put Merthiolate on my scratches and calamine lotion on the bug bites. They were worse than I'd expected.

A couple of days' sleep would have been nice, but I'd have to settle for a short nap. I put on clean shorts, climbed into bed and passed out immediately.

***

The phone rang as I awoke. I looked at my clock. It was 4:30. I hopped out of bed, made it to the hallway, and answered before my grandmother or Ida could get there.

"Is your TV on?" It took me a moment to recognize Bright Wilson's voice.

Annoyed, I asked, "Is your refrigerator running?" I was in no mood for silly jokes.

"No! Seriously!" he said.

"What's happening?"

"Find one of the Tampa stations."

"I can't. We're too far away. What's going on?"

"I was getting ready to come up there to interview you this morning when I got an anonymous call. They were transferring Frankie Tavares to Tallahassee. Word had it he was cooperating with state authorities. I got to the jail just as they walked him out in handcuffs. Suddenly, his head exploded like a ripe watermelon, blood and brains all over the sidewalk. They must've used hollow points or dum-dums. Police think it came from a nearby high-rise."

"Oh my God!" All I could picture was Colleen on her way to a meeting that would never happen.

"I didn't see your girlfriend with him, just a couple of deputies."

"Yeah, she was supposed to meet him in Tallahassee."

"Well, it's a good thing she wasn't there. I'm telling you, man, I almost shit my britches. It was like the Kennedy assassination all over again, one shot, and it was all over... You know, when people kill like that, they're not just *killing*. They're making a statement."

"How'd you know he was getting out?"

"Somebody called and tipped me off."

"Did you get his name?"

"Nope"

"Anybody else there?"

"Couple of TV guys"

"Bright, it was a setup. They wanted the media there to cover it."

"Yeah... Damn!"

"Look, I've got to call Colleen. I don't suppose you'll be up here today."

"No. I need to see if I can reach Frankie's family, get some reaction. Maybe I can be there tomorrow."

"Thanks, Bright, I've got to go." I hung up before I realized I had no way to contact Colleen.

As I stood pondering this, the phone rang. For the longest time the only sound on the other end was sobbing.

"Hey. I just heard. I am *so* sorry."

"What do I tell his parents?"

"It's not your fault."

"I should have been with him, Tom. I was his lawyer for Christ's sake."

"What could you have done... besides getting yourself shot?"

She sighed. "I don't know. I just feel like I should've been there."

"Baby, there's nothing you can do for Frankie now but help the authorities catch whoever did this. Stay there. I can be in Tallahassee in a little over an hour."

"No, you can't! *You stay right where you are.* I'll be okay. Do *not* give that hick sheriff another reason to arrest you."

I took a deep breath and let it out slowly. "Okay. I understand. Why don't you get some rest and then come back here tomorrow? You need some time off. You've put in a lot of hours on this case."

After a long pause she said, "Frankie never had a chance to tell anyone where the dope is coming in."

"It could be that landing strip near Pleasant Springs... Win said they began grading it weeks ago. Surely they've finished by now."

"It could be. Do you think you can get a closer look at it?"

"Probably"

"Just don't get yourself killed." She sniffed. "I can't afford to lose any more clients. The partners frown on that sort of thing."

"Don't worry."

"I'm going to stay here tonight. I'll get a hotel room and take a long, hot bath."

"Great! That's exactly what you need. Try to get some sleep."

"I don't see that happening. I'll call my office and tell them I need a couple of days off. Do you think I could stay at your grandma's tomorrow night?"

"Sure."

I figured she could sleep in the third bedroom, where Ida stayed the night before. It had a door adjoining mine. We'd have to be quiet. My grandmother's hearing wasn't great, but even if she were stone deaf she could hear Colleen.

"I'll see you in the morning. I should be there some time before noon," she said.

"Good. I can't wait. I love you, baby."

"I love you too."

I found my grandmother in the living room reading the newspaper and kissed her on the forehead. She looked up and smiled.

By now it was five, and I decided to phone the hospital. The duty nurse seemed surprised to hear from me so soon after the sheriff took me away in handcuffs.

When I asked about Win, she said they'd replaced the dressing Doc Green put on his arm and gave him three pints of blood.

"Mr. Stevens will be fine," she said, "but he's gonna be weak for a few days, and that arm's gonna be real sore. The doctor wants him to stay another night. He should be releasing him tomorrow morning about ten o'clock."

She paused for a moment then whispered, "But I don't think he'll be going home."

"What do you mean?"

"That Sonny Jeter, the sheriff's nephew, is out there in the lobby. He and his brother have been taking turns watching Mr. Stevens' room. It looks like they're waiting to arrest him as soon as he leaves the hospital."

"Is Ruby Johnson there?"

"She is, but she's helping a nurse with another patient right now. Can I have her call you?"

"Yes. I'd really appreciate that."

"I'm glad Win's gonna be alright," said my grandmother when I returned to the living room. "I haven't seen him in a coon's age, but he sure was a good friend to your daddy." She stared out the window and for a moment I thought she'd start crying again.

A few minutes later the phone rang again. It was Ruby. I explained Win's situation, that he'd be leaving the hospital the next day and, under no circumstances, could we let the sheriff arrest him. There had to be a way to get him out of there without either of the deputies seeing him.

"Let me figure out something," she said. "I'll call you back."

I was helping Ida with lunch when the phone rang again. My grand-mother answered before I could get there.

She gave me a puzzled look. "Tom, it's for you. It's Ruby."

"I just called her to find out how Win was doing." I waited until she returned to the living room.

"Hey," I whispered, "what did you find out?"

Ruby sounded scared and, judging by the background noise, had called from a pay phone outside. "Just be here by 9:45 tomorrow. Wait out back behind the kitchen entrance. Don't be late."

"Okay. I'll see you then. In the meantime, I think I'll come visit him when we finish eating. Will I be able to get in?"

"Sure. Just watch out for those deputies. They've been sleuthing around here all day."

"Don't worry."

When she hung up, my grandmother asked, "What did Ruby want?"

"Nothing much… She said Win isn't leaving the hospital until to-morrow morning. I think I'll go by and see him."

"That'll be nice. Maybe I can come with you."

"Uh, I don't think so. They said he can only have one guest at a time. Maybe you can go by later."

She pursed her lips and gave me a suspicious look. "Okay."

I went back to my bedroom and pulled out my notebook. I added to my list the things I'd found out from Win about the landing strip and the possible connection to Frankie Tavares. When I opened it I noticed a couple of brown spots where I'd spilled my Coke at Sandy's a few days earlier.

I recalled how June startled me as I sat there, and in an instant I knew hers was the voice I heard on the phone at the hunting club. For the life of me I couldn't imagine what she had to do with the Suggs brothers, but I intended to find out.

Chapter Thirty

I arrived to find Bubba Jeter sulking in a corner of the crowded waiting room staring at an old hunting magazine. He glowered at me as I passed.

Unable to resist, I grinned and waved. "Evening, Bubba," I said, so loudly it echoed down the hall.

He neither spoke nor returned my smile but went back to looking at the pictures. I marveled that he wasn't holding the magazine upside-down.

I found Win sitting up in bed wearing a hospital gown and watching the grainy, black-and-white image of a game show featuring audience members in ridiculous costumes yelling and vying for attention from the broadly smiling host. Win looked like he would lose his mind. It was late afternoon and the hospital had already served supper, most of which still sat on his tray.

"Hey, they tell me you're gonna live," I said.

"Not if I don't get the hell outta here soon. They won't even let me smoke in this place. Right now, I'd kill for a cigarette." Strands of white hair clung to his pale face. He, no doubt, craved a drink as well.

"I understand they're not releasing you until tomorrow."

"That damned doctor! You'd think I was in a coma or something."

"You'll need a ride home. I'll come by and pick you up."

"You don't have to do that."

"It's no trouble. I don't have anything else to do. Besides, there's something we need to talk about."

His eyes narrowed. "What?"

I glanced out the door at the empty hall. Moving up close I said, "The sheriff and his nephews plan to nab you the moment you leave. I think I can get you out of here tomorrow without them seeing you, but we'll have to go somewhere besides your place."

"Ah shit!"

"Another thing... Do you think I could borrow your boat for a bit?"

"Sure. It's not like I'm gonna be using it. It's on a trailer attached to the Gulfstream with a logging chain. The gas tank's in the shed and the key to the padlock's in my pants pocket over there."

I fetched it from the torn, stained khakis someone had folded and laid in the corner. "I want to go back up to that spot you told me about and get some pictures."

"No problem. Just don't get yourself shot. You can take my tackle box and a spinning rod. Anybody asks what you're doing up there, just tell 'em you're fishing."

"Thanks. Good idea."

"And I mean it. Don't get yourself hurt. You know ... you handled yourself pretty well out there last night."

"Thanks, but I wouldn't be here without you. I never got a chance to thank you for helping me track down those assholes."

"Don't mention it. Just find out what Emmett's up to."

"Yep, I'll pick you up some clothes and stuff while I'm there."

"Thanks... whatever you can find."

"Another thing, what do you know about June Skinner?"

He gave me a surprised look. "Why do you want to know about her?"

"I'm starting to think that was her on the phone last night at the hunting club. Why would she be calling Lester Suggs?"

"I don't know. She was a year behind your daddy and me in high school. It seemed like she was kinda sweet on your daddy, but he never even noticed her. June had a reputation... if you know what I mean. Your daddy, and Bill and George and I, went off to college and I didn't see her again for several years. She married a truck driver named Buck Skinner. Beat her up a lot. Then, one day he turned up dead. Somebody bashed his head in. Rumor had it June did it, but I couldn't see that. She got a job working for Sandy. That's all I know."

"How would that have involved Lester Suggs?"

"I don't know." Win ruminated for a moment. "You know, Lester was the kinda guy you went to when you wanted somebody killed and couldn't do it yourself."

"The caller who told you about my parents' accident at the Pelahatchie Bridge, could it have been June?"

"Hell, I don't know. I guess so. It's been a long time."

***

When I unlocked Win's Gulfstream and turned on the light, I had my first good look at the place and saw why he kept it dark. It looked the way you'd expect a trailer to look ... one that's fallen off the hitch of a truck.

I stepped over litter and dirty clothes on my way to the tiny bedroom. There in a chest of drawers I found some reasonably clean clothes. I pulled out what looked like enough for a few days and put them into a grocery bag I'd picked up at the IGA, thinking Win might not be coming home for a while.

With a little effort I attached the outboard, rolled the trailer down to a low spot on the bank, lowered the boat in the water and jumped in. The motor purred softly as I turned upstream. In a waterproof bag I carried my Nikon, a zoom lens, an extra roll of film and a Polaroid.

The Pelahatchie narrowed and deepened above Win's place, its banks as high as five feet in spots, its dark waters swirling with tannin. Sandbars loomed in the shallows like buttermilk-colored ghosts. About a quarter mile up, the river suddenly broadened. A thin creek issued a sickly yellow sludge. When I was sure nobody was watching I killed the engine and let the boat nose up onto the beach.

Pulling my cameras from the bag, I knelt under an overhanging bush. When I peered over the bank what I saw took my breath away. It was just as Win had described it. For the better part of two miles there was not a tree in sight. Across the terrain crouched high mounds of yellow-white clay. Aquamarine ponds dotted the landscape, breeding countless millions of mosquitoes.

Amid all this lay a long, recently paved asphalt strip. If I had any doubts as to its purpose the large Beechcraft coming at me from the opposite end quickly dispelled them.

As I snapped pictures it left the ground and passed a dozen feet overhead. With the Polaroid I captured the markings on the tail section.

Thinking the pilot might have seen me and radioed my description to his base, I grabbed my gear, jumped in the boat and tried to crank it as it swung downstream. For one heart-stopping moment it refused to catch.

I was almost back to Win's place when the plane slowly circled above. I pulled under a canopy of willows and sat for several minutes wondering what to do. If I got out at Win's, the pilot would easily spot me. He might even notice the white Mustang parked nearby.

Finally, he left. The men at the airstrip were probably in pursuit already. I made a quick dash hoping I could get to Win's before they caught me. With no time to tie up the boat, I tilted its motor out of the water and pushed it back into the current. As it rounded a bend, I heard another one approaching, grabbed the camera bags and ran.

From the shadows beneath the Gulfstream, I saw the heads of two men as they slowed near the spot where I'd jumped ashore. I got a couple of shots of them with my Nikon. Whether they saw my footprints on the beach I couldn't tell. Not wanting to find out, I ran for my car, started the engine and sped away as a bullet tore the fabric roof inches above my head. Another ripped through my rear window and struck the back of the passenger seat. Heart pounding, I hit the highway and didn't look back until I got home.

***

Ida had already cooked supper and left for the day. My plate sat on the stove covered with Saran Wrap.

"I was wondering if you were coming home," called my grandmother from the living room. "I never know anymore."

"Okay! Okay!"

"I'm just glad you're not on the news like that poor man they shot down in Tampa."

I saw no reason to tell her the "poor man" was Colleen's client.

"They showed his parents. They looked like real nice people. Lord, have mercy! What they must be going through. You know his daddy's a big politician down there."

"Yeah. I heard about it earlier."

I retreated to the kitchen and ate my meal. I'd just finished and was washing up when the phone rang. It was Colleen.

"Hey," she said in a soft voice.

"Hey. Feeling any better?"

"Some"

I told her about my visit to Win and my trip upriver, pulled the Polaroid from my pocket and gave her the plane's tail number.

"Good. I'll pass it on. That might be where the dope's coming in or it might not. The important thing is that *you* stay away from there. If the feds show up and start shooting, I don't want you standing in the crossfire."

"No problem. When do you think you'll be here?" I asked.

"Well, that's the thing. The feds want me to stick around another day or so in case I remember anything else about Frankie's involvement with Salazar."

"Another day or so...?"

"I don't know how long it'll be, but I'll keep you updated. You just stay out of trouble. *I mean it.*"

"Okay. I'll have to figure out how to get Win out of town."

The evening news showed the Atlantic storm making landfall near Hallandale on a track that would take it south of us. During commercial breaks I washed a load of clothes and hung them on the line hoping they'd have time to dry. Thunderheads loomed in the east, reflecting the brilliance of the setting sun.

While my grandmother wasn't looking, I packed some clean clothes and put them in the car in case I needed to leave town in a hurry. I retrieved the .45 from beneath the magnolia, along with Win's gun, put them in plastic bags and hid them in the trunk behind my suitcase.

With nothing better to do, I pulled out my notebook. Again, I saw the small brown Coke stains and wondered about June Skinner. Then I recalled a comment someone had made.

My plans for the next twenty-four hours took a sudden turn. I called Colleen back and told her to stay put. If I could get Win to Tallahassee, then maybe her friends could help us. Exhausted, I turned in. I'd figure it all out on my morning run.

Chapter Thirty-One

The sky had darkened overnight, and a moist southeasterly breeze enveloped me. As I ran the neighborhood streets, the leftover soreness from my exploits at the hunting club eased, but I still couldn't work out a way to get Win out of town without abandoning my grandmother and again running afoul of the law.

On returning, I showered, pulled my damp clothes off the line and hung them in my room to finish drying.

Sitting at the breakfast table with my grandmother, I mentioned, "Win's getting out of the hospital today. He has no way of getting home, so I told him I'd pick him up."

"That'd be nice. I hope you won't be gone long."

"I should be back by lunchtime."

"Good"

"I'll try to stay out of trouble this time," I added with a smile.

"Well, I certainly hope so," was her only reply.

Ida gave me a suspicious look as I ducked out the back door. "What are you getting yourself into now?"

"Nothing, Ida… but when the deputy tries to arrest Win at the hospital, he won't be there."

"Just don't you get *yourself* arrested again. Your lawyer ain't here to bail you out this time."

"I hear you."

It was 9:30 when I arrived at the hospital. As I passed the entrance I slowed, peered through the glass and saw Sonny Jeter pacing the lobby. I parked behind a dumpster out back and left the engine running.

A tall Black man in a white orderly's uniform met me at the service entrance and ushered me past Housekeeping to a spot near Win's room.

Glimpsing Sonny at the end of the hall, I ducked into a storage closet, eased open the door and peeped out.

Doc Green ambled down the corridor and entered Win's room with Sonny trailing behind. Ruby passed me, never glancing in my direction, stood outside Win's room and gestured to someone up front.

A scream echoed in the lobby, and Sonny and Doc rushed out. The orderly rolled a large cart into the hallway, blocking their view, and Ruby stepped into Win's room. She reemerged, pushing him in a wheelchair and I followed them out to my car.

Win hopped up gingerly and trotted to the passenger side. "Let's go," he shouted.

In seconds we were pulling out, surveying the front parking lot as we passed.

"No sign of the sheriff," he said.

Reaching under the seat, I retrieved a small grocery bag and handed it to him. "I bought you a present in honor of the occasion."

He smiled as he pulled out the carton of Marlboros.

"Roll down the window," I said, "and don't get ashes in my car. I have a quick question for you. Why would June Skinner have told George Martin she saw me making notes about Arcadia Development?"

"How do you know she did?"

"She's the only person who could have. I was having lunch at Sandy's, and she saw me."

"So?"

"So, she must have seen my notes about Arcadia and the hunting club. What do you know about her?"

He considered for a moment. "Well, after George and Bill and your daddy returned from the war, George married Jo Anne Robbins. There were rumors he was seeing June on the side."

"Anything else?"

Win paused as though choosing his words. "I heard later that June had gone to Jacksonville for an abortion."

"When?"

"Maybe a week or so before your mama and daddy died."

"My grandmother told me my dad was upset about something the day before the accident but didn't want to talk about it. Could that be what made him so mad?"

"Could be. Abortion's illegal."

"Would the baby have been George's?"

"Maybe."

My plans for the rest of the day suddenly came into focus. First, I had to stash Win somewhere. I knew better than to take him home or to my grandmother's, those being the first places the sheriff would look. But where to go? I had to think fast.

Stopped at the traffic light in front of Sandy's, I glanced in my rear-view mirror at the car behind me, a spanking new Plymouth Gold Duster. Through the windshield I saw the smiling face of Bright Wilson.

I motioned him to follow, and turned onto a side street, pulling in behind an abandoned packing house whose parking lot, overtaken by kudzu, had cracked and buckled over the years, its only occupant the rusted-out hulk of an abandoned transfer truck.

No one had followed us from the hospital, but by now Willingham and his nephews would be scouring the county for us. Fortunately, they'd be looking for a white Mustang, not a Plymouth Duster.

Bright was a decent writer. With his straight teeth, wavy blonde hair and winning smile he'd have made a much better television reporter. He was the only newspaperman I ever knew who showed up for work impeccable in a dark blazer, white dress shirt, and tweed slacks. Today he sported a gold Izod shirt and navy-blue chinos, as if headed to the links.

As I explained my dilemma he bounced around like a kid on Christmas morning. I promised him the details on Arcadia and Salazar later, but first he had to get Win out of Monrovia. I gave him directions to Tallahassee and the phone number for Colleen's motel room. He was to call her from a pay phone, as soon as he got into town, and then find rooms for himself and Win under assumed names. The newspaper would pick up the tab.

Once they checked in, he could call me at my grandmother's, and I'd fill him in on the rest of the story. Meanwhile, he could interview Win for background on the Suggs brothers and the murders of my parents. I didn't mention the Tavares case or the airstrip near Pleasant Springs, not knowing how much the authorities wanted to keep under wraps until after the bust.

Passing him the film from my Nikon, I said "Get these developed as soon as you can. They'll be useful in your story," then jokingly added, "At least give me credit for the art."

"Sure, man. No problem."

He and Win jumped in the Duster and departed.

***

By now the wind had picked up. Stopped at an intersection I watched traffic lights sway. On the sidewalk a whirlwind lifted a plastic bag and sent it dancing across the street to a silent minuet.

Bubba stood waiting for me on our front porch chatting amiably with my grandmother.

"Alright," he said as I pulled up. "Where is he?"

"You talking about Win?"

"You know damned good and well…" He caught himself, glancing apologetically at my grandmother. "You know who I'm talking about."

263

"I dropped Win off a few minutes ago at his place. He's probably still there."

"He'd better be." Bubba scowled and bumped me as he strode to his car and sped away.

I silently prayed that the sheriff wasn't already at Win's, knowing I'd lied and helped him escape.

"What was all that?" my grandmother asked.

"I picked up Win at the hospital. The sheriff wanted to arrest him for murdering the Suggs. A friend of mine met us at the old Shane Tobacco Company and got Win out of town."

"They wanted to arrest him for murder? They ought to give him a medal for killing those animals."

"I'm afraid the sheriff doesn't see it that way. Anyhow, Win's safe by now, and, hopefully, I am as well."

"You'd better be."

We sat quietly in the living room watching television. A weather update showed the storm shifting northward on a direct course for Monrovia. My grandmother watched quietly, worry lines furrowing her brow.

Two hours later Bright called to say he and Win were in Tallahassee and that he'd spoken to Colleen.

I filled him in on what I'd learned about my parents' deaths and Jimmie's lynching and explained most of what I'd discovered about The Little River Hunting Club, leaving out the dope shipment and Salazar. I'd give him those details later, just in time to scoop the TV stations in Tampa.

From the other end of the line came a scratching sound as Bright took furious notes. "Damn!" he exclaimed.

"Take care of yourself and Win too, I said. "And don't let anybody but Colleen know where you are. I mean *nobody*." I hung up.

***

We'd just finished supper when a heavy knock shook the front door. It was Willingham.

"Good evening, Sheriff, what can I do for you?"

"Where's Win Stevens?" he bellowed.

"I have no idea, Sheriff." I'd avoided asking Bright for the name of the hotel so I could answer this question truthfully.

He leaned close to my face. "If I find out you've been aiding the flight of a suspect I'll come over here and arrest your ass myself. You understand me?"

I smiled as he turned to leave. "You have a good evening Sheriff."

My grandmother took her medicine and turned in early. I waited until I was sure she was asleep, knowing the pills would have her slumbering peacefully through even the worst storm.

Pulling the .45 from my trunk, I reloaded it, jacked a round into the chamber, and put the handcuffs in my pocket in case I needed them.

I looked up and down the street to make sure Willingham hadn't returned.

As I pulled out of the driveway, fat raindrops pelted my windshield. With the storm coming there would be few cars out, but I took backroads, anyway, lest someone recognize my car. I now knew, or at least thought I did, who hired the Suggs brothers to murder my parents.

***

Arriving at the Arcadia site, I found the wrought iron gate locked and the guard nowhere in sight. By now the squall had arrived in earnest. I parked on the shoulder, climbed the fence and walked, half-blinded by rain, for what seemed a quarter of a mile down a magnolia-lined brick drive. Landscape lights on either side guided my way.

The house, a two-story, red-brick colonial with a white-columned portico, loomed, brilliantly lit, as I rounded a curve. I couldn't imagine one man living alone in such a place.

Beyond it a smooth, manicured lawn ran down to the placid waters of the springs. From what I could tell, George's house sat at the precise spot where the Pleasant Springs AME Church once stood.

I'd always liked George and thought I knew him. He was direct and often brusque, with a dry sense of humor, all of which I'd *mistaken* for honesty. He tripped himself up with his comment about me writing in my notebook. He could only have gotten that information from June Skinner, whom I'd now tied to the Suggs brothers.

As I reached the last magnolia, a guard emerged from the house. Gazing in the other direction, he failed to notice me. I jumped behind a tree, crouched low and peered at him, wiping water from my face. He strolled about for a few minutes, stared into the woods, and then bent to light a cigarette under the hood of his yellow slicker.

He was a couple of inches shorter than me, but noticeably bigger through the arms and chest. At one point he looked straight past where I knelt, apparently unable to see me in the shadows. In the light I recognized him as the man I'd seen at the gate a few days earlier.

As he rounded a corner of the house, I moved closer and hid behind a large azalea with a view of the back yard. An exterior light cast his shadow across the lawn.

Closer to him stood a row of cabbage palms, recently planted and anchored with two-by-four supports about four feet long. Their fronds whipped in the rising gale like jacks on a patrol boat. Carefully, I pulled one of the boards from the soft soil and took up position at the corner of the house near where the guard stood.

At my feet lay a rock garden with smooth, white stones about the size of my fist. I chose one, peeped around the corner, and hurled it into the palmettos at the edge of the yard. He didn't move.

I threw another one, much larger, and this time he turned, staring into the brush for several seconds before tossing away his cigarette and walking over to investigate. I flattened myself against the side of the building, waited until he passed me and padded across the thick grass behind him.

When he stopped, I brought the two-by-four down on the back of his head with all the force I could muster.

He staggered forward a step or two and then turned to face me. Slowly his eyes rolled back, as he toppled to the ground. I turned him over and tied his wrists behind him with a length of nylon cord I'd brought. With another I bound his ankles and hogtied him so that he arched backward.

I thought about gagging him, but I hadn't brought any tape, and by the time he came around he could scream all he wanted. I'd be inside having a polite conversation with George, and the nearest neighbor lived at least a mile away.

Starting toward the house, I had another thought. Not far from the man stood a small statue, like the ones in front of so many Southern homes. It was a lawn jockey in red and white livery and matching cap holding out an iron ring. For good measure, I dragged the guard over to him, pulled out my handcuffs, and locked him to the ring.

Glancing up, I caught an eerie reflection on the surface of the lake. The water seemed to move in a way that had nothing to do with wind or rain, and the ground trembled as I ran toward the house. It lasted but a second, and I shrugged it off as a figment of my heightened imagination.

Rounding the swimming pool, I crossed the patio to a large set of French doors. Through the glass I saw George seated at a desk with his back to me perusing a stack of documents. A few feet away a fire blazed in a large hearth despite the warm weather. He gave no reaction as I turned the knob and stepped softly into the room, instead tossing the papers onto the fire. When I was about halfway across the carpet he looked toward the front of the house and called out, "Lou? Is that you?"

"I'm afraid Lou's tied up at the moment." I pulled the automatic from my waist band and pointed it at his forehead.

George jumped in his chair. "What the fuck…?"

"How long have June Skinner and the Suggs brothers been working for you, George?"

"What are you talking about?" He scowled, but his voice quavered as his eyes rested on the gun.

"June called the hunting club the other night while I was there, asking for Lester. The other day you mentioned my writing about Jimmie in my notebook. That information could only have come from June."

"I don't know what you're talking about."

"You're a lying sack of shit. What did June have to do with the Suggs?"

George shrugged, as though deciding to come clean. "June and I had an affair years ago. Jo Anne discovered it and left me. When June became pregnant, I paid for an abortion. Buck Skinner found out, beat June senseless and was coming after me… I had the brothers take care of him."

"Yeah. And the Suggs also admitted killing my parents. Was that your doing too?"

He didn't answer.

I took a deep breath and scanned the room. "You know… you have a nice place here, George. You and Bill have done well for yourselves, running folks off their land and bilking the people of Monrovia out of their meager savings. First you sold off the phosphate rights. That must have been pretty good… while it lasted. Then you set up this development scam. People here are so desperate they really believe you're building a resort and retirement community that'll make them rich. Now you've launched another little enterprise, and you're not about to let anybody mess *that* up. That's why you sent those goons to kill me… just like they killed my parents."

"You don't know what you're talking about. Your parents and I were good friends."

"Oh, yeah? You had them *murdered*, George. Is that how you treat your friends?"

"I had nothing to do with that. That was the Suggs' doing. Your daddy found out we were using the hunting club to scare off the colored folks so we could buy up their homesteads. It was 1953, and farming was still pretty good. This was prime land and some of us wanted to grow tobacco here around the springs. Only, the Blacks wouldn't sell it to us on account of it having been theirs since Reconstruction. Your daddy was going to arrest the Suggs. He was going to offer them a deal to tell him who they worked for."

George began to plead. "I couldn't let that happen, Tom. I never wanted to hurt your mama or your daddy. I just thought maybe… the Suggs could somehow scare him off."

"You knew my daddy all those years and thought you could 'somehow scare him off?' You knew exactly what the Suggs would do. And with my daddy out of the way and that ignorant, corrupt Willingham as sheriff you could get anything you wanted. When did you get in bed with Rico Salazar?"

"I've said all I intend to."

"Then I guess I'll shoot you and be on my way," I said.

He shook his head slowly, staring at his desktop. "We did well for about ten years. We even cultivated that land we bought from your grandmama. But in 1963 we started losing money. Costs kept going up and tobacco prices kept falling. That's when we discovered the phosphate. We sold the mining rights to a company downstate, but that didn't last long either. In just five years they've taken it all out. Then Bill came up with the idea for Arcadia Development."

"Yeah, yeah... So how did Salazar get involved?"

"A few years back Bill met a banker down in Miami Beach. They started putting together some strange deals. I guess you could call it money laundering. This guy turned out to be an agent for Salazar. At Salazar's request the bank loaned us money to buy more land.

When the mining company told us they were pulling out, I called Salazar and told him we couldn't make the payment on our note." George chuckled as though sharing a funny story with an old friend. "That was *not* a pleasant call. Those boys don't like being told they're not getting their money. I thought Bill and I would end up like Bugsy Siegel. Instead, Salazar made us an offer that would wipe the slate clean."

"You're talking about the dope smuggling?"

"Hell, Arcadia was nothing but a pipe dream, another of Bill's harebrained schemes, but it's amazing what folks will believe when they want to. Bill loaned me money from the stock offering to build this house and the landing strip. Salazar said he wanted to use it for an *import operation*."

George grinned. "I knew that was you out there taking pictures. You never could leave things alone, always sticking your nose where it didn't belong, just like ..." He stopped before he said it.

"Just like my daddy?'"

"Your daddy was a good man, Tom, a good man. He just couldn't see reality through all his high ideals."

"What about Bill? Was he involved in the murder of my parents?"

"That sanctimonious dipshit? Oh, he was great at putting together schemes, but he never had the stomach for dirty work. He probably suspected I was behind the Suggs killing your parents. But he never had the guts to tell anybody."

"Why'd you lease the hunting club back to the Suggs?"

"We had an arrangement. They ran security for us. In return, they'd get the local drug concession, selling it to the Blacks. The Suggs planned to use the money to rebuild their Klan operation. They were useful idiots."

The shit got deeper and deeper, and the more I thought about it the angrier I got. Glancing about, I took in the expensive furnishings, art and book collections.

Easing back toward the doorway where an ornate vase stood on a pedestal, I lifted it with my free hand, finding it heavier than I expected.

"Careful!" he pleaded. "That's genuine Ming."

"Oops!" I opened my palm and let it crash on the tile floor. As I did the entire house shuddered.

George gaped like a caged animal. "What the hell was that?"

I ignored it. "I guess it was the vase. Tell me about Dana, George. Why did you have to kill her?"

His expression changed, a wry grin spreading across his face. "I didn't kill Dana, son. She had nothing to do with this."

"Then who did? We both know it wasn't Jimmie Lee."

"Tommy Boy, you don't even want to know."

"Tell me the truth and I might spare you. Whose white Cadillac was that parked outside the bank the day before Dana got killed? And don't give me your bullshit about it coming from a dealership in Ft. Lauderdale. It probably came off your lot."

"Nope, it was a recent purchase by an old friend of yours. Bill just helped finance it."

He spoke rapidly now, his eyes darting back and forth between my face and the .45. Slowly, almost imperceptibly, he shifted his weight to one side. In the heat of the moment, he'd forgotten the mirror on the wall behind him. In its reflection I saw him reach into a partially opened drawer and clutch the butt of a gun.

Without so much as a thought I squeezed the trigger. As I did the entire place lurched, like an earthquake, jarring my arm. My shot went wild, shattering the mirror. From throughout the house there rose a chorus of shattering glass and cracking timbers.

George's first reaction was sheer terror, but he quickly recovered. His hand came up with a sawed-off shotgun. It was almost level with me when another jolt hit, crushing the windows behind me and spraying shards across the room. Taking careful aim before he could recover, I put a slug in the middle of his forehead.

The floor beneath him gave way, and he disappeared through a large hole, toward which the room began to list. On instinct I lunged through what remained of the French doors, tumbling onto the patio.

Struggling to my feet, I sprinted across the lawn to Lou. He'd regained conscious and began screaming something I couldn't make out above the noise. I knelt, uncuffed him, and cut the cords from his ankles. "Run!" I screamed,

His kick missed my head by less than an inch. He glowered at me as he struggled to his feet and was about to yell something when his eyes suddenly focused on a point behind me.

Over the roaring storm came the cries of the dying house. I jumped back from him and turned to see little more than the front wall remaining, the rest of the structure tumbling into a yawning abyss. The far edge of the sinkhole merged into the springs as it filled with water.

"Let's get out of here!" I shouted.

When we got to the entrance I held the gun on him with my left hand and cut the ropes from his wrists so he could climb the gate. From the look on his face, his only concern now was escaping.

"I just saved your life," I said. "You're not going to give me any problems, are you?"

He glared at me. "No."

Slowly I returned the gun to my waistband, where I could grab it again if needed.

"What the fuck was that?" he asked in a thick Brooklyn accent.

"*That* is a sinkhole. There are underground streams all over here. That spring over there is the mouth of one of them. There must've been a cavern beneath George's house. I guess he built it in the wrong place. Come on. There's no telling how big it'll get. Do you have a car here?"

"No. I was using George's truck. He kept it in the garage. It went down with the house."

"How's your head?"

"I've felt better, but I'll live."

"Look, I'm sorry about that, but I had to talk to George. It's a long story, but several years ago he paid a couple of rednecks to murder my parents. He got what he deserved tonight. Are we okay?"

He leaned against the fence catching his breath. His eyes had trouble focusing and his face took on a greenish cast. "Okay," he said. "It's alright. Besides, I was sick of working for that bastard anyway. He didn't pay me shit, and I didn't want any part of this stuff going on here."

"Where were you staying?"

"In a room over his garage"

"Yeah. Well, I can drop you off at the hospital, so they can look at your head."

"No. I'll be alright."

From his ashen face, I knew better.

As I helped him into my car, Lou introduced himself and said he'd worked at a bar in Manhattan where he met Bill Emmett. Emmett was in New York on business and got him a job as George's personal bodyguard. Before that, Lou said he'd never been south of D.C.

I asked him where he might go now that George no longer needed his services. He said he wasn't sure.

He told me Salazar visited George several times, saying he wanted the landing strip finished right away for a major shipment. Lou also mentioned Willingham and his nephews leaving the house several times with bags full of money.

"Look," I said, "If you want to live you need to come with me. You know too much. Salazar isn't about to let you just walk off the job. He can't take the chance you'd testify against him."

"I don't want to go to any hospital. My head will be okay. I need to disappear before Rico shows up."

"Okay, so let me help you. My fiancé's a lawyer. She's in Tallahassee right now working with the state attorney general's office and the FBI. If you'll come with me they can protect you."

I had no idea whether this was true, but I needed to get him to Tallahassee. With his testimony, and some luck, the feds could put both Rico *and* the sheriff behind bars.

The only thing still gnawing at me was George's final remark about Dana's murder. I'd shot him before he could tell me who owned the white Cadillac. I pounded my steering wheel in frustration. *Now I'd never know.*

Chapter Thirty-Two

Lou rode with me to my grandmother's house, where I parked my car out of sight. We entered quietly, so as not to wake her, and stayed in the kitchen.

Lou sat while I carefully checked the lump on his head. It looked like a split, overripe pomegranate oozing blood, but I figured he'd survive the trip to Tallahassee. I applied some iodine and gave him a plastic ice bag to hold against it.

Meanwhile I changed into some dry clothes. I started to offer Lou something to wear, but nothing of mine would fit. So, instead, I grabbed a couple of towels for him to dry off.

***

When I reached Bright at his motel, he said he was typing his story from the information I gave him earlier, embellishing it, no doubt, to make it seem like the scoop of the century.

He said Win was asleep in the room next door. I filled him in on most of what had happened and had him book the Howard Johnson's last empty room for Lou.

My next call was to Colleen.

"Hey," she said, "I met with the AG and an FBI agent and told them what you found out. You cannot repeat any of this, not yet at least. I could lose my license. They sent some guys down to Jasper County tonight to stake out the landing strip. They also have an arrest warrant for Bill Emmett."

"Emmett isn't the main player. George Martin is… *or was*. Now he's dead. It's a long story. I've gotta get out of here. I'll call you when I get to Tallahassee. I should be there in about an hour. I'm bringing someone who can corroborate Frankie's story and give the feds the details about Rico and the landing strip."

I hung up and left a note for my grandmother saying I had gone to see Colleen in Tallahassee, making no mention of George Martin. Eventually somebody would figure out what happened to him. But it would be a long time before they found his body, if ever.

I looked in on my grandmother and found her snoring softly. I felt bad, leaving her alone, but I knew she'd be okay. Ida would be there in a couple of hours.

Grabbing my overnight bag, I helped Lou into the car and took some back streets to make sure nobody saw me. A couple of blocks from our house a narrow side road joined Tallahassee Highway near the Pelahatchie Bridge. From there I retraced the journey that brought me here a week earlier, back to the town of Capps, where I turned onto Highway 27. It seemed an eternity had passed in that short time.

As I drove, I processed what I'd learned. There was still one loose end.

"Lou, do you recall ever seeing Emmett, or Salazar, or *anybody*, driving a white 1959 Cadillac?"

He thought for a moment. "No. I'm pretty sure I'd have noticed a Caddy that old."

"Oh well, it was a long shot. Just thought I'd ask."

His eyelids began to droop, and I almost panicked. "Lou, you've had a concussion. You've got to promise me you won't fall asleep. Okay?"

For the rest of the trip, I talked to him constantly, asking every question I could think of, which seemed to irritate him, but before long I knew his life story. Twice on the trip I stopped by the roadside so he could puke. The second time he didn't make it out of the car. The rain let up, and I put the top down, partly to get rid of the smell, partly to keep him from falling asleep.

***

Bright met us in the lobby at the Howard Johnson. He called an ambulance and told them a friend had taken a nasty fall in the parking lot. When it left with Lou, I banged on Win's door until I finally woke him. I filled them in on the details of George's death and the collapse of his house into the sinkhole, skipping the part about the bullet hole in his forehead.

Colleen met us at a nearby Shoney's accompanied by her friend from law school, an Assistant Attorney General named Dick Sterling. He appeared close to fifty, with shaggy, prematurely white hair and a drooping mustache. His charcoal grey suit looked like he'd slept in it, and, from the volume of coffee he drank, Colleen must have wakened him from a sound sleep.

"Mr. Williams, Mr. Stevens, Mr. Wilson, I want to convey our profound gratitude for your cooperation. Naturally, we'll need to conduct independent investigations into the deaths of the Suggs brothers and George Martin. Suffice it to say that won't involve Sheriff Willingham or his deputies. In a few hours, if everything goes as planned, I'll be meeting with officers from the Highway Patrol and a couple of FBI agents. They'll accompany us back to Monrovia to take the sheriff and his nephews into custody. It's my understanding that Governor Kirk will be calling a press conference to announce the appointment of an interim sheriff. Right now, I suggest you all go back to the motel and get some rest."

Colleen and I waited in the motel parking lot while the others went inside. Then I followed her to her room.

As we showered together, I took her in my arms, and we began to make love.

"Hold on," she said. "I have a surprise for you."

I toweled off, climbed into the double bed, and lay waiting for her as she closed the door behind me. From the bathroom I heard the sounds of her putting on clothes. Finally, the door opened.

Silhouetted in the light, she leaned against the doorframe and drew up one knee in a provocative pose. Her blonde curls fell across her shoulders, and she gave me the look of a mischievous teenager. She wore a crisply starched white blouse, green plaid skirt, and white knee socks.

"Your school uniform..."

"I'm not exactly in uniform," she said. "I decided to forego the black patent leather shoes... Oh, and a couple of other items..." She smiled, opening her blouse, and slowly drew up her skirt. Without warning she bounded onto the bed, ripped back the covers and climbed on top of me.

Afterward, she removed the uniform, laid it across a chair, and crawled back under the covers, where I held her as we drifted off to sleep. For what must have been the thousandth time since I'd met her I realized how lucky I was.

***

We met back at Shoney's the next day. Win, Bright, Colleen and I were having coffee and Danish when Sterling rushed in. He'd received a call from an agent he'd staked out the landing strip the night before. At about three that morning several men arrived and laid flares along the runway as a large plane landed, apparently the Beechcraft I'd seen earlier. The officers waited until the pilot disembarked before they raided the facility, arresting fifteen people, all members of the Salazar organization. One of them made the mistake of pulling a weapon and died in a hail of gunfire.

Anxious to get to Monrovia before anyone could tip off Willingham, Sterling and an FBI agent took the lead vehicle, a black Lincoln Continental… apparently an homage to Efrem Zimbalist, Junior. Colleen and Bright took their cars. I cleaned up the mess Lou had made in the Mustang and returned to Monrovia letting Win drive as I wrote furiously in my notebook. Six highway patrol cars preceded us and a seventh followed.

The hospital had released Lou, who, under no obligation to return to Monrovia, chose to sleep off his headache at the Howard Johnson's, compliments of the FBI. Win made the drive to Monrovia in record time, keeping pace with the patrol cars ahead of us.

At Capps a small crowd of onlookers gawked as we merged onto Highway 19. I glanced at Win. Eyes focused on the road ahead, his expression left no doubt he was back in his element after all these years.

When we got to Monrovia we went straight to the jail. Four of the cars parked out front, while the other two navigated the tight alley. For a moment I visualized the fat sheriff and his nephews hightailing out the back door, patrolmen in hot pursuit. Win parked across the street behind the courthouse in a space reserved for Judge Adams.

Before long, a gaggle of townsfolk had gathered in the middle of Crawford Street. They didn't wait long. Three highway patrolmen came out escorting Willingham and his nephews in handcuffs. They stared at the ground in bewilderment. Behind them came Sterling, who stopped at the top of the steps and made a statement for the benefit of the crowd.

"Ladies and gentlemen, as you can see, we have today placed Sheriff Howard Willingham and his deputies, Cantrell and Josiah Jeter, under arrest on charges of bribery, extortion, aiding the transportation of illicit narcotics, and theft by taking. At approximately ten this morning,

Governor Kirk will hold a news conference to announce his appointment of an interim sheriff, pending a special election. We will not be issuing any further statements at this time. Anyone having business related to law enforcement in Jasper County will please address your concerns to my assistant, Mr. David Wright, who will be available here at the sheriff's office."

In his haste, Bright had neglected to bring a photographer from Tampa, so I retrieved my camera from my trunk and captured photos of Sterling and the onlookers. Bright interviewed everyone else and then me. I gave him as much information as I could, carefully avoiding details about George's death until I could discuss it with Colleen.

I asked Colleen if she'd like some real breakfast. As we strolled the short distance to Sandy's, she explained that Governor Kirk's temporary sheriff would be a man named Willis Pettibone. Pettibone had been a cop in Louisiana before joining the Wackenhut Corporation as a security specialist. Sterling would remain in charge until Pettibone arrived in a few days.

"As soon as things calm down back there," I said, "I need a private word with Mr. Sterling."

"About what?"

"About some unfinished business… First let's eat."

As we reached the corner opposite Sandy's, Colleen stopped. "Oh! I almost forgot. I may have found the owner of your white Cadillac."

"What?"

"One of my investigators looked up the sale of a white '59 Caddy in Ft. Lauderdale in the summer of 1958. The funny thing was… she only owned it a couple of days."

"*She?*"

"Yeah... Do you know a Clara O'Connor?"

Something seized up inside me. This had to be another nightmare. *It made no sense.* I lowered my head, recalling my visit to her classroom, and then… just as suddenly, *it came to me.*

"What is it, baby?" Colleen asked.

Struggling to keep my head from exploding, I said, "There's something else I need to discuss with Mr. Sterling."

***

I found Sterling on the phone going over recent arrests with the local district attorney. Meanwhile a couple of men from the AG's office reviewed records of open investigations. I waited outside until Sterling hung up.

"Mr. Sterling, I was wondering if I could speak with you a moment."

"You'll have to make it quick."

"Ten years ago, an angry mob lynched a young Black man wrongfully accused of murdering a white woman. I think I now know who the real murderer was, and I believe I can prove it. I know you're busy. I just need to borrow one of your men and see if we can find the case file."

At length he agreed.

For nearly an hour I combed through records in a hot, musty room, while Colleen watched patiently. I began to worry that Willingham might have removed the evidence or destroyed it. Then I found a manila folder labeled "Padgett, Dana S," its tab worn and dogeared, its inscription barely legible. I buried my face, wondering if, after all these years, I could go through this again.

When I opened it, out spilled several glossy black-and-white photos of Dana's nude body, some at the crime scene and others on a tabletop at the morgue. I avoided the more gruesome ones but noticed a close-up of her throat with bruises on either side in the shape of a person's fingers and scratches in the center of her chest like fingernail marks.

I pored over Doc Green's report listing the cause of death as "manual asphyxiation." The last piece of paper in the file contained a notation about the necklace Willingham found, supposedly on Jimmie Lee Johnson, with no mention of how he knew it belonged to Dana. At the bottom was a blank line for the signature of whoever came to pick it up. Mike Padgett never claimed it. A reference at the top indicated its location in the property room. I went back through the photos, among them a shot of the necklace itself with a jade stone shaped like a jagged piece of broken heart.

The final enclosure was a three-page document detailing Jimmie's interrogation, never mentioning the beating he received from the sheriff and his nephews, the results of which I saw that night staring back at me through the bars.

I replaced the file, explained to Sterling what I'd discovered and asked if one of his patrolmen could accompany me to the school.

Chapter Thirty-Three

By now it was mid-afternoon, and school had let out. The day had turned hot and humid following the previous night's storm. I asked the patrolman to drive, hoping to get there before Clara left. The busses were pulling out, but a few remaining students milled about on the grounds and in the halls talking and laughing. I heard one of them mention the sheriff. In a town the size of Monrovia word travels fast. They quieted as the patrolman stopped and waited outside Clara's door.

I found her gathering up her schoolwork, apparently preparing to leave. Startled to see me, her voice quavered. "Tom! I understand you've had a busy day, and yet you have time to visit. Well, I'm… glad to see you're okay." Above the fake smile her eyes studied my face. "What brings you here? I'd have thought you were on your way back to Tampa to turn in your big story. I can't believe the things I've heard about Sheriff Willingham … and George Martin. Who would have known?" She sounded breathless as she prattled.

"This is the most important business I have today, Clara." I paused and took a deep breath. "Do you remember when I came by the other day, and you made the comment about my digging up old ghosts? I assumed you were trying to protect me from getting into trouble by asking too many questions."

Her head lowered, but she remained silent.

"I've been wondering, Clara, why you hadn't retired before now. You know… it's funny the seemingly trivial things we sometimes recall. Back in the summer of 1958 you told me you were thinking of packing it in and moving to Sanibel with a friend. It never occurred to me, as a sixteen-year-old kid, just how many kinds of *friends* a person can have. Whatever happened to her, Clara?"

Absent-mindedly I picked up several pictures from her desk. She was about to protest when I carefully replaced all but one, the black-and-white shot of a smiling Clara at the teachers' banquet, wearing her white dress *and a necklace.*

"Jade in the shape of a broken heart," I said. "You know what? I'll bet the new sheriff will find this an exact match to the one you gave Dana. Dana once told me a *friend* gave it to her. You should have gotten rid of this photo, Clara. But you probably weren't thinking clearly when you ripped the other necklace from Dana's throat and strangled her. My guess is you threw it out the car window, where the sheriff and his nephews later found it."

"Your guesses are worthless in a court of law," she said, her expression morphing from feigned outrage to pure hatred.

"I know, but you'll be amazed how long fingerprints can last on a piece of jewelry. Mike Padgett never claimed the necklace, and that dumbass Willingham apparently never examined it. In fact, it's sitting up there in the property room at the jail right now."

As far as I knew, Willingham had wiped the necklace clean or smudged any fingerprints beyond recognition, but Clara wouldn't know that.

"People talk about all sorts of things when they have sex, Clara. Dana once told me she planned to leave Mike and move to Sanibel with a friend."

In fact, she'd never said any such thing, but I was on a roll.

"Dana enjoyed the presents you gave her, Clara, but she eventually tired of you and decided to break off the relationship. You picked her up that night in your new Cadillac, and rode around town trying to talk sense into her, winding up at the country club. First you tried to reason with her, and then you pleaded. And when she laughed at you and made hurtful remarks, you became angry, and grabbed her. You snatched the necklace and strangled her. With all those years of sports activities and yard work, you had hands as strong as any man's. When you finished, you stripped off her clothes to make it look like she'd been molested. You dragged her body out of the car and hid it in the woods."

I glared at her. "You left her there like a bag of garbage under that pile of leaves. You drove home, cleaned up your car, and took it back to the dealership in Ft. Lauderdale. And then you went about your business as though nothing had happened. You let Jimmie Lee Johnson, who never hurt anyone in his life, hang from a tree for a murder *you* committed. You might as well have lynched him yourself, you and the Suggs brothers and their friends. The dealership in Ft. Lauderdale may be out of business now, but the DMV can still track the registration back to you, and Benny Stillman will identify it as the one he saw that night at the club."

As I spoke, she gazed out the window as the tears flowed, her voice cracking. "Do you have any idea what it's like to have someone you love with every fiber of your being tell you she only endured you for the things you bought her. Dana was reckless with other people's feelings, only caring about the pleasure they gave her. She used me and *betrayed me*," Clara shouted. "*Do you know how that feels?*"

"I know *exactly* how betrayal feels, Clara. I can describe it very well right now."

She choked and sobbed. "I was already on the road to Ft. Lauderdale when they arrested Jimmie. I had to get rid of the car before anyone connected it to Dana. You *have to* believe me. I didn't find out about the lynching until I got back, and by then it was too late. Afterward I told myself it was all over. Nobody would believe Jimmie was innocent, no one, that is, but you."

She lay her head on her desk and moaned, "Can you imagine what I've lived with all these years?"

285

I leaned down and screamed in her ear. *"Can you imagine what Ida and Ruby Williams have lived with all these years?"*

When she finally lifted her head, the patrolman stood beside her desk. He pulled a card from his wallet and read, "Clara O'Connor, you are under arrest for the murder of Dana S. Padgett. You have the right to remain silent…"

I stepped outside for fresh air. Looking back, I saw him escort Clara from the building, a sweater draped over her wrists to hide the cuffs.

Declining his offer of a ride back to my car, I sat on a bench under a crepe myrtle watching a cow-killer ant make his way across a mound of brown sand. Then I heard a familiar voice.

"Hey, you need a ride somewhere?" Colleen asked, gazing at me from the open window of her car.

"Home"

Exhausted, I wasn't sure whether I meant my grandmother's house or my apartment in Tampa. Colleen drove me to my car and then followed me back to my grandmother's.

***

We found Ida alone in the kitchen. Softly I told her about Clara and Dana, while Colleen joined my grandmother in the living room.

When I'd finished, Ida sat staring at her clasped hands, shaking her head in disbelief. But for the tears on her cheeks, she was the picture of constraint. She looked up, gazed at me and said, "Now everybody's gone know what I've known all this time. My boy didn't kill nobody… and you know what *really* makes me mad?" her voice rose. "Not one of them crackers who hanged Jimmie will *ever* come to justice, and this whole town will act like nothing ever happened. That was a human being that never counted for *nothing* to them people."

There was nothing more I could say. Even the public apology that I knew would never come couldn't possibly have been enough.

Colleen remained in Monrovia long enough to enjoy an early supper with us before returning to Tampa. When we finished, Sterling came by and accompanied us to what had been George Martin's place. We found the gate open, but across it hung a streamer of yellow crime scene tape.

Sterling parked, and we walked the long driveway as I had the night before. In less than twenty-four hours this had become a very different place. The sky had cleared, and there was an uncanny stillness, stirred only an occasional westerly breeze. Mockingbirds called from nearby trees and dragonflies hovered above the Johnson grass nearby.

As we rounded the final turn I stopped dead in my tracks. The trees and shrubs were still in place, except for the palm whose support I'd used to club Lou. Nothing remained of the house. The lake, now completely still, had engulfed it. This could have been an idyllic park somewhere or just another neighborhood awaiting development.

A man in a wet suit stood at the edge of the water, holding one end of a yellow nylon rope. From the way it moved and the occasional burst of bubbles, I could see another diver was searching the springs below.

As we approached, he emerged, shook his head and spoke to his partner holding the rope. "I can't see a damned thing down there. It drops straight off and there's too much silt. If there was ever a house here you sure couldn't prove it by me."

Sterling let out a sigh and turned to me. "We'll keep at it, but I'm beginning to doubt we'll ever find anything. If we do I'll get in touch with you."

"Sure." I handed him my card.

***

Colleen and I never saw Sterling again. A couple of years later Colleen would receive a call from a mutual friend saying he'd succumbed to lung cancer and was buried with honors in a small cemetery outside his hometown of Quincy, just west of Tallahassee.

No one ever located George's body. As far as I know it still festers somewhere deep in the Florida aquifer. The state eventually dropped the investigation of his death.

By nightfall everybody in Monrovia knew Arcadia had been nothing but a hoax and the money they'd invested was gone. An employee of the Monrovia State Bank arrived for work early the next day and saw Bill Emmett's car parked in its usual slot. When he went to Emmett's office he found him slumped over his desk, his face resting in a pool of congealed blood. His right hand clutched a .22 revolver. He hadn't left a note.

The bank, under new ownership, eventually foreclosed on the land around the springs and sold it to the state for a park. The IRS took the rest of the property, including the phosphate pits and the landing strip.

Rico Salazar, along with several associates, went to a federal penitentiary for tax evasion. He would die there, years later, of an undisclosed illness rumored to be syphilis. The CIA-sponsored drug smuggling from Southeast Asia, however, went on for years before a televised exposé launched a congressional investigation.

For some reason neither the bank nor the IRS expressed any interest in the Little River Hunting Club property.

There was one final detail I needed to clear up, but I would bide my time, given all the publicity surrounding the deaths of the Suggs brothers, George Martin, and Bill Emmett.

I waited seven weeks.

***

Following my return to Tampa I wrote a companion piece to Bright's story, which the *Sentinel* carried in its Sunday edition. I went about my duties, covering local politics, including Langford Styles' sudden withdrawal from the state senate race for what he called *health reasons*. Gradually all the media attention and notoriety subsided, and for this I was grateful.

It was a Tuesday afternoon, the day of the California primary. I finished my work and left early, awaiting election results. That night I would write an analysis to go with the wire story. In fact, I'd already made my notes, assuming a victory for Bobby Kennedy.

Colleen was in Tallahassee appealing a murder conviction and wouldn't return until the following day.

Leaving the Mustang at my apartment and my phone off the hook in case anyone called, I rode a city bus all the way to South Dale Mabry, where I rented a 1965 Ford Fairlane, paying for it in cash. It was a nondescript, light blue sedan just reliable enough for a six-hour round trip. I showed the rental agent a fake driver's license I'd purchased from one of my sources.

As my business in Monrovia didn't involve my grandmother or require an overnight stay, I decided not to call her. This would be my final tribute to Jimmie Lee Johnson.

At a Shell station on Buffalo Avenue, I stopped to fill up a cheap gas can I'd purchased a few days earlier at a Western Auto on the other side of town. At a Gulf station on Fowler, I filled up another one. I laid out a plastic tarp in the Fairlane's trunk and set the cans on top of it, in case either of them spilled, bracing them between the spare tire and a wooden crate I'd found.

A few miles out of town I pulled onto an unpaved road crossed by a shallow, muddy creek a few yards from the highway. When there were no other cars in sight, I ran the Fairlane back and forth through the stream, spinning the tires and slinging mud on the sides and rear, leaving just enough to obscure the license plate without drawing the attention of a curious highway patrolman.

By now it was eight thirty and the sun would set before I reached Monrovia. I could return to Tampa before anyone noticed my absence and somehow make it through the next day on a couple hours' sleep.

My out-of-the-way route brought me into Jasper County from the east through Mabry. Instead of passing through town I took a narrow lane connecting to Pleasant Springs Road. The few houses I passed were unlit tarpaper shacks whose residents would scarcely notice an old mud-spattered Fairlane.

The logging chain still blocked the hunting club driveway with what appeared to be a new lock and a sign reading, "Private Property – No Trespassing." I drove past it to the bridge where I'd parked weeks earlier. Using a penlight clenched between my teeth I carefully removed the gas cans from the trunk and, following the now familiar trail, carried them to the log cabin. I found the place dark and deserted. A half moon, peeking through the clouds, provided all the light I needed.

I broke out several windowpanes and poured gasoline through each opening, saving just enough to splash around the foundation. Then I doused the front steps and porch and threw the cans through one of the broken windows.

From my pocket I pulled a book of matches I'd taken from Sandy's, lit it and tossed it through the window, jumping back just in time to avoid being knocked off my feet by the explosion. I reeked of singed hair and eyebrows, something I might have to explain later. Too late I considered the possibility that the flames might spread to nearby brush and create a forest fire.

In the flickering light, I found my way back to the car, glancing back once at the cabin, now fully ablaze. As I crossed the bridge out of Jasper

County my only thought was that somewhere Jimmie Lee Johnson was smiling his big toothy grin. I said a silent prayer, hoping no one ever rebuilt the place.

My route took me north to Mayo, where I turned back toward I-75. By the time I reached Tampa it was two a.m.

I pulled the car into a deserted gas station north of town with a faucet and hose. After washing off as much mud as I could, I crossed the street to a brightly lit 7-11 and went inside for a Coke.

The cashier, a heavy-set woman about twenty years old, stood with her back to me, staring into the grainy image a black-and-white portable TV perched on a shelf. Shoulders trembling, she sobbed as a reporter, standing amid a stunned crowd, tried to make himself heard.

"Oh my God!" she wailed as she turned to me, her eyes red-rimmed from tears. They shot him. The bastards shot him."

"Shot who?"

"They didn't want him to be president, so they shot him." She collapsed into a folding chair and wept.

It finally sank in when the television image cut to a grim-faced anchor.

"If you are just joining us we have confirmed that Senator Robert F. Kennedy has died from apparent gunshot wounds following a victory celebration at the Ambassador Hotel in Los Angeles. This occurred just hours after his defeat of Vice President Hubert Humphrey in the California Democratic primary." Cameras cut to the image of Roosevelt Grier ushering a stunned Ethel Kennedy through a crowd.

The wind rushed out of me, and I completely forgot where I'd been and what I'd done earlier. For the next hour and a half, I consoled the cashier and jotted interview notes. Her parents had brought her to the U.S. in 1960 following Castro's takeover of Cuba. She learned to speak English from watching television and finished high school in Tampa.

Working nights to help support her family, she saved enough money to attend Hillsborough Junior College.

In November she would vote for the first time in her life. Though her parents favored Richard Nixon, she was an ardent Kennedy supporter, seeing him as the best hope of a bright future for all Americans, native-born and immigrants alike.

She gave me permission to use her name in my coverage of local reaction to the assassination. I returned to my apartment, showered and prepared for a busy day. At the last minute I remembered to put my phone back on the hook. Colleen had, no doubt, tried to reach me for hours.

Epilogue

The following year Colleen and I married at a small cathedral in Cambridge, Massachusetts. My grandmother and Ida came. It was the first time either of them had been out of Florida or flown on an airplane. Neither of them knew what to make of a Catholic ceremony, but they adapted well.

"That sure was a beautiful wedding," Ida commented. "But I never saw so much getting up and getting down in all my life. It just about wore me out watching them people."

In the winter of 1971, my grandmother died after a brief bout of pneumonia. I buried her in the small cemetery beside the New Hope Baptist Church, between my grandfather and my parents. Ida died the following summer from breast cancer. Ruby and I exchanged letters for a few years, but eventually lost touch.

Cephas T. Adams stepped down from the bench in 1972, after forty years. Six months later he too went to his final reward.

Win Stevens wrote me that he'd sworn off drinking. He went back to his old job as deputy under the interim sheriff and ran unopposed in the special election.

Clara O'Connor, who'd had a major influence on my decision to become a writer, spent the rest of her life in the women's penitentiary in Tallahassee, where she died of uterine cancer in 1975.

Colleen and I now live in Midtown Atlanta in a fully restored Victorian home built in 1908. Here we've spent the last several years, me working as a free-lance writer and Colleen as partner in a prominent local firm. We've raised two beautiful daughters, Edna Kathleen a pediatric oncologist at Emory-Crawford Long Hospital, and Ida Marie, who followed in her mother's footsteps as a criminal defense attorney.

One evening, a few years back, as Colleen and I waited in line for a performance at the Alliance Theater a woman's voice called out from behind me.

"Tom? Tom Williams?"

There stood Jenny Maxwell. She introduced me to her husband Don Waters, and I introduced them to Colleen. Jenny and Don lived in a fashionable neighborhood in Cobb County overlooking the Chattahoochee River. We exchanged phone numbers and promised to get in touch. But we never did.

On a recent Sunday morning I retrieved a copy of the *Atlanta Journal Constitution* from my front yard and opened to the "Living" section, which I seldom read. It featured a photo of the Jasper County Courthouse with a row of beautifully renovated shops in the background. The article described the discovery of this charming community by a group of investors, who planned to restore its past glory as home to millionaire tobacco farmers and Coca Cola shareholders. Improvements included a golf course and retirement community on the outskirts of town by the scenic shores of Arcadia Springs, recently acquired from the Florida Department of Environmental Protection.

The picture showed a group of people standing on the courthouse lawn engaged in a ribbon-cutting ceremony. Its caption read, "Monrovia Mayor Alphonso Watkins celebrates restoration of the courthouse square historic district, accompanied by his lovely wife, Panky Carter-Watkins."

I gazed at the image for several minutes before turning to the sports section.

The End

About the Author

A writer, lecturer and consultant, Ray Dan Parker lives in suburban Atlanta with his wife of more than forty years. When not writing, he spends his time working outdoors, teaching and serving in his community.

As a student at the University of Georgia, Mr. Parker studied literature and history and wrote for several campus publications. It was there he developed his love of writing.

Mr. Parker's first novel, *Unfinished Business*, is the story of Tom Williams, a young newspaper writer who returns to his hometown in 1968 to investigate the deaths of his parents and the lynching of a friend for a murder he didn't commit.

Coming Soon!

RAY DAN PARKER'S

FLY AWAY:
The Metamorphosis of Dina Savage
A Tom Williams Saga
Book Two

While enjoying an outdoor concert at Atlanta's famed Chastain Park, Tom and Colleen Williams chance to meet renowned artist Liam Sanstrom and his mysterious date, Dina Savage. The next day, Tom learns that their amorous outing has led to a drug-fueled night of horror for Dina.

As Tom follows Liam's ensuing trial, he finds that no one seems to know anything of Dina's past or even cares. His determination to learn who she really is leads him into a world of corporate espionage and, ultimately, to a small town in Mississippi and the discovery of a grisly, unsolved murder from twenty years earlier.

For more information
visit: www.SpeakingVolumes.us

Now Available!

IVAN BLAKE'S
THE MORTSAFEMAN TRILOGY
BOOKS 1 – 2

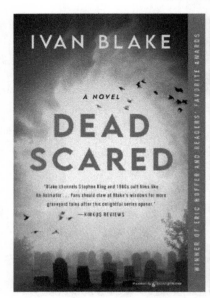
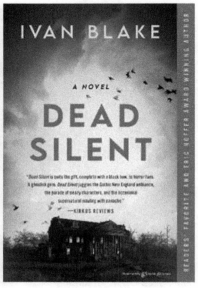

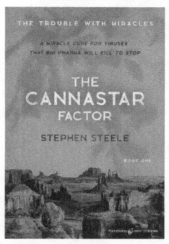
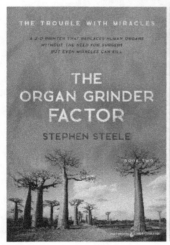
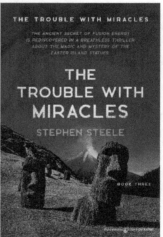

CPSIA information can be obtained
at www.ICGtesting.com
Printed in the USA
LVHW101929090423
743885LV00001B/162

9 781645 409090